W9-ATL-646

DRINK THE TEA

DRINK THE TEA

a mystery

THOMAS KAUFMAN

MINOTAUR BOOKS

New York

A THOMAS DUNNE BOOK FOR MINOTAUR BOOKS.
An imprint of St. Martin's Publishing Group.

DRINK THE TEA. Copyright © 2010 by Thomas Kaufman.
All rights reserved. Printed in the United States of America.
For information, address St. Martin's Press, 175 Fifth
Avenue, New York, N.Y. 10010.

www.thomasdunnebooks.com
www.minotaurbooks.com

Design by Kathryn Parise

LIBRARY OF CONGRESS CATALOGING-IN-PUBLICATION DATA
Kaufman, Thomas.
    Drink the tea / Thomas Kaufman. — 1st ed.
        p. cm.
    "A Thomas Dunne book."
    ISBN 978-0-312-60730-2
    1. Private investigators—Washington (D.C.)—Fiction. 2. Missing
persons—Investigation—Fiction. 3. Daughters—Crimes against—
Fiction. 4. Washington (D.C.)—Fiction. 5. Corruption—Fiction.
I. Title.
    PS3611.A843D75 2010
    813'.6—dc22
                                                    2009041126

First Edition: March 2010

10 9 8 7 6 5 4 3 2 1

Dedicated to Jim, Joanne, Martha, and Pete

ACKNOWLEDGMENTS

My thanks to George Pelecanos and Walter Wager, two great writers whose advice and encouragement helped me all the way through. Thanks also to Ruth Cavin and Toni Plummer at St. Martin's Press, and to Robert Randisi of the PWA. Many thanks to Peter Banks of the National Center for Missing and Exploited Children; Steve Hamilton; S. J. Rozan; Montgomery County, Maryland, Detective Terry Ryan (Ret.); Sari Horowitz, Scott Higham, and Peter Milius of *The Washington Post*; Willard Carroll; Matt Nicholl; Michael Cuddy; Larry Klein; Ed Read; Cass Peterson; Alexander Milenic; Patty Zubeck Means; Anne Morgan Gray; Kate Dell; Dr. Meg Chisolm; Maggie Magill; my wife, Katie, for her constant love and support of my writing despite a boatload of rejections; and our kids, Emma and James, who have congratulated me on not being able to take a hint.

PART ONE

If anyone wishes to enter the Way of Tea,
they must become their own teacher.

—RIKYU

CHAPTER 1

Steps Jackson leaned across the table and said, "I want you to find my daughter."

I stared at him, my coffee cup halfway to my lips. "You've got a daughter?"

"Why would I ask you to find a daughter I don't have?" A wave of irritation crossed his face. Steps looked like a rich man whose son has just fallen into the punch bowl.

"You never mentioned a daughter before." I felt defensive, as though Steps had accused me of being a poor listener. "Didn't you tell me once you had no family at all?"

"True enough when I said it." He sighed. "Look, Willis, you're the only private investigator I know."

I made a time-out sign. "I'm just one guy. You have a missing person, you go to the cops. They've got the manpower."

He looked down at his cup. "It's not just any missing person, Willis. It's my daughter. I thought, maybe you could help me out. And I figured, I don't know, someone with your particular background would *wanna* help me."

My "particular background." Cute. If anyone else had said that I would've spit in his eye, or punched him out. Maybe both.

3

But I didn't have so many friends that I could afford to lose one. So I took a deep breath, slid my cup to the side. "I can listen."

Steps looked relieved. He sat back, shifting his gaze to the window. "D.C. has changed, man. In every way but one. The women. Never *seen* a city with so many women. Now, there used to be this club on Fourteenth, near U Street? Name of Middleton's. Ever hear of it? Course not, way before your time. This was back when U Street was the place, man. Everyone who came through town played there." Steps looked up as Chella, our waitress and the Zamboanga Café's owner, came by with fresh coffee.

Despite its name, the Zamboanga's fare was pretty straight ahead: burgers, fries, and Cokes. The salads were iceberg lettuce hacked into quarters with a goodly portion of Thousand Island dressing slathered on top. Bare fluorescent tubes buzzed from a grid fourteen feet above.

The specials—and I use the term generously—were block-printed with a felt marker on sheets of manila paper thumb-tacked to bare walls. A long countertop wound through the place, and five creaky booths stood like dominoes along the windows looking out on F Street.

While Chella poured the coffee, she asked Steps where was he playing. He said he'd comp her some tickets. I looked outside. Traffic crawled along F Street, stranding tourists on the median strip. Ten in the morning, with the humidity racing the temperature to one hundred. Typical summer day in Washington, D.C.

Once Chella went behind the counter, I said, "Middleton's."

He nodded. "When the rest of the clubs'd close, we'd all meet at Middleton's. Alvin, the owner, seemed like a sweet guy who loved jazz. Did some of my best playing there, mostly in the wee hours of the morning for the other musicians on the stand."

"Mostly black crowd?"

He smiled. "I recall some faces as pale as yours. So, we'd play for hours, then cut out to breakfast. Most times, Alvin'd come with us, and his daughter, Colette, she'd tag along. See, that's how Colette and me got together. We just started joking with each other, you know, flirting? Well, she was just eighteen, with the kinda skin that makes satin feel like sandpaper. You know what a young woman's skin feels like?"

I told him I knew.

"Well, I figured that's all it was, flirting. But I guess Colette had her own ideas, 'cause the next night she comes into the club where I'm playing and sets down right in the front. I was soloing on 'Devil Moon' at the time."

"You remember the song? How long ago was this?"

"Twenty-five years. Shit, Willis, if I thought it would help, I could tell you which notes I played." He looked up at me. "Funny, but there're only a few moments like that in a man's life, you know? Where something important's going down and you know it, right when it's happening. Colette just came in and sat down, crossed her legs, lit a cigarette, and then lit into me with those brown eyes of hers.

"I nearly fell off that stand. Musta hit a few odd notes, too, 'cause I heard the bass player and drummer laughing behind me. I finished my solo with as much dignity as I could muster and let the pianist take over. I turned away from Colette, set down the sax, took out my handkerchief, and wiped my palms and face. Then I turned back to look at the piano player, listen to his solo. I wasn't just being polite, my heart was beating so hard up there, I didn't want to chance looking at her."

"That surprised you?"

"That I felt that way? Yeah. It was more than just her being

5

so fine, you know? She had some kinda pull, it just reached out across the floor towards me, I could feel it. And even though it scared me, I liked it, I didn't want to spoil it by looking at her too close, too soon.

"So the piano player finishes and the trumpet player lets fly, and I turn kinda casual and, man—she's looking right at me, more gorgeous than ever." He shrugged. "That was the longest set of my life."

Steps sat back and took a deep breath. His body seemed to grow larger right in front of me, seemed to take up most of the booth. I guess I'm bigger than Steps, but I was young when I met him and he's always seemed like a giant to me. Definitely easier to picture him changing a tire than tapping the keys of his sax. His kinky hair was short, with more gray than the last time I'd seen him, and his skin had a warm brown glow like eagles' feathers.

"What about your daughter?"

Steps opened his eyes, focusing on me from years away. "I'm getting there. Colette stayed till the last set, and we split for my hotel. It was only six blocks away, but I took a cab. Guess I wanted to impress her. We got to my room, and Colette, she didn't disappoint me."

"Anything else? Besides a lack of disappointment?"

"You gonna let me tell this?" Steps looked away. "I'm not gonna say something stupid like I was in love with her. Willis, I'm sixty-five—I can honestly say I don't know what love is. Maybe nobody does."

"Maybe not."

"But even if I did love that chick, I never got the chance to tell her. Never saw her again. See, that morning I had to catch the train to Philly, then out West. I thought about asking Colette if she wanted to come. You know, Duke Ellington used to say of his female companions, 'This lady is traveling horizontal with me.' " Steps gave me a bitter smile. "But I got distracted. Different city, different women, you know?" He sounded more apologetic than macho. "Look—I wanted Colette, wanted her pretty bad, but I figured to wait till the next time I came to town."

"And that was?"

"Just shy of a year. I was at Club Indigo and picked up a local band. After our last set I said we should go to Middleton's. They just looked at me like, haven't you heard? Alvin closed the club months ago. Right after I left town, turns out. So I ask around, but nobody knows where Alvin's got to. Or Colette. Two weeks at the Indigo, man, and every night I'm looking out at the faces coming in, hoping I'll see her. No such luck. Daytime I'm going around asking every cat in town where Alvin and Colette might've got to. By the time I had to move on, I'd given up."

"And your daughter? When did you first hear of her?"

"Two weeks ago. Some hip-hop guy in New York wanted to sample my sax lines over 'Cantaloupe Island.' When I get there he says he just missed me in D.C. at the Money Jungle. I ask him how's the food—see, they'd just got a new chef. So he looks at me like I just said the secret word and says so I know already. Know what? I ask him. 'About your daughter,' he says.

"I say what the hell is he talking about? He says that the chef's a young guy, one of these nouvelle cuisine types making a fortune off his grandma's recipes. Anyways, this chef loves jazz, talked about his favorites, and said he went to high school with Steps Jackson's daughter."

I took out my notebook. "Did you call him? What's his name?"

"Tony Hancock. I tried to, but the guy's hard to reach, doesn't return my calls. Must have left a dozen messages." Steps sat forward. "So can you help me? Help me find this girl?"

"You haven't told me her name and birthdate."

"I'd tell you if I knew." Steps looked worried, an expression I had never seen on his face before. "You just gotta help me, man."

Now I got it, why Steps hadn't filed a missing-person report. We were in D.C., Dysfunction City. I could just imagine the cops' reaction. Somehow I didn't think they'd spend a lot of time looking for someone without a name or a birthdate, even if she was Steps Jackson's only child.

In jazz they talk about a sense of time, how a musician can take a beat, divide it and subdivide it, cracking time into pieces and skipping them like stones across a lake. Everyone knew that Steps was a master, had a phenomenal sense of time. And now his asking me about his daughter showed good timing, too. For three years I had been operating my own detective agency—part-time. So far I had no office, no gal Friday, and damn few clients.

I did have a cell phone. And a license. The D.C. government had given it to me. Which kind of surprised me, how they'd handed it over when all they knew about me was that I had the twenty-dollar fee.

They could have handed me the license for free and I'd still have had two problems. The first was how much work I'd been getting—close to none—and the second was the kind of work I'd been stuck with—divorce cases, with a few subpoena deliveries thrown in for good measure. This wasn't the kind of work I could build a reputation on, at least not the kind I wanted.

Maybe that could change, now that Steps was dropping this case in my lap. A chance to do something worthwhile. I liked the idea of helping my friend. I liked the idea of working on a case where maybe, possibly, some good could come of it.

Plus what Steps had called my "particular background."

He was right. It was all I needed to make me want to help him, even if he hadn't been my friend.

"Okay," I said. "I'll find your daughter."

CHAPTER 2

I saw only one problem in finding Steps's daughter.

I had no idea how to do it.

Now, finding a person who's been missing for the past twenty-four hours is one thing. But for the past twenty-five years? That's different. Also, my only recent sleuthing had been figuring out who was drinking the coffee and not paying for it at Shelly Russia's place. That was my other job. My day gig, as Steps would say. Working for Shelly made me wish my detective business were doing better.

Shelly Russia owned a record warehouse, maybe the biggest in the D.C. area. When I say records, I mean records like those big black things we bought before CDs came around. Every music distributor in the country had switched, except Shelly. Shelly sold polkas.

He sold polka recordings from Poland and Romania and

Russia. Slavic melodies squeezed through an accordion. Also the polka modernists, spin-offs from the Brave Combo wave, who converted recent songs to polkas. You really haven't lived till you've caught "Candle in the Wind" as an accordion riff.

I was Shelly's manager, handling orders, overseeing twenty employees, and making sure that all of them, regardless of race, creed, or musical preferences, paid for their own goddamn coffee. I'd been there two years, a long time for me. My average job interment is six weeks. Since Shelly allowed me a large amount of autonomy, things had worked out.

Even in the cosmopolitan city of Washington, D.C., you'd be amazed at how many polka records we sold each week. Now, there's nothing wrong with accordion players. I just happen to prefer jazz. Not the new jazz, it's too technical. Listening to it is like a trip to the dentist. But if you go back in time, you see the stars come out: Miles, Coltrane, Bill Evans, Bud Powell, and my all-time favorite, Steps Jackson.

I never really appreciated jazz until I heard Steps. Whenever he came to town I found some excuse to skip work and light out for whatever club he was roosting in. He was playing at Red Pepper's in D.C. I got up the nerve to approach him and say hello. In the dim light in the back, near the double doors to the kitchen, Steps was snarfing a burger and fries. I walked up to him, introduced myself. Told him how his music had changed my life, how I'd never really understood or enjoyed jazz before hearing him, how I had listened to his albums so many times there was a pile of black vinyl dust by the tone arm of my record player.

During all of this Steps had dropped a french fry. I was spilling my guts while he flipped his napkin over, then stood and turned around, searching for the missing fry. He'd bent down to look around his chair when I came to the end of my chatter and, sensing from the lull I had reached an impasse, he looked up at me for the first time.

"That's cool," he said. He had stopped his search for the missing fry and I had stopped my "I'm your biggest fan" spiel. We looked each other in the eye. Then we started laughing. Steps waved me over to the chair next to his, and soon we were talking like old friends.

Now he wanted me to find his daughter.

So here I was on F Street, thinking how best to approach a chef who claimed to know her but refused to return Steps's calls. I walked past kiosks containing *The Post* and *The Times*. Their headlines claimed that a Senator Broadfield had announced his resignation. A slow news day in D.C. I dodged a bus and crossed F Street, passing a restaurant that signaled its abandonment with yellow D.C. CLOSED BY DEPT HEALTH signs gaily festooned over its empty windows.

Peeling off the least weathered sign and rolling it into my pocket, I began heading to my car. There were no Metro train stops in Georgetown; the folks there had wanted to discourage the wrong element.

I figured to come anyway.

CHAPTER 3

I kicked my car to life, chugged toward Eleventh, then west on K Street. My first obstacle was Shelly Russia—he expected me to show up for work. The obvious answer: call in sick. As I took K Street beneath the Whitehurst Freeway, I tapped in Shelly's number on my phone. He answered with his usual charm.

"Who the hell *is* this?" He snarled as though I'd just phoned three times in a row and hung up each time.

"It's Willis."

"Gidney, what the hell do you want?"

"I've got a little family emergency. I won't be in today."

"Don't fuck with me, Gidney. I know Steps Jackson's in town. You think I can't read a fucking paper?" Uncanny. Over the years I had, in fact, begun to doubt that Shelly could read. "You get your ass in here today, you got that?"

"Shelly, Shelly, I'm way ahead of you. Everything's been shipped for the week and it's only Tuesday. Check it out. If I show I won't have anything to do and you know it."

Silence. Then: "If you weren't so fucking good at this, I'd've canned your ass years ago." I waited. "Okay, fuckwad, take the morning off. But if you don't show by noon, start looking for a new job."

"I'm part-time, Shelly. You want to replace me with one of the mental defectives you've got there, go ahead. You'll be paying them double and they won't get half as much done." Shelly hung up, so I didn't hear the string of expletives that would inevitably have followed such an exit line. I turned right onto Wisconsin Avenue, heading into the heart of Georgetown, if there is such a thing. Georgetown, I've been told, was once a quiet and pleasant community. Must've been before my time. Racing past me were wealthy, beautiful children driving sports cars, accelerating through their lives and the streets much too fast. An amplified thumping sound—would they call that music?—poured out of every car. It had the beat of a galley-ship drum, signaling the oar strokes for the wretches below decks. Somehow, I guessed these kids saw themselves differently. I parked below the alley to Money Jungle. On the corner I passed a coffee shop that had once been a toy store.

I like toy stores. I like to walk in, wind up some silly contraption, and watch it skitter across the floor. I guess part of the fun of being a parent must be playing with your kid's toys. I'd tried to convince Karla about having a child. Not in this lifetime, she'd said. Down the alley, the Money Jungle's door was open. As I stepped in I was shocked. I'd seen the club only at night, with its colored lights and excitement and shadows and mystery. Walking into the club now, I saw that Money Jungle had all the mystery and excitement of a hangnail.

A young black woman asked if she could help me.

"I'm with the city," I told her. "Raoul Walsh, Department of Health. For the inspection?" I spoke in a rapid, bored voice, then raised my eyebrows at her.

"Um, what inspection would that be?"

I sighed. "Lemme see the manager."

The young woman hesitated. "Certainly, sir. May I tell him what this is about?"

"Sure, tell him it's about a week between the time I close a kitchen for violations and the time it reopens."

Her eyes widened at that. While she hurried off I took a stool at the bar, wondering if single-batch bourbons tasted better than a two-dollar shot of Early Times.

"Yes, may I help you?"

I turned and saw a man older, shorter, and fatter than myself, which made me like him immediately. Too bad, since I was playing the heavy just now. "Sure," I said, pulling out the yellow Closed sign I had lifted from the failed F Street restaurant. "You can get me some Scotch tape."

He turned a nice shade of green. "Is there a problem?"

"You could say that. We've scheduled an inspection of your kitchen and I'm cooling my heels at the bar. I'll just phone for more of these," I said, fanning myself with the notice.

He sputtered, then coughed, then wiped his head, which was suddenly hobnailed with sweat. "Wait, wait . . ." He gasped. He began making a jerky motion of his arm.

"That the way to the kitchen?" He nodded. "Great." I hopped off the stool, rolling the notice back into my pocket. I marched through the double swinging doors and into the fluorescent-lit kitchen. Clean walls, clean stainless-steel surfaces, and spotless utensils. The floor wasn't just clean enough to eat off, it was clean enough to have surgery on. A black man in his mid- to late twenties, immaculate in white pants, shirt, and apron, scowled as I invaded his domain. When he saw his boss hustling behind me, his expression grew puzzled.

"Can I help you?" he asked.

"Not unless you're an electrical contractor."

"Sir?"

"Your AC outlets. Those cute little holes in the wall? D.C. code says there're supposed to be two GFI outlets every eight feet. These look like Edison installed them." A bit of a stretch, me a health inspector faulting them for a wiring problem. But for the life of me I could find nothing else wrong in that kitchen. "Where's the phone?"

"Um, in my office."

"Good, 'cause I need to call *my* office."

"Now, wait a minute, Walsh. Can't we, uh, isn't there something we can do?"

I gave him the fish eye. "Something we can do?"

"Well, Walsh, maybe we can work something out, you know, we scratch your back . . ." His voice trailed off under the glare I was giving him. If I were going to agree I would have chimed in by now. I didn't. Instead, I drew myself up and made my face beet red; people tell me I'm really good at this. The manager recoiled exquisitely.

During this little exercise Hancock looked from me to his boss, then back to me. Now Hancock came around the counter, making soothing gestures with his hands. "Please, Mr. Walsh, we didn't mean anything like that, we're just a couple of D.C. boys."

"You?" I sneered at him. "I heard you were some hot-shot chef from New York City."

He laughed, still trying to ease the tension. "No, sir, born and raised right here. Graduated from Cardozo High."

"Cardozo? That's a great school." I beamed at him, all my anger forgotten. His boss was behind me, and I could imagine him looking bewildered at my change of mood. "Lot of famous people from Cardozo."

"Really?" Hancock was walking a tightrope, trying to maintain his self-respect while kissing my butt. I admired the near-genuine look of interest he gave me.

"Sure," I said, and reeled off the names of half-a-dozen famous people. I had no idea if they actually had gone to Cardozo. I think I could have named King Tut without fear of contradiction. Hancock chimed in with names of his own. I nodded and said, "I think Steps Jackson went there, too."

"I knew his daughter," Hancock said with pride.

"Oh? What's her name?"

"Bobbie, Bobbie Jackson."

"Really?" I leaned against the counter. "Tell me all about her," I said.

CHAPTER 4

For all my play-acting at Money Jungle, I got only two pieces of usable information—an address for Bobbie in the Shaw neighborhood of D.C., where she had lived a year ago, and the name of a mutual friend who worked on the Hill. I decided to try the Shaw address first.

Shaw is a little too real to be in sight of the U.S. Capitol. You see the big white dome, glimmering through the heat waves like every state senator's wet dream, and you think that everything around it would be like Disneyland. South of the dome you find the trendy spots, the restaurants where a guy like myself might take his future ex-wife for a proposal of marriage. Shaw is north of the dome, a different world.

I parked in a line of auto carcasses that lined the street. The buildings were abandoned. The apartment building corresponding to Bobbie's address was ugly and looked to have been built that way. Now it was in limbo, between city neglect and the wrecker's ball.

Like the buildings on both sides, the front doors and windows were blinded by weathered plywood. I heard voices—from inside? Around back, through a shattered window I glimpsed two black kids having some kind of tussle. I stepped through a sagging chain-link fence covered with rust and into a yard so desolate that even the weeds stayed away.

The back door was missing. I went in.

I heard the voices more clearly. Which meant that these two were flyweights. Back at Bockman's, my juvenile home that was part of the "particular background" Steps had mentioned, the arguments were short and pointed, like homemade shivs.

In the dim light I drew closer. The shouting died. I stepped lightly as I came around the corner. I saw a table and two chairs, one of which had been knocked to the floor.

Then I saw why it had gotten so quiet. The bigger one was tall, skinny, not quite twenty. A wool cap rode low on his head, and a hard, mean smile lifted his face. He gripped a pearl-handled knife. He seemed to enjoy using his right hand to press the knife point into the smaller kid's neck, releasing a pearl of blood, while he removed the kid's roll of bills with his left. The blade hadn't done much damage, but you'd have had a hard time convincing the smaller kid.

He looked to be twelve. His eyes were wide with panic, his breath quick and shallow. His arms were held out straight, as though he were balancing on a tightrope. In one hand he clenched a plastic bag with several glass vials clinking inside.

I moved behind Wool Cap. "You pay taxes on that?"

Wool Cap started and spun around, backhanding the knife

toward me. I grabbed his wrist, twisted it, using his motion to carry his arm behind his back. Then I yanked up. He screamed and dropped the knife. The smaller kid grabbed his cash and his baggie and darted out the door. Didn't even say goodbye. The knife thunked into the floor. I kicked it to the left and threw Wool Cap to the right. He landed and rolled, the rings on his hand rapping against something metallic in his jacket.

He was a puckish little weasel.

At Bockman's you learn that a fight is never over till somebody's out. I pushed my foot against the table and launched it into Wool Cap. He still had his hand in his pocket when the table's edge slammed into his stomach, followed by my elbow smacking his head into the wall. His eyes rolled up as he slid down the wall.

I approached him, making sure he was well and truly out. Then I reached into his pocket and took out the gun, a stainless Smith & Wesson 9-mm that looked new. So he had wanted to scare the kid without killing him. Maybe. I dropped the gun into my pocket, then dug out Wool Cap's wallet. Inside were three driver's licenses with the names Dante Thomas, Dante Lee, and Dante Marsh. Each license carried a similar picture of Dante scowling at the camera. Three American Express cards with the same three names kept the licenses company. The Marsh name had a gold card, for those special occasions, like impressing the other dealers. Maybe you could buy dope from Dante and charge it.

Next I found a sheaf of bills big enough to choke a sewer pipe. Walking around money. There wasn't much more. A plastic membership card from Blockbuster Video, a paper card with holes punched in it from the Riverside Roasters on Capitol Hill that promised a free coffee after you bought ten (Dante had two more to go), a matchbook from a bar called Rusty's, and about three feet of dental floss rolled into a spool.

I put everything back and stuck the wallet into Dante's jacket. I wondered if he flossed in the morning or the evening. I once knew a guy who flossed after every meal. That seemed a bit excessive, but then again he was a Jesuit.

The apartment provided nothing that would point to Bobbie's whereabouts, just trash. I was moving past Dante for a look upstairs when he started. His eyes blinked open, he saw me, he went for his gun. I showed it to him. He started to get up. I kicked his legs out from under him. "Chill, Dante. Let's talk about Bobbie." If Dante was scared, he sure hid it well. He glared at me, then said:

> *"Fat policeman goes*
> *Too far too quickly.*
> *Spring flowers will trace his grave."*

I said, "Nice. Now tell me where Bobbie's hanging these days."

Dante smiled.

> *"While he asks questions*
> *Cold winter prepares itself*
> *To freeze his fat ass."*

I stuck the end of the Smith in his ear. "And here we were getting along so well." I cocked the gun. "You sure you don't want to tell me where to find Bobbie?"

His eyes still had that mean look. This is what's wrong with D.C. Here I had the gun and he wasn't smart enough to be scared. Annoying. When he snarled, his teeth looked clean. Maybe he was a morning flosser after all. I shifted the gun so its muzzle pressed against his teeth. "Dante, if you don't tell me what I want, I am going to shoot your teeth out. You'll face a lifetime of exorbitant dental bills."

Now he looked agitated. "Hey, man, what's wrong with you? I don't know 'im, I don't know no Bobbie, okay?"

Not exactly the information I wanted, but at least he'd stopped speaking in haiku. And the pleading tone to his voice convinced me—this was as close to the truth as I was likely to get.

I stood. "Dante, if I find out you're lying, I'll be very angry."

He stood and pulled his wool cap down. Recovering his dignity. He held out his hand for the gun. I shook my head. He glowered at me, chin down, looking from the tops of his eyes.

> *"White nigger gives gun*
> *Or Dante will rain down death*
> *Like Texas hailstones."*

I shrugged. When he saw that I was keeping his piece, he edged past me, keeping his distance. It hadn't been a great exit line, but I admired his defiance. I watched his wool cap glide past the shattered side window, then climbed the stairs and went through the second floor. I found nothing. Shit. A TV detective would've hit something cool before the commercial.

The top floor was the same, until I reached the rear apartment. It looked like it had been lived in more recently, though I couldn't say how recently. And, unlike the rest of the building, this apartment had been cleaned out, there was nothing in the corners, no trash, no papers. Only some torn black plastic trash bags.

The middle room was the smallest, the heat stifling. Two small windows offered a spectacular view of a garbage pile next door. A ragged line chewed its way around the windows, like some paint-eating bug giving it the once-over. The electrical outlets were different from the ones in the rest of the building. They looked new, had provisions for ground plugs, and were the type you could reset, like the ones at Money Jungle.

The ceiling had a series of holes drilled through the drywall and into the studs, as though something heavy had hung there. On my way out I found the breaker box in the kitchen. Most buildings have fifteen-amp circuits, twenty amps tops. But these lines had been upgraded to carry forty amps.

So why would someone bother to heavy up the wiring on a building that was all but condemned?

CHAPTER 5

Downtown, I went past Fisherman's Wharf to Vital Records, a modern building nearby, all glass and striking angles, four stories high with open spaces and pillars. With the smell of the Potomac River filling my nose and the sight of some fine seafood shacks enticing my eyes, I parked on Ninth Street. I locked Dante's gun in my glove compartment. Then I noticed the parking meter. It looked like someone had whacked it with a sledgehammer. The top part, which kept time, seemed intact. But beneath it the coin box was missing, like a face with no mouth. I stuck in a quarter and turned the handle. I got twenty minutes' time and the quarter dropped out of the meter to my feet.

I picked it up and headed to the entrance. The usual gang of smokers sucked on cigarettes in the sunshine. They also had to endure planters of red and yellow tulips, white and purple pansies, and a red feather maple. Poor devils. Meanwhile, the healthy folks indoors helped themselves to recycled air and fluorescent lights.

In the lobby, a woman cop with a utility belt Batman would have envied had me sign in, then told me what I already knew—the line starts here. The records room was just big enough to accommodate a long, long line of all kinds of people. Mostly working-class with a sprinkling of lawyers. Hispanic and black, Asian and white, men and women, old and young. A wall-mounted TV showed a square-jawed news anchor, then flashed to a picture of Senator Broadfield. Next came a shot of a younger man waving and smiling, presumably toward people off-camera, while at the bottom of the screen "ETHICS VIOLATIONS?" scrolled across. Next, a commercial about pain and how to relieve it. Everyone in line watched. The Brotherhood of Pain Relief. Maybe waiting in line was painful.

It would have been for me, so I took the elevator to the basement. The lock on the alarm-system door offered little resistance. As a youngster I would've needed an hour to pop the lock, but that was before I had perfected the art of Tampering. Now, I could have simply triggered the fire alarm for the building, but don't you think the fire department has enough to do?

Besides, when was the last time anyone actually tested the alarm? With the warm feeling that can come only from civic-mindedness, I thumbed the Test button. Immediately a klaxon shrieked through the building. When I returned, the records room was nearly empty. A miracle. As the staff left, I snagged the elbow of a black man wearing rimless glasses and a thoughtful expression.

"Hey, Clavus, what's up?"

He looked at me, blinked, then his shoulders sunk. "Again?"

"I hate lines." With my hand guiding his elbow, we walked back behind the counter.

"What you looking for today?"

"Birth certificate."

His logged on to his screen. "You know, I could just mail you form FRM300."

"But then we wouldn't get a chance to see each other." The alarm was still going strong, it grated my nerves. Still better than waiting in line, though. Life is a series of trade-offs.

He sighed. "Right."

"How's Octavia?" That was Clavus's sister. I'd met them the day they landed in Bockman's. She was a cute little twelve-year-old that a gang of older guys wanted to know better. Clavus had been happy to have my help discouraging them.

"Good, she's good."

"Tell her I said hi."

"All right. What's the date of birth?" His fingers poised above the keyboard.

"She was born about twenty to twenty-five years ago."

He shot me a look. "You don't know the birthdate?"

"No."

He shrugged. "I can search using her name."

"Don't have her name either."

Clavus turned from the screen. "Am I hearing you right? You wanna find someone, but you don't know the name or birthdate?"

"I think I have the gender right."

"And you *think* she was born in the District?"

"A hunch."

He nodded, as if that made a difference. "Just what name are we looking for? If the name's special or unusual—"

"Jackson."

He whistled low. "I don't think our standard search would help you much."

I pulled out two bills that bore Andrew Jackson's likeness, wrapped them around my business card, and slid them toward him. "Someone smart as you could find a way."

He hesitated taking the bills. "I really don't know if I can do this."

The alarm stopped. "You've taken my money before."

"Not that. I don't know if I can do a search that would show anything."

"You'll figure out something."

"When?"

I acted surprised. "Today, Clavus." I tucked the cash into his shirt pocket. "Call me later today."

As I walked away Clavus said, "Hey, Willis. You know what you never ask?"

"What?"

He smiled. "You never ask me about searching for God."

Right, me and God.

I told Clavus, "I don't think Vital Records is set up that way."

CHAPTER 6

Finding God would be difficult, but finding lunch was easy. I left Vital Records, past the customers, smokers, and staff, who traded resigned looks as they realized the alarm had ended with no fire trucks in sight. I put the same quarter in the same meter and got it back. I was starting to like it here. Down the street a meter maid ticketed a car. She glared at me. I flipped the quarter and caught it, George Raft-style, then leered at her.

My stomach growled in anticipation. I crossed Maine Avenue and bellied up to the counter of Custis and Brown's, where I slammed down two bowls of Maryland she-crab chowder, then placed a call to Lieutenant Emil Haggler, a D.C. homicide cop I knew. A male voice answered second district. I asked for Haggler, was put on hold, then a voice came over the phone and said, "Haggler."

"It's Willis."

"Well, well. Where you been, son?"

"Here and there. I wonder could you do me a favor?"

"No more parkin' tickets, Willis, I done told you before."

"This is different. I'm trying to find someone for a friend of mine and I wonder could you help me?"

"Oh, yeah, the part-time *detective*," he said. "Somebody late on their alimony?"

"No, missing person, and it's the first case I've had this year that doesn't involve infrared video and telephoto lenses."

"Glad to hear it. I can think of another cop who'd approve."

He was talking about Captain Shadrack Davies, who had been Emil's boss and one of my foster fathers. This was my cue to say something about Shad. Instead, I kept on target. "Right. So how about a search on Jackson, Bobbie?"

"Man or woman?"

"Woman, African American, about twenty to twenty-five years old."

"Where you looked so far?"

"Just a request at Vital Records."

"Okay. I could check our files, see she has a criminal record."

"Good. Could you also check DMV?"

I could hear him scribbling away. "Anything else?"

"Phone and utilities. Oh, and bank accounts."

"Christ, you want me to wipe your ass for you, too?"

"No, I'm doing pretty good with that now."

"Could have fooled me." Then he hung up.

I was lucky I'd caught him on a good day.

CHAPTER 7

My next stop was Stephanie Chilcoate. According to Hancock, she was a high-school friend of Bobbie's who now worked as assistant to the District's shadow delegate to Congress. As I tooled down North Capitol Street I wondered how one assisted a shadow. But hey, this was the U.S. Congress, the international model for screwed-up institutions everywhere.

Her office informed me that Ms. Chilcoate could be found in Rayburn room 2405.

I wasted time looking for parking. I took a right on New Jersey Avenue, then saw the police lot. Empty spaces beckoned. Nearby sat an unmarked cruiser with an official-looking cardboard slip on the dashboard that read POLICE. The driver's window was open. I put the cardboard slip on my dashboard. It would be a shame to get towed from such a convenient place.

Inside the Rayburn House Office Building, I stepped through the metal detector, then watched my phone glide across the grainy black-and-white TV screen, a fuzzy gray shape on a grayer background. It reminded me of the first time I'd ever seen a security monitor. I was a kid, inside a Metrorail guard's kiosk.

I don't have what you'd call a linear memory of childhood. Tiny pieces, like flecks of light filtered through tree leaves, shifting, winking on and off, so jumbled I couldn't tell you what was real and what I dreamed. Fragments of images, ghost sensations. I see myself in a baby's crib, under a porch light at night. A woman—my mother?—walks past me into the house. Why am I outside? Why doesn't she pick me up, take me in with her? Did it really happen? I have sense memories of a woman holding me, a dog barking, the smell of sulfur and snow falling.

Another jump cut, and I'm older, on the streets of Washington, looking at the U.S. Capitol simmer in the heat and thinking it was a merry-go-round. As a kid, each day I spent on the street I figured I was stealing, getting away with something. I had no way to see what I was losing. You live on the street, the first thing you lose is your identity. If you're young, this happens fast.

There's lots of reasons why. Number one is the people around you. Men and women and boys and girls who've passed through society like phantoms through an alien dimension, existing only in a stranger's peripheral vision, filler for the paper's Metro section. These folks are your peers, your friends, the village that's raising you, except it's not really a village. It's a pack. So you do what they do. This time I'm telling you about, when I got busted, wasn't the worst of it, not by a long shot. It's just the first time I got caught.

And God is definitely part of my first, true, linear memory. He had some scam using a Xerox and a five-dollar bill, slipping the copies into the fare-card machines of the Metro. He knew the bill readers in those machines couldn't tell a copy from the real thing.

God, a ten-year-old black kid whose full name was Godfrey White, had been my mentor for a month. I'd bunked with him beneath the Whitehurst Freeway, in a cardboard box that had once held a GE refrigerator (two-door, self-defrosting, icemaker included). With God's help, I knew I could stay out of Junior Village and Bockman's. I'd never been to either, but my mental image was, if they caught me, I'd get chained to the wall and gnawed by rats.

Later, I found I wasn't far off the mark.

Getting me into the Metro guard's kiosk had been part of God's grand plan. I had paid attention while he explained how he would feed the Xerox copies of his five-dollar bill into the Metro fare-card machines. The amount $5.00 would light up. Then God would tab the Minus button until the fare showed $.05, jab another button, and down the chute would tumble $4.95 in change. Not a bad return on a ten-cent Xerox.

The only trouble with God's fare-card scam was that the bottom of the coin return was metal. All that change tumbling down made a racket. The Metro guard who sat in a nearby glassed-in booth might begin to suspect something, particularly if he heard that kind of sound ten times in a row. God figured that $49.50 was all the change he could carry away in his paper sack.

My job—distract the guard.

"How?" I asked.

"Cry and tell 'im you're lost," God said.

I was a despicable little brat and took to my role with gusto. I played the lost little boy with an intensity that would have expelled me from the most amateur play. I was too young to know better. I thought I was great. I cried mommydaddymommy-daddy as I approached the Metro guard, and he recoiled exquisitely. I was incoherent with fear and pain, in hopes he would open the door to the booth and I could get inside.

He didn't want to leave his booth. He tried speaking to me through his little microphone. I wasn't having that. I cried harder, my pale little face beet red, the tears streaming down— real tears. I was playing an abandoned kid. Method acting. I beat my little fists against the window to block out the sound of change gushing down the chute. God told me I'd get half of the take and that was all the motivation I needed.

Finally, the guard, a kindly-looking white guy with a salt-and-pepper goatee, opened the door. I practically fell inside. I hugged his knees and cried, my voice bouncing off the glass walls of the booth. So far, God had used four of his copies. "Whassa matter, boy?" the guard asked. I wailed even louder, my earsplitting voice reverberating off the glass walls. It was even giving *me* a headache. "Did you lose your mommy and daddy?"

My mouth open, I screamed and nodded. Outside, a steady stream of change clanged. "Where'd you lose 'em?"

I heard another crash of coins—that would be eight—and took a breath. The guard thought he was calming me, but I was building toward my big finish. In heartrending sobs, I said that the subway doors had closed behind my parents and the train had pulled away without me.

"Which way was the train goin'? I'll call ahead," the guard said.

"Not here." I sobbed "D-d-downtown." The stutter was a nice touch. Meanwhile, God had finished and, hefting his swag, staggered toward the exit. I held up my hands to the guard. I said I was all right now, I'd find my folks, don't worry. I figured he'd be glad to get rid of me.

I was wrong. He started to come after me, his hand out, a solicitous expression on his face. I backed away, realizing I might have overplayed my part just a tiny bit. I retreated into something and fell, and there was a crash and God's bag of coins hit the tile floor and coins were bouncing off the floor like water drops on a red-hot skillet.

The last time I saw God, he was hotfooting it out of there as the Metro guard grabbed my arm, his fingers tight. I can still feel his fingers there.

Now, as I walked through the metal detector at the Rayburn Building, I tried not to look guilty. The cops only nodded at me. I grabbed my phone and keys and turned to study the building directory. Room 2405 was on the fourth floor, because the 2 meant this was the Rayburn Building. Only in Washington. Around the corner were two sets of elevators. One for civilians like me, the other for congressional staff only. I pushed both Up buttons and waited.

I was awash in a sea of charcoal-gray lobbyists, men in suits and tasseled loafers. A few women brightened the group, mostly office staff. It's the custom to bring your staff from your home state. A shapely redhead in a sleeveless kelly-green top and matching skirt pushed the staff Up button and gave me a suspicious look.

I tried to guess where she was from. Then I wondered what she looked like with her clothes off. Then I wondered if that was sexist of me. Probably. To be politically correct I'd have to mentally undress all these male lobbyists, too. Didn't seem worth the trouble.

The elevator doors wheezed open. We rode silently to the fourth floor, where we parted company. At the landing I turned left and was nearly knocked down.

"Hey, sorry, pal." A guy with a ruddy complexion and red hair was pushing a canvas laundry hamper. He wore a faded red T-shirt, khaki shorts, thick wool socks, and hiking boots. Around his waist he wore some kind of tool belt, through which he had looped a rope with rolls of adhesive tape in different widths and colors. The hamper he pushed creaked under the weight of metal stands, extension cords, and rubber mats.

"No problem. Laundry day?"

"Huh?" He looked at the hamper then and smiled. "Nah, we're doin' a political spot." He'd jerked the hamper to the side so he wouldn't knock me over, and some cables had fallen onto the floor. I slung the cables over my shoulder, falling in step with him.

"A spot? Like a commercial?" I asked.

"That's right." He was nearing the end of the hall. Six other hampers lined the hallway, each full of gear. Thick black cables snaked across the floor, covered with a rubber mat that had been taped down. The cables ran to a junction box that supplied electricity.

I pointed at the cables. "I see you're well connected."

He laughed. "Nah, our lights draw a lot of juice, so we gotta tie in to the mains." He pointed to some metal clips shaped like alligator jaws, at the ends of the cables, attached directly to the electrical lines.

The other ends of the cables ran through an open door. Shifting light rays shot out of the door like a UFO landing. Two Neanderthals in uniforms watched us as we approached. The bigger one had a scar across the bridge of his nose. On their shoulders were patches with the words TARGUS SECURITY and a lighting bolt going through. They saw me carry cables, waved me past without any trouble.

Inside, technicians swiveled enormous lights mounted on tripods, shooting blue light through sheets of milky white paper four feet square. The paper diffused the light, and basking in the cold glow on the other side was the man I had just seen on the TV at Vital Records—Congressman Jason McHugh.

McHugh looked to be in his late fifties, with small, black, deep-set eyes and dark eyebrows and dark hair. His smiling face was wide and rubbery and smooth, almost like a doll's. His smile didn't quite reach his eyes. Three feet above the congressman's head, a banner proclaimed AMERICA FOR THE AMERICANS!! in red, white, and blue.

On his desktop were tiny American flags. He wore a flag baseball hat set square on his head, a flag necktie, and a little flag pin on his lapel. Flags draped at diagonals from the walls, swayed from the ceiling, stood at attention on flagpoles. The stars-and-stripes motif covered napkins by the bar, jackets on the coat rack, a pair of boxer shorts hanging in a picture frame. A stack of cardboard boxes containing flags reached nearly to the ceiling.

It seemed like a lot of flags.

Facing McHugh was a teleprompter screen and behind it a camera. McHugh spoke earnestly to the prompter screen, as though it were his best friend. I couldn't make much sense of what he said, but he didn't mention any ethics violations. A man with a stopwatch standing next to the teleprompter shouted, "Cut!" McHugh frowned at him.

The stopwatch man was heavy, maybe 220, most of it fat, with the kind of boyish face that never seems to age. He wore an expensive-looking suit and had the regulation tassels on his shoes. But somehow none of it worked. He looked like a kid playing dress-up.

"Sorry, Jase, but your script runneth over. This is a thirty, so we have to do it in twenty-eight seconds, twenty-nine tops, okay? Maybe we should lose the basic-values part." He waved the stopwatch.

McHugh looked at him the way you'd look at your shoe after strolling through a cow pasture. With a nearly imperceptible southern drawl, McHugh said, "Brice, does that stopwatch work in your office as well as mine?"

Brice looked surprised. "Why sure, Jase."

"And do the laws of the physical universe apply to your office as well as mine?"

"Well, sure."

"Then why didn't you time the spot before you waddled over here?"

Brice's mouth opened and shut. The congressman's staff and the film people who had been milling about when Brice hollered, "Cut," now came to a stop. In the silence McHugh sighed and, rubbing the bridge of his veined nose, closed his eyes. When he opened them, he saw Brice still standing there. McHugh looked disappointed. He said, softly, "Do you think you might want to shorten the copy before we shoot another take?"

"Sure thing, Jase." Brice gave a cheery smile. As he passed me he made eye contact and said, "Asshole."

"Oh, and, Brice, while you labor to repair the obvious, maybe we could clear these," and here McHugh made a gesture that took in all the technicians, "these bottle washers out of my office for a while? I'd like to get a *little* work done today."

The cameraman, an older guy with salt-and-pepper hair and a beard to match, switched off his camera and stretched. "Okay, everybody take ten." A young man came over. He wore the standard issue flag tie. When I told him I was looking for Stephanie Chilcoate, he led me away from there and into an inner office, saying, "Have a seat, she's meeting with Ayzie."

"Who?"

"Azalea Trace, she's the congressman's administrative aide." I could hear this kid capitalize the C in *Congressman* when he said it. A true believer.

From where I sat I could see through a series of doorways to the main hallway, where a procession of lawyers and lobbyists slid past on one another's slime trails. Two desks flanked the hallway door, with an older woman to the right working at a computer and a younger woman on the left answering the phone. Her voice had a pleasant southern lilt to it, except when she said the congressman's name. It's hard to say "McHugh" with a lilt.

The room suffered a flag shortage, I counted only twelve.

Time for a nap. I'm good at napping. I let the murmur of office work and muted voices envelop me. I closed my eyes. Then

I heard raised voices and opened my eyes to see two women come out from the back.

One of them was black, in her twenties, wore a tight black dress and had long black hair parted in the middle. Another time her face would have looked like an angel's, but now it was contorted by rage. She worked at keeping her voice down. "Ms. Trace, I came here in good faith."

"Stephanie, you came here without an appointment at the worst possible time."

I took a long look at Azalea Trace. She was worth it. Early thirties, about five foot two, tanned, with auburn hair. Her face was heart-shaped, with high cheekbones and a chin that came to a little point. Her eyes were clear and blue and knowing. I thought of John Lennon's line, "she's not a girl who misses much."

A few freckles left over from childhood were sprinkled across the bridge of her nose. The nose wasn't straight, it had a funny kind of bump in it that took her out of the magazine-cover type of beauty and into the real world. She wore a business suit that was cut elegantly but still showed plenty of curves. Without getting all worked up about it, she looked good.

"And what about the District's timing, Ms. Trace? Your boss is making commercials about keeping America racially pure, while the lack of adequate housing is killing us."

"Stephanie, we've been through this before. The congressman is working closely with the several NGOs to locate buildings that are economically feasible renovation targets. Before the next committee meeting I'll suggest to the congressman—"

"Suggest?"

"—that we take up the matter."

"All you'll do is suggest?"

Trace's eyes got a hard look to them. "Considering what we've received from *your* mayor, that's all we're willing to do at the present time." She turned to me and said, "Can I help you?"

I said, "Gosh, I hope so. I've got the day off and want to violate some ethics."

Trace didn't bat an eye. "You're here for a reason?" she asked. "Or just amusing yourself?"

"Sorry, I'm here for Ms. Chilcoate." I turned to her and said, "Your office directed me here. I'm looking for an old friend of yours named Bobbie Jackson."

"Just a minute." Chilcoate turned back to Trace. "Ms. Trace, I know the District won't make any difference to the congressman's run at the Senate, but Delegate Armstrong needs his help now."

I looked at Azalea Trace. She was looking at me. Without taking her eyes from mine she said, "I can't do a thing until the next subcommittee meeting." She turned abruptly and hurried back to her office.

Chilcoate's eyes narrowed as she watched Trace's backside. Then she turned and looked at me. "I haven't seen or talked to Bobbie for ten years."

And then she walked away.

CHAPTER 8

I spent the better part of an hour waiting in Stephanie Chilcoate's office.

She knew I was there, and she knew that I knew that she knew. But whenever she came out she didn't look at me. No matter, I could wait. That's two things I'm good at, waiting and napping. Of course, napping is a skill you're born with. Waiting I learned as a kid.

Take Juvie Justice, for instance. You're a lot better off waiting until eleven o'clock at night to commit a crime. An adult in D.C., it doesn't matter what time of day you're busted. But if you're a kid, wait until night. Once the clock strikes eleven, all the social workers have gone home, so the cops are stuck with you. And since it's nearing the end of their shift as well, they're much more likely to let you walk.

I had been counting on this when I was brought in for ripping off the Metro fare-card machines. I figured I'd be in custody for an hour, then meet up with God for my share of the take. I was thinking 50 percent wasn't enough. Maybe 60. The Hispanic cop who was processing me wanted to ditch me, I could tell. I was making him uncomfortable. Good. Maybe he'd never processed a kid before.

"What's your name, son?"

Instead of answering him, I grabbed a pencil off his desk and some paper.

"What're you doin', kid?"

"Writing down your badge number."

"My—what for?"

" 'Cause you've blown the case. Sloppy procedure." I wasn't sure what that meant, but I'd once heard a cop chew out another over it, and it had sounded good.

"Sloppy?"

"You haven't charged me with anything."

"Um, you're a minor, I don't think I have to."

"Oh, yeah, you do. And you haven't Mirandized me, either. Who's your supervisor?" He began to look upset. Maybe I should ask God for 70 percent after all.

"Jesus, kid, just tell me your fucking name."

"Swearing at a minor." I scribbled as an older, black detective walked past.

"Who's the little terrorist, Lopez?"

The cop straightened in his chair and said, "He won't give his name, Lieutenant Davies."

"Who brought him in?" The lieutenant picked up my paperwork and looked it over.

"Uh, Officers Gidney and Willis, sir."

"Okay." He squatted down to my eye level. He had a seasoned look to him. A bushy black mustache under calm brown eyes that had seen it all. "What's your name, son?"

"Donald Duck." I wasn't about to admit that I had no idea.

"Yeah. Well, we're not putting that on the report, the captain would ream us out." He tapped the report with a thick forefinger. "You like the name Willis Gidney?"

"I hate it."

"Well, it's better than Donald Duck, so you're stuck with it. Unless you want to tell me your real name."

I didn't say anything.

"Okay, Willis. Where do you live?"

"I can't remember."

He nodded. "We'll find a place for you until you do." He made some notes and handed the report back to Lopez. That's how a cop named Davies opened the door for me, sending me on my odyssey through the D.C. Department of Corrections. Sometimes it seems like my life has been a series of doors opening and closing.

Just then another door opened nearby. Stephanie Chilcoate came out for a moment and pretended to notice me with an are-you-still-here? kind of expression.

I stood. "Ms. Chilcoate, I'm sorry you and Ms. Trace had a disagreement, but I'm not going away till you speak with me."

"You'll have a long wait."

"I'm used to long waits. I like them. Did you know it took my mother twelve months to carry me to term? It nearly ruined her. She said next time she'd rather give birth to an elephant."

I saw a smile flicker. She said, "I really don't know why I should help you. And your little joke with Ayzie was very ill timed."

"I'm sorry, but McHugh reminds me of a used-car dealer."

Chilcoate crossed her arms. "Don't underestimate him. The politicians who thought he was some kind of hick have either defected to his side or lost their places in office."

"I heard the ethics probe will hurt his chances."

She smiled without humor. "The probe will probably come to nothing but a slap on the wrist. It'll probably help him with his voters down South, they love to rally around an underdog, even one who may have links to organized crime. But that doesn't explain why you're here."

"Look, Ms. Chilcoate, you have no reason to help me. But you might want to help an old friend—Bobbie."

She thought about it, shrugged, and took me back to her office. It was a windowless room, slightly larger than God's cardboard box, with just enough space to sit down. "So you're a private detective. I thought they were shady old guys with beer guts."

"I'm the newer model. Smart, sexy, and winsome."

"And big enough to stop a runaway truck. What's your connection to Bobbie?"

"I'm just helping a friend find her."

"You know, even if I wanted to help you, I have no idea where Bobbie might be."

"Let's start at the beginning. What can you tell me about her?"

"Well. Let's see. Bobbie was smart, did well in all those classes the rest of us struggled with. She was good at English and science. Math, she got As in math. She was a careful person, always, I don't know, cautious. If there was a party or something, she'd have a good time, but part of her was always a bit detached, always watching from the outside, you know?"

I nodded. "Any boyfriends?"

She thought for a moment. "I don't remember her having one. Like I said, she was always cautious. But I could be wrong."

"Did you have any mutual friends?"

"Can't think of any." We sat in silence for a moment. Outside, I heard phones ringing and faxes coming in and heels against the marble hallway.

"Would you have a picture of Bobbie?"

"No. Wait a sec—" She rose and went to the bottom of her

bookshelf, where larger-format books leaned against one another. Out came a maroon book with a large CHS on the cover. I stood next to her while she went through the pages, talking about the kids she knew. Something happened to me, looking at her yearbook. I began to feel jealous. Of her, her high school friends. Her history.

I could picture little Stephanie skipping home after school, having a snack with Mom, doing her homework when her dad came home. I wanted to grab the book from her and fling it out an open window. Or, better still, a closed one.

Me, I never got to high school, though I've always been a reader. I'd taken an equivalency test and gotten into college, but it hadn't worked out and I'd stopped after a year.

Chilcoate stopped at the page with Bobbie's picture. A dark-skinned girl looked back at me. I didn't see a resemblance to Steps Jackson, but that didn't mean anything. What I saw was a child. All the kids in the book looked like children to me, but there was something about Bobbie's face that seemed earnest and vulnerable.

"May I borrow this?" I asked. "I'd like to make copies of her picture."

"Well, so long as I get it back."

I held up my fingers in the Boy Scout pledge. "Promise." I handed her a business card with the slogan, "I cheat the other guy and pass the savings on to you." After she took the card I asked, "Of the people in this yearbook, who were Bobbie's closest friends?"

"I just remember this one guy, BG. He was, you know, this total nerd. A science nerd."

Flipping back through the book, I found a picture of a boy

named Buford Goodwin. Buford? Maybe his parents hated him. This kid looked pale and his hair was slicked back and shiny. His horn-rimmed glasses threw enormous shadows across his eyes. And his eyes had a strange look to them, the left eye was staring straight at the camera, but the other one was looking away, off and toward the right. As if part of him were there and part weren't. His teeth were slightly bucked, and acne had pitted his face. His interests included biology, chemistry, debate. He looked apologetic, as though his violin lesson had run over and he'd shown up late to chess club.

"Yes, that's BG."

"Was he Bobbie's boyfriend?"

"No, they were friends, classmates. But that's all. I really don't think Bobbie had anyone special. She kind of kept to herself."

"Would you have Goodwin's address or phone number?"

"God, no. I haven't really kept in touch with my classmates."

"Why not?"

"Have *you* kept in touch with your high school classmates, Mr. Gidney?"

Most of my "classmates" were dead or in jail. "Thanks for your time, Ms. Chilcoate."

I was nearly out the door when she said, "May I ask who you're helping find Bobbie?"

I didn't see any harm in answering her. "Someone who hasn't seen her in a long time. Her father."

Stephanie Chilcoate stared at me. "But, Mr. Gidney, that's impossible."

"Why?"

"Because Bobbie's father died before she graduated high school."

CHAPTER 9

With Chilcoate's yearbook under my arm, I returned to the Capitol Hill police lot in time to see a D.C. tow truck remove the unmarked police cruiser from which I had removed the cardboard POLICE slip. I really had intended to return it, but now it might raise a few eyebrows if I did. Oh well. I could make much better use of the POLICE slip than they could. As I drove away I called Steps at the Willard Hotel.

"Willis, what's the word?"

"I've talked with someone who was friends with Bobbie at Cardozo High."

"Bobbie? Oh, that's her name?"

"According to Hancock. I've got a picture of her I'd like to show you."

"Quick work. You are fabulous, man."

"Well, maybe she's your daughter, maybe not." I told him what Chilcoate had said, about Bobbie saying her father was dead.

"Well, shit. That doesn't mean anything. Maybe she was mad at me for not being around, so she said I was dead."

"Maybe. When's your first set tonight?"

"Nine."

"Okay, I'll come by with the picture."

I saw that I had three voice mails. The first message came from Clavus. "Hey, Willis, I figured a way of searching our database. We got a lot of Jacksons for the years you specified, but no baby girl with first name Bobbie, or Roberta. As near as I can tell, there was no Bobbie or Roberta Jackson born in Washington during that period. I'd say that if I could be of further assistance, please call me back during business hours, but you know to do that anyway."

Meaning that my bribe money was used up.

The second caller did a superb imitation of Jerry Lewis as the Nutty Professor: "Uhhhh, Mr. Gidney? This is Seth? From, uhhhh, Pencil's Neck? Your computer's been fixed and the wireless link is working, but it's been like sitting here? Like forever, ready for you to pick up?" He left the address.

My computer was at home, taking up desk space, thanks just the same. Which meant that this one was Karla's, a leftover from when we split. Great.

The last call came from Haggler. "Willis, I have a prelim on Bobbie Jackson. No criminal record. Nothing from DMV. Too late in the day for the banks, I should get something tomorrow. Nothing from Verizon. Checked utilities and found a Pepco bill in her name at 427 Seventh Street Northeast. Call me."

The address was the same building in Shaw where I had interrupted Dante's pas de deux. I called Haggler's precinct and he came on after a minute.

"Hey, Willis."

"What's up, Emil?"

"Pepco turned up something that's a little strange on Jackson's electric bill."

"How do you mean? Like inconsistent?"

"No, that's typical. Town like D.C., people have gas heat in the winter, then run A/C all summer. The bill goes up. No, this bill was normal, then in winter it skyrockets to seven, eight hundred dollars a month."

"Does it say what apartment she was in?"

"Number eight."

That was the one with the ceiling holes and beefed-up electric panel.

"Seems like a lot," I said.

"Yeah, you know that ain't right for an apartment in Shaw. A tanning salon, maybe. 'Cept there ain't no tanning salons in Shaw." He laughed. "Then she ordered a cut-off, May twelfth. But she didn't leave no forwarding address, if that's what you're thinking."

"How'd you know to ask for the amounts?"

He chuckled. "Shit, how long you think I been doing this?"

I pulled over on Seventh, parking near what had once been the Lansbergh building and was now expensive condos. The meter was missing its lower half. I walked down to E Street to Pencil's Neck—a computer geek's dream come true. Inside, dark cherry paneling reflected warm halogen track lights. Racks upon racks of the latest magazines about computers. And an espresso bar the size of Congress but with less hot air.

Men and women draped themselves over wrought iron chairs, speaking the poetry of programming code. Two or three male customers were getting pretty steamed up about cryptology and freedom of speech. One of them got so angry that he actually sloshed coffee over the brim of his cup. Exciting times.

Past them were aisles and aisles of computer gear, and finally the repair desk, where I paid $164.78 for the privilege of liberating Karla's laptop. Maybe I could use it as a doorstop. On my way up front I saw a young woman seated at a workstation with a CD-ROM that boasted more than 200 million phone numbers.

I gave her a smile. "Hi, do you work here?"

45

"Sure. Need some help?"

"This phone-book program, does it include Maryland, Virginia, and D.C.?"

"Yeah, the guys who wrote the program have their business here, so the listings for this region are pretty good. But it's got phone numbers from all fifty states."

Hard to place her age, but I'd guess late twenties to early thirties, with coffee-colored skin and large eyes. I couldn't quite figure out what shade of blue they were. Blue green? She wore her hair in dreads, some black and others bleached a very light brown. She had a small silver ring in her left nostril, and smile lines running down to the corners of her mouth. Her shirt was a faded purple, left untucked over baggy gray cotton pants. It gave her body a dumpy, shapeless quality.

"Can you help me find a number?"

"I can try." She turned to the screen and I leaned over her shoulder.

"Bobbie Jackson."

"Well, you just enter the last name of who you're looking for. Like this." She typed faster than I could follow. The screen filled with Jacksons and she scrolled down to the Bs.

"Too bad, I don't see it." She turned to me. "Is that your name?"

"No, I'm Val Lewton."

She squinched up her nose at me. "Oh, right. And I suppose you're like here to direct the sequel to I Walked with a Zombie."

A fellow film buff. "Yeah. But instead of adapting Jane Eyre, I'm using the life story of Bill Gates. Can I try that?"

"Sure." She let me sit down.

"Can you search on a first name, too?"

"Uh-huh. Like this." It was her turn to lean next to me. Her hair smelled of sandalwood. She turned and her face was a few inches from mine. "What first name?" As though asking me an intimate question.

My throat had gone dry. I managed to say, "Colette."

"Nice name." She typed and again the screen filled with names.

"All these people live around here?"

"Oh, this is the entire United States. You wanted Maryland, D.C., and Virginia, right?" A few more keystrokes and only three names were left. "There. Just the local Colettes."

"Can you print that out for me?"

"Sure." Another lightning keystroke, and a nearby printer spit a sheet of paper at me. She handed me the paper and walked away, saying, "Let me know if you need any help."

For the next half hour I used my phone and the computer. The first Colette sounded to be twelve, but I guessed she was probably close to twenty. The next Colette answered the phone with a French accent as thick as a wheel of brie. I tried ordering a snail sandwich to go and she hung up on me.

The third Colette's number was answered by yet another woman with a French accent. I thought about getting the jump on her by hanging up first. Instead, I asked if she was Ms. Colette Andrews. She told me to wait and in a moment I heard a strong, no-nonsense voice tell me she was Colette Andrews.

"Ms. Andrews, this is Federal Express. Did you send a package to Duluth recently?" A hell of a lot more clever than asking if her refrigerator was running.

"No, I'm sorry." Then she hung up.

Along with their phone number, the computer had printed

Vance and Colette Andrews's address on Foxhall Road NW. I kept the printout.

Now I started scanning the CD-ROM for Buford Goodwins. About two million Goodwins, but none with the first name Buford. I felt happy for them. I did find twelve listings with first initial B. I called them all, but not a Buford was to be found.

Maybe Bobbie had married and for some reason used her maiden name for the Pepco bill? If she had a phone, it could be listed in her husband's name. Or maybe Bobbie had divorced and kept the phone in her married name? I tried not to think about it.

Instead, I thought about what Chilcoate had said. Assuming she was telling the truth, why would Bobbie tell Chilcoate her father was dead, then tell Hancock that her father was a jazz musician named Steps Jackson?

I smelled sandalwood. Standing next to me was the shapeless young woman.

"Have any luck?"

"Hard to say." I smiled and got up, collecting Karla's stuff.

"Well . . ." She let the word hang in the air, smiling at me. "I hope you find who you're looking for."

"Thanks. And thanks for your help."

"Anytime."

As I pulled away from the curb my phone started chirping.

"Willis, you're still coming over tonight, aren't you?"

"Hey, Jan. Yeah, things are a little crazy just now—"

"Willis—"

"—So I don't think tonight would be good."

"—That's what you said last time."

"I know."

It's always nice to hear a friend's voice, but I wasn't about to admit I'd forgotten our dinner date. In the background I could hear Emily, Jan's four-year-old, tearing around the house. The racket I heard made me feel adrift, a ghost tethered to Jan by a wireless link.

"I'll try to come by later, okay? Before Em's bedtime. I bought her a bath toy." I had purchased it last week and really wanted to unload it. People might get the wrong idea if they knew I carried a bright green plastic frog in my pocket.

Jan cursed me in a friendly way and hung up. Before I had a chance to stow my phone, it rang again. I answered and heard a guy say, "Yeah, this is Varga." His voice had a rough edge, as though it had been a long time since the drinks at lunch.

"How can I help you?"

The voice took on a friendlier tone. "Yeah, you got a minute? Are you familiar with Kerberos?" I said I was. "So, you got a few moments to meet today? You know our building in Georgetown? We'd like to discuss something with you that would be to our mutual benefit."

"You're making me curious."

"Good. When can you get here?"

"I'm practically sitting across the desk from you," I told him, and pointed my car toward K Street.

CHAPTER 10

I parked in the cavernous shade beneath the Whitehurst Freeway. The streets were hot and dusty, filled with tourists and jog-
gers and Georgetown University students.

The Kerberos building was brick. So were the sidewalks and
planters and stairs leading up to the glass doors. The top three
floors had a brick overhang, jutting out over the Potomac River,
which was something of an architectural triumph. At least that's
what the newspapers said when the building opened.

The glass doors swung open, then whispered shut behind me,
hushing the dusty heat and noise from outside. In front was a
horseshoe-shaped desk of brick. Three little pigs in black uniforms answered phones, made notes on clipboards, and looked at
TV monitors. They didn't have as many cameras as CNN.

As I drew near, I saw they were equipped with the standard
Glock 9-mms, plus extra clips and handcuffs and night sticks.
From a distance they looked like D.C. cops. Their badges looked
authentic too, until you got close enough to see the word
Kerberos.

One of them inspected me. "Ah, Mr. Gidney. Here to see Mr.
Varga. Sign in here, please, then take the elevator on the left to
the third floor."

I had no idea how he knew who I was, but I didn't like it. At
the best of times I feel distrust toward large organizations. Right
now alarms were going off in my head. But I had made the trip
here and I was curious, I admit it. So I signed in and rode the

elevator. Another black uniform was waiting for me. He had me sign a clipboard to show that I had, in fact, taken the elevator to this floor. Then he told me to walk this way. Some straight lines aren't worth a response. I shrugged and walked that way.

Heavy wooden doors with names in raised silver letters lined the hallway. No sounds came from behind those doors. The hidden lighting was so muted that we had no shadows. We drifted down the carpeted hallway like ghosts until we came to the office of Security Chief Frank Varga. The uniform gave a quiet knock on the door, opened it. I walked in.

Sheets of plate glass angled from floor to ceiling. The air beyond the glass was hazy in the Washington heat, obscuring the view. I could barely see the outline of the Washington Monument. Without that to guide me, I would've guessed we were on another planet.

"Have a seat, Gidney."

I had to walk twenty feet over a thick beige carpet to Varga's desk. It looked like it was made of stainless steel. The desktop was clear of papers, pens, pictures, and phones. Centered in front of Varga was a single file folder. In front of the desk were two identical chairs of steel and black leather. Varga extended his hand to me without getting up. I had to lean over to take it, off-balance. His hand was dry and hard. He gripped my hand and used it to steer me into the chair on the left.

Varga looked like he had once been a powerhouse. Now he was old but solid. He had thick gray hair brushed back from his forehead. His hairline ran straight across his forehead, then straight down both sides, giving his face a blunt, squared-off look. He had a fleshy nose networked with red veins, and a block of concrete for a chin.

A door to the left opened. Two men came in, neither wearing

a black uniform. The first was heavyset with mean little eyes surrounded by scar tissue, above a nose that had been broken and set to the right. His hair was dark and cut short. He wore black jeans and an untucked gray polo shirt over a hard, round belly. He had trouble standing still.

"This is Westy." Varga nodded toward the agitated man. Westy scowled at me, cracking the knuckles of each hand, shifting his weight from foot to foot. I could have taken him with a ball of yarn.

"And Mal."

Mal was trouble. He was a foot shorter than Westy, skinny, with a pale, weasel face. The creepy part was his eyes, green serpent eyes that never blinked, like a camera that would never shut off. His blond hair looked bronzed and was permed into tight curls all the same size, like a cap.

Varga turned back to me. "Today's my kid's birthday, Gidney. He's sixteen. Great kid, got terrible acne all over his face. I'm buying him a guitar. He's got one already, a Gibson Les Paul Goldtop, cost me fifteen hundred bucks. Which is a hell of a lot, you ask me. But he's the only kid I got, you know? So I'm getting him a Fender, uh, a Stratocaster. You know guitars?" For a moment he actually seemed interested in what I'd say.

"Hendrix played a Stratocaster."

He looked a little disappointed. "Yeah, well, whatever. Point is, he's gonna be knocked out when he sees it. It's a pre-CBS model, made in 1962, so it costs more. Six grand, to be exact. Today's a big day for him. And me. So guess where the last place on earth is that I wanna be?"

I waited.

"It's right here talking to you. So let's get down to it. We," and here he made a gesture that took in the office, himself,

Westy, and Mal, "we are the fucking professionals in the security business, and I'll tell you why." He held up his index finger. "Firstly, we protect shipments of valuables and cash."

"I don't think *firstly* is a real word," I said.

"Shut the fuck up," Westy said, rocking on the balls of his feet.

"Second," and here Varga touched—what else?—his second finger, "we supply bodyguard services to visiting dignitaries, important members of Congress, like that. You unnerstand what I'm saying?"

I rubbed my chin. "Wow, you really put a guy on the spot, don't you? Let's see. Yeah, I think so. That's two things. If you get past ten, do you take off your shoes?"

Westy said, "Keep it up, fat boy."

Varga said, "We know all about you, Gidney, we got computers to investigate people, even losers like you. You're a half-assed private eye. And being a half-assed private eye, you waltz right into Jason McHugh's office. We own Targus, those were our guys you breezed past."

"I was working. What's the problem?"

"The fucking problem is that some of these congressmen need a little help seeing why extra security is important. Some of them don't think they need it, since there's, what?" He turned to Mal. "Ten different police jurisdictions here?"

"More like twenty," Mal said, giving me the no-blink look.

"Ten, that's ten." Westy cracked his knuckles.

"Has Westy skipped his meds?" I asked.

Westy said, "Let me stomp him, Mr. Varga."

Varga ignored him. "What we don't need is some loser showing up at Jason McHugh's office asking questions. Our guys heard you talking to that D.C. bitch Chilcoate." He sat forward in his chair, his hands flat on his desktop. He gave me the hard look and said, slowly and with emphasis, "You are annoying me, Gidney. Don't go there again." He leaned back in his chair. "In fact, stay off the Hill from now on."

"Okay if I cut my nails once in a while?"

"Cut your fucking throat, for all I care. Just stay away from McHugh and his staff."

"I can help with that." Mal spoke quietly, as though reminding Varga of his presence. Varga looked at Mal for a full ten seconds. The look was full of curiosity, tempered by distaste. Then Varga shook his head. Mal looked down, pouting, which made Varga smile.

I looked from Mal to Varga. "'Mutually beneficial,' you said." I held up my palms. "So far I don't feel like I'm benefitting at all."

"By us letting you walk out of here, on your own two feet, that's how you benefit." Varga tapped the file folder with a blunt finger. "Gidney, you're a fuck-up. You couldn't hack college, you can't keep a job. Somehow you made it through the police academy but couldn't cut it as a cop. I read something here, you killed a cop when you were a kid? Is that right?"

He meant Shad. I felt the blood rush to my face. "No," I told him, "it isn't."

"Yeah. Well, I've said my piece." Varga sat back.

"Here's mine. I'm in business, too. I try to get along with people. But I'm willing to make an exception. So I'm telling you now, stay out of *my* way. Or I'll bring the three of you down."

Westy said, "That's it," lunging toward me, his right fist whistling at my head.

I stepped inside the punch and slammed the heel of my left hand into the bridge of his nose. He staggered back as blood gushed down the front of his shirt and onto the carpet. He saw the blood, then roared and rushed me. I let him take a step, then snap-kicked him in the head. His eyes rolled up as he dropped.

Breathing hard, still in my fighter's stance, I looked up. First at Varga, then at Mal. Varga was frozen, Mal's eyes were bright. My breathing was the only sound in the room. I backed to the door. "You'll have to do better than Westy. Or get a different-color carpet."

As I left I could have sworn I heard Mal giggle.

CHAPTER 11

Outside Varga's office, I tried to steady my heartbeat. My hands had been shaking so bad, I couldn't hit the Down button on the elevator. A passing secretary had to help me. Now, walking back to my car, I wondered why I'd been showboating with that high kick into Westy's nose. I could have kicked him in the kneecap and brought him down just as easy. But after Varga's crack about Shadrack Davies, I'd been pissed off and not thinking clearly.

About fifty feet from my car, I brushed past two Kerberos employees in black uniforms on their way to headquarters. They didn't seem to notice me, which was good. I'd had enough exercise for one day.

Driving to Colette Andrews's house, I stopped at a Kinko's to copy Bobbie's picture from the yearbook. The kid managing the shop took time out from his comic book to set me up, then

I watched as copy after copy of Bobbie's face slid past, looking not as much like a high school photo as a mug shot. D.C. Juvie Justice took Polaroids of us whenever we got checked into a new facility. Like the first one they took of me. A classic. My first day at Junior Village.

Junior Village was designed like an army barracks, but without the frills. Bunk beds, fluorescent tubes flickering behind wire mesh, and that dysentery-green color on the walls that shows up at only the very best institutions.

The District owned this asylum for lost boys, but placed it just outside Columbia, Maryland. We were far away from families, lawyers, courts, and judges. When we needed to go to D.C., we were transported by bus, giving us lots of escape routes. At any time, about a fifth of our merry band had gone missing. The adults running the place barely knew we were gone.

This was a system I grew to love.

The five fenced-in barracks were built to house 120 kids. The 297 children I joined were a noisy group. Some were still in diapers at age six. The older ones, up to age fourteen, were potty-trained, but that was probably the only training they would ever have. Most kids, like myself, had no parents. Others had parents who neglected them or abused them or couldn't control them. We were a diverse, sprightly lot.

Some of us were mentally ill, like Mike Calhoun, who reportedly had bitten the nose off an older kid who'd bothered him. Some were born with drug addictions, like Forty-watt Williams, who spent most of his day in the rec room watching TV—the back of it, not the front. Some said Forty-watt wasn't very bright.

The remaining group were delinquents who could cheat, steal, and lie with straight faces. Naturally, I aspired to be included in this third group. Their undisputed king was a thirteen-year-old named Eddie Vermeer. If you needed or wanted something—and could pay—the guy to see was Eddie Vermeer.

The bleeding hearts among you might decry our deprivations, which included education, affection, attention, wealth, values, and role models. But that's nit-picking, isn't it? I would point to the rich collective experience we shared. Junior Village was a laboratory of sociopathic behavior, a celebration of thievery and duplicity that would have made Fagin's gang look like Girl Scouts.

The D.C. judges who had placed us there tagged us as PINS. Persons In Need of Supervision. And I seem to recall a small number of bewildered adults among us. They were the cream of the public-servant crop, if you thought the cream consisted of slow-witted, dishonest, monosyllabic cretins who couldn't have supervised water down a drain.

This suited me perfectly. I took a good look around, deciding where the market demand was, then took steps to fill it. Common sense told me to start small. Cigarettes were always in demand, as were comic books, gum, and candy. If I were a kid there today, and Junior Village hadn't been closed by a court order, I'm sure guns would top the list.

I decided on comic books as a starting point. First, they could be reused. Second, I was something of a connoisseur, being a voracious reader of this fine illustrated literature. And third, I knew where I could get my hands on them. Just outside the fenced-in perimeter of our little village of barracks and bunk beds lived the warden of Junior Village and his family. I can't for the life of me remember the warden's name. His title probably wasn't warden, but that's how we thought of him. His two children, Angela and Mobley, I remember well. I often spotted them through the Cyclone fence that separated our two worlds.

Mobley was a whale of a boy who howled at the slightest bruise or tumble. What interested me was his extensive collection of Marvel and DC comics. Often I'd see him, beached in the shade of his back porch, poring over his collection with a Baby Ruth in one hand and a Coke in the other.

His older sister, Angela, was a dark-haired vixen of sixteen who was the uncontested fantasy girl for all of us and the start of a number of fistfights among a few of us. No one had ever spoken to her. She liked to parade past us in the most revealing outfits, seemingly unaware of the sensation she caused. Her current fistfight champion was a hulking fifteen-year-old named Greg Howler, or Greg the Keg as he was known. When the supervisors passed out Thorazine, the Keg was always first in line, which helped explain the nervous tics that exploded across his face.

Now, there was no way I could get to Mobley. He was terrified of the monsters in his father's zoo. Angela was different. She seemed fascinated with us PINS, the way children are fascinated by ants before crushing them.

On a particularly hot summer day I played near enough to the fence to speak with her, but not so close as to draw attention to myself. Right on schedule, she came striding by in a halter top and white shorts. I leaned close to the fence and said, "You coming to the movies this Friday?"

She stopped and turned, her eyes half closed and her chin raised. A smoky look of lust and contempt. I wondered how many hours she had practiced that look in the mirror. "What movies?" she said. I noticed she spoke out of the side of her mouth. Perhaps she had mentally placed a cigarette on the opposite side. Planning for the future.

"First Friday of every month we get movies, sometimes good ones. But I guess you couldn't come to see them, huh?" I kept my eyes wide and innocent, the picture of guileless youth. She wasn't the only one who practiced.

"What movies?" she asked again. I guess snappy dialogue wasn't her strong suit.

"Well, this month it's *The Godfather: Part II*." I had taken to reading *The Washington Post*, they had a great funnies section, and I had seen the ad for this movie in the style section.

She looked at me with disdain. "That's a *new* movie, you little creep. They're not gonna show it to a buncha morons like you."

I didn't understand why we couldn't see a new movie inside Junior Village, but I accepted her statement at face value and improvised. "Sure. But Marlon Brando's great-nephew is stuck here, so Brando arranged for the screening." I realized as the words tumbled out that I might have stretched the truth danger-ously tight. But I kept my gaze steady and true.

I could see that Angela was hooked. "Whadda load a crap," she said, hands on hips. She looked left and right, then back at me. "So whatzit cost to get in?" I remember looking past her at brother Mobley and his comic books.

The kid who managed Kinko's made a ridiculous noise, a parody of a person clearing his throat. I looked down to see that my cop-ies were finished. Obviously I was keeping this guy from catching up on the latest issue of *The Dark Knight*. As the kid took my money I tilted my head, amazed to see what DC was charging these days. Holy markup, Batman!

Then I drove to the Georgetown library and spent two hours scrolling through *The Post*'s database. My hard work was rewarded by some astounding discoveries: Vance and Colette Andrews were a rich interracial couple. They traveled. They went to art-gallery openings. They played golf. They gave to charities and attended inaugural balls. My back hurt. I stood and stretched, trying to get a picture of who these people were and coming up blank.

So I drove west on Reservoir Road, then wound around the curving slopes of Foxhall Road. Mansions on the right and a country club on the left swept past until I approached a wrought-iron gate with the name Andrews in twisted metal that looked like script. I turned in from the flow of traffic onto a driveway of light-colored sand and pebbles. The Andrewses lived in the kind of house you'd see in the movies, the establishing shot of some wealthy hero's home. Or wealthy villain's. But they'd never film *this* house—the Andrewses didn't seem to need the money.

In the wide, grassy lawn someone had placed a tiny corral. A sign above it said WELCOME BACK, ANDREWS!! Inside the corral were two lambs with collars bearing the names Colette and Vance. I hoped this was a joke, I'm lousy at questioning quadrupeds.

I parked. The driveway led to a front door that would have stopped a horde of Visigoths. It was tall and massive and gleaming with years of oil. Probably had a team of door oilers come through once a month. A door knocker in the shape of a lion's head rested in the middle. I knocked. A minute later the door was opened by a young white girl in an honest-to-God maid's uniform. Maybe they were filming a sitcom inside.

Speaking with the same French accent she'd had when I'd

phoned an hour before, she said, "I'm sorry, but Mr. Andrews is at State and Mrs. Andrews does not see anyone without an appointment."

"Of course. But would you please tell Mrs. Andrews I'm from Perth Gallery?" According to *The Post*, this was a favorite of hers. "I need to speak with her regarding a recent acquisition in which she had expressed an interest."

In a minute the maid came back and asked me to walk this way. Today was really my day to resist temptation. I followed her without reply.

As soon as I entered the house, I started casing it. It doesn't mean anything, I had no plans to rob the Andrewses, it's just kind of automatic with me. As a kid in a new foster home, I'd always look to see how I'd escape and what I'd take with me. My version of *Name That Tune*, like, I can break out of this foster home in two minutes. Later, as I grew more adept at stealing, I'd figure how long it would take me to break *into* a place. I'd spotted the locks and alarm system coming in. I figured I could get into the Andrews place in fifteen minutes, tops.

We went down a dark, carpeted hallway of six-foot-high portraits in gilded frames, past a case of tennis trophies, and into a bright room with an enormous window made up of two thousand diamond-shaped pieces of glass held in place by strips of lead. The window looked out onto a backyard the size of Kenya. Everything was perfect. Sunlight poured through, as though delivered precisely on schedule.

The maid closed the door. Walnut-paneled walls with ivory inlay gave the room a warm feel. A Steinway baby grand looked lonely in the corner, hoping someone would play it. The overstuffed couches and chairs in bright primary colors should have looked too modern for this room, but somehow it all worked together. Several paintings by different artists divided the wall space, three by someone named Delling. Across the room, in a space all by itself, a little watercolor hung crookedly. I was straightening the frame when Colette Andrews walked in.

She moved with an athletic grace. Her skin, nearly the color of the walnut panels, felt warm and smooth as she gave me her hand. I wondered if it was as soft as Steps remembered it. Her eyes were brown, the whites very clear. Her voice confirmed what I had guessed about her age, but that and the fine lines near her eyes were the only giveaways. Her hair was jet black. From a few feet away you'd guess she was in her late twenties.

"Pleased to meet you, Mister . . ."

"Gidney."

We shook hands and turned so that we both faced the picture. "Nice, isn't it?" She seemed to radiate pleasure, just looking at it. I watched her face, wondering what it must be like to live like this.

I said, "Watercolor seems to have fallen out of favor with our artists these days. And abstract watercolor at that, it's a rare treat."

"It's representational." She looked at me with an amused challenge in her eyes.

"Sorry, I couldn't even guess."

"It's a rock quarry." She pointed. "There's the edge of the cliff, and trees growing on top and a little water reflecting the sky at the bottom."

I nodded. "It's lovely. Who painted it?"

"Cézanne."

I did my Stanley Kowalski voice. "Oh, yeah, I hearda him."

She laughed. "I was only just aware of him when my father gave it to me."

From what Steps had said, I couldn't picture a club owner like Alvin Middleton as a collector of Cézannes. "When was this?"

"My freshman year at Sarah Lawrence. I had it hanging in my dorm room."

I looked at the painting again. "Awfully darn nice of old Dad."

"Oh, he didn't really want it. See, there's a small bit of water damage in the upper right corner." She made a gesture with her palm up, very noblesse oblige. "Won't you sit down?" She sat near the end of a bright magenta couch. I took the purple armchair. "Now, what's this mysterious acquisition Byron sent you over to discuss with me?"

"It's a portrait of a jazz musician, a sax player." I hoped for a reaction, but she looked as placid as ever. I added, "His name is Steps Jackson."

"And?" Her lack of reaction could have made a less stalwart detective doubt his reason for being there.

I said, "And it's by Delling."

"Funny," she said in a way that wasn't funny at all. "I talk with Chris Delling all the time, and he's never mentioned it."

"Maybe it slipped his mind."

She stood. "And now I recognize your voice; you called earlier today. Some bullshit about a package. You're a fraud. I think you'd better leave."

"One more thing," I said, reaching into my pocket and taking out Bobbie's picture. "Would you tell me what you think of this?"

I handed her the picture. She looked at it. She blinked. Maybe that was a big reaction for her. Then she handed the picture back to me. "So?"

"She looks just like you, Mrs. Andrews."

"I'm sorry, Mr.—Gidney, is it? You're asking the wrong person, and you're in the wrong place."

"She's your daughter, isn't she?"

"Will you leave, or do I phone the police? We get very good service here."

"Go ahead, phone them. That's a nice watercolor you've got, I liked the story behind it, too. But we both know your father didn't hand out Cézannes. And I think Bobbie's your daughter."

Colette's face mottled. "You're a dirty, stupid man doing a dirty, stupid job. You can tell your employer I said so."

"Why won't you help us? Steps only wants to see her, talk to her."

For a moment her anger faltered, and in that moment fear flashed in her eyes like summer lightning. "The only thing I'll help with is swearing out a complaint if you don't leave this instant." She wasn't quite shouting. The strain showed in her face, the tightness around her mouth. She picked up the phone.

"All right, Mrs. Andrews, I'm going." I put a business card on her table and some menace in my voice. "But I'll be back. Maybe I'll bring Bobbie's high school friend with me. Stephanie Chilcoate remembers you very well. Maybe she can help jog your memory."

I put the photo of Bobbie by my card, then slammed the door behind me and stomped down the hall. A moment later I went back and nudged the door a crack. I felt childish doing it, but did it anyway. She still stood there, just as I had left her, looking down at the phone handset but not really seeing it. Slowly she put it down. Then she sat on the bright magenta couch, held her head in her hands, and started to cry.

I closed the door softly and drove away from there.

CHAPTER 12

I drove home thinking about Colette Andrews. On the way I hit a 7-Eleven on Columbia Road for some essentials—corn chips, Twinkies, Cheetos—then drove to my former love shack, a brick row house on Webster Street off Sixteenth. The house where Karla and I had lived formed part of a row of houses, identical to the row across the street. Which in fact were identical to rows of brick houses one street up or down. At the front door I hefted the laptop and snacks and keyed the lock, hoping I was actually on my own doorstep.

Inside, all the lights were on. As was the television, spraying our empty living room with video. I picked my way across the floor so as not to trample Karla's clothing, sidestepping my way into the kitchen, where I put the uneaten junk food in the cupboard. Wedged it in, actually, the cupboard was anything but bare.

I walked back into the living room. I could've switched off the TV, gathered up her shorts, shirts, socks, bras, and shoes, and set them on a chair. I could've rolled up shades, turned off lights, closed windows, and straightened picture frames as I went up the stairs. I didn't.

Everything was just as it had been four months ago—that long?—when she took off. I carried the laptop into what had been her office, a little sunroom off our second-floor bedroom. Like setting cheese in a trap. She'd be back in no time.

Gidney, you insidious devil.

I locked the house and drove away with no clue where I was going. The cross-breeze made it feel a little cooler. Heading down Sixteenth, I saw the sun floating toward the horizon, getting ready for the big plunge. It felt as hot now as it had this morning on the third floor of Bobbie's house in Shaw. I thought about the torn plastic garbage bags. Could she have taped them to the window of the middle room, then pulled the paint off the wall when she took off the bags? Made sense, but what had she been doing? Trying to make the room even hotter? Trying to keep the light out?

I needed another crack at Dante. I couldn't locate Bobbie, and so far he was the only connection I had with her house. I took out the matchbook I had lifted from him. It still read RUSTY'S BAR. I pointed my car that way. By now it was getting on toward eight o'clock. I thought about calling Shelly Russia at home, decided against it, and called Haggler.

"Christ, what now?"

"A quick question. You ever hear of a company named Kerberos, a guy named Varga?"

"So he phoned you? He wanted a reference, he was thinkin' of offerin' you a job."

As a punching bag. "And you told him what?"

"What's to tell? I just confirmed you were the same Willis Gidney he was interested in hirin'. He seemed to know a lot about you already, except for what a pain in the ass you are."

"Now he knows."

Haggler chuckled. "Why am I not surprised?"

"Give him any information?"

"What, am I your agent? 'Cause if I am, you owe me ten percent."

"Ten percent of nothing's still nothing."

He laughed and hung up.

If Varga thought I was muscling in on Kerberos, I could understand why he wanted me to back off. But the real question was, how did Varga know to contact me in the first place?

I spent two hours looking for Dante at Rusty's Bar and at Riverside Roasters. No one admitted to knowing Dante, where he was, or where I could find him. I went to Blockbuster and showed the manager Dante's card, pretending it was mine and that they were charging me for a rental I hadn't made. He went and made a printout for me showing a zero balance. The printout also showed Dante's address, on Morse Street near Brentwood Park. I thanked him and left.

At first I figured to stake out Dante's house, but I was ravenous. Man does not live by Cheetos alone. Then I remembered I was near The Doves, the restaurant where I had proposed to Karla. The food was good there. You might say the romantic atmosphere of The Doves was responsible for Karla saying yes.

When I married her I hadn't had lots of experience with women, which may sound funny to you. But remember, I was in a guys-only setting most of the time. So I was more perplexed by girls than attracted to them.

For instance, I remember hanging with the other guys when they spied a new girl and remarked upon her anatomy. I shouted my full-throated accord. But truthfully, it wasn't until I was seventeen or so that I really admired a woman's backside without the prompting of others.

Take Angela. I was meeting her once a month by the Junior Village fence at eleven o'clock at night. Waiting for her, I had been thinking only of the comic books she would steal from her brother. But when I saw her approach, her dark hair and pale skin in the moonlight, my young man's fancy turned to thoughts of pimping her.

Look, I'm not particularly proud of myself as a kid. I suppose I was trying to be successful, imitating those around me. And I prospered. My comic-book business was taking off, and I had begun branching out into other consumable items. No durable goods, like guns or knives, but one could always dream.

Maybe Angela could help me there, too. She was more gullible than she looked. She hadn't seen a movie yet, but here she was delivering my third payload of brother Mobley's comic books in as many months. Perhaps it was my boyish charm, which I had in abundance. Maybe it was a credit to my growing ability to lie convincingly. I was learning at Junior Village.

My education wasn't limited to lying: I was also learning to pick locks, and to suborn the trustees. I couldn't quite drive a car, but I knew how to hot-wire one. I spent a lot of time fighting. At first I was getting beaten almost every hour. Like a time clock, that's how I'd been getting punched, but I was learning.

As I carried my new load of comics to my barracks, I wondered if Angela had any girlfriends who'd like some extra cash. Something sounded behind me. I turned and Greg the Keg drove his fist into my stomach.

I dropped the comics, put my hands over my stomach. Not smart. The Keg drove an uppercut into my chin, which lifted me off my feet and onto my back. His face erupting in Thorazine-induced nervous tics, he screamed at me, called me a little shit, said Angela was his and he was going to kill me. Two months before I would've panicked, but this was not two months ago. When the Keg rushed me, I drove my foot into his crotch, grabbed his shirt, and flipped him over me and into the wall of our barracks. His back made a pleasing *thwack* as he hit the wall and slid to the ground.

"Not a bad move, kid."

Now I panicked, thinking there were two of them. I scrambled to my feet, fists out, and the same voice laughed. "Take it easy, kid. I'm on your side."

I could taste blood on my mouth and wiped my hand across it. My jaw throbbed. It would hurt for a week. I looked at the Keg, who was lying on his side in the dirt. "You could have helped," I said to the newcomer.

"You didn't need it."

I turned to get a look at him. It was dark, but I could make out a good-looking kid with an easygoing smile. He put a hand on my shoulder. "Come on, I'll buy you a beer."

I've heard that a good con man either has an open, honest face that people just naturally trust, or is the kind of guy you'd want as your friend. Eddie Vermeer was that rare phenomenon, a person with both qualities. I was sitting in his private room on a bed that actually had clean sheets and a box spring under the mattress. He handed me a can of Bud.

"How old are you, kid?"

I shrugged, looking around his room. I couldn't keep the wonder out of my voice. "How'd you land the cool digs?"

He glanced around as if noticing for the first time the difference between his private room and the communal hell the rest of us lived in. "Clean living."

I'd been swigging beer and laughed and beer went up my nose. I thought that was funny, too, and fell over laughing. Eddie watched me. When I recovered, he said, "You got here four months ago." It wasn't a question.

I drank more beer. He shifted in his easy chair, a monstrous green vinyl lounger with the footrest permanently extended. "You've done pretty well, apart from pissing off the Keg." This wasn't a question, either. "It's too bad, in a way."

"What is?"

"That Junior Village is shutting down. Court order. If anyone around here read more than the funnies, they'd know that."

"So?"

He nodded as if coming to a decision. He stood, taking a key ring from his pocket. "I wanna show you something." He walked over to what I had thought was a closet door and unlocked it. He motioned me to take a look inside.

The closet was no closet. It was a second room, nearly as large as Eddie's. There was no furniture inside, only shelves lined with new stereos, TVs, kitchen appliances, power tools, all the stuff we American males dream of. All in boxes, like a department store.

I thought it was the most beautiful sight I had ever seen.

Just as quickly as he had revealed it, Eddie shut and locked the door. He pocketed the keys, saying, "Kid, there's two types of people locked up here. The dumb ones and the smart ones. The dumb ones escape, the cops pick 'em up, and they wind up back here no better off than they were before."

"And the smart ones?"

His smile flashed at me. "The smart ones come and go, quietly. No one knows they've gone. Being here is a great alibi, you know."

"They don't come back empty-handed, I bet."

He grinned. "They don't at that. But everything's about to

change, now that we're all moving. All of that stuff, my, uh, inventory, will have to be moved, too."

I started to see it. "You'll need help."

"I will at that."

I held out my hand. "Say hi to your new partner."

CHAPTER 13

Eddie Vermeer hesitated. "Junior partner, kid. You've got a lot to learn."

"Like what?"

"Well, I've just given you the elements for a con. Figure it out, and we're partners. Ever work a con before?"

That's how I became friends with Eddie Vermeer.

Years later, the night I proposed to Karla at The Doves, I'd found myself thinking of Eddie. All the tables were small, but they'd hung fabric from the ceiling, so that each table was enclosed in soft, swaying walls of cool greens and blues. I could almost feel Eddie's presence nearby—stuck in my memory, a boy who would never grow old, smiling and shaking his head. Marriage—Eddie would think I was a first-class idiot.

As for Captain Shadrack Davies, would he agree? Since Shad was the D.C. cop who'd given me my name and sent me on my odyssey through Junior Village, he'd probably have an opinion, too. And his opinion always had the same basis.

Do the right thing.

I was trying. I'd had several beers that night at The

Doves— that's what Karla told me the next day. But I must've done okay, because a month later she married me.

This time when I parked outside The Doves, I took a clipboard and a baseball cap from the backseat of my car. I entered the foyer. A chinless man with a receding blond hairline and a supercilious expression approached me. Did I have a reservation?

I tapped the clipboard with a ballpoint pen. "Pick up for Esther Claire." A few diners nearby glanced up at me. Esther Claire was the four-hundred-year-old food critic for *The Post*, a woman who scared the pâté out of everyone in the restaurant business. More than a few restaurants had been forced to close after her reviews. If the maître d' had had a chin, it would've quivered. Tiny beads of sweat popped from his forehead.

"Uh, I'm sorry, you're picking up what?"

"An order of perleau? For Ms. Claire? For her review on the best of Capitol Hill?" It drives them crazy when you end your sentences as questions.

"I'm so sorry, but we haven't—" He stopped and turned. "Oh, Richard," he called, his voice as steady as a blind man on roller blades.

A second man appeared, nearly identical to the first except for the tortoiseshell glasses he wore. He smiled and said, "Yes, Davey," his glasses catching the light. He reminded me of a guy I once knew. I wanted to snatch the glasses and twist them in a knot.

"This gentleman is here for Ms. Esther Claire's order of perleau. For her article on the best Washington restaurants," Davey said.

Richard raised his eyebrows. "This is the first I've heard of it."

I put on a big, friendly smile. "No problem, we'll try it next year." I waved the clipboard at them and headed toward the door. I might as well have told them they were to be guillotined at dawn.

"Now, you, you wait just a minute," Richard said, his head jerking and the lights bouncing off his glasses. "Just wait one minute. I'll check in the kitchen."

It was more like eight minutes. But, sitting in my car and washing down the last bit of perleau with some Chardonnay they were kind enough to provide, I decided the wait was worth it.

Maybe I should have asked for a glass when they gave me the bottle of wine. Eddie would have appreciated that. But why push it? Soon I'd go to see Steps at the Willard. For now I leaned my car seat back and felt the warm air come in off the Chesapeake Bay. The sky was the kind of royal blue that comes just after sunset.

I remembered my dream from last night, a dream about fire and children screaming and a man with rimless glasses. I grabbed a warm Coke and tore off the tab, thinking about how Dr Warren E. Waters had entered my young life and nearly destroyed it.

That was the week I had figured out a con. A good one. One that would make Eddie proud of his new Junior Village partner. I turned it over and over in my mind and saw no problems. I kept returning to the same set of facts: we were leaving Junior Village, and Eddie had a lot of merchandise, probably too much to transport.

What I didn't understand was that Eddie was teaching me to think in a way that I'd never thought before. I mean, I knew lots of ways to convince people that I was telling the truth. And I was a practiced rip-off artist. But how the hell do you steal from someone and end the affair with none of them the wiser?

Part of the credit goes to Greg the Keg. Apparently, kicking him in the balls was exactly the sort of move that won his respect. Thorazine was still his drug of choice, since it was free here. In addition to the facial tics and yellowed skin, the Keg also appeared to be developing breasts. I was too polite to mention it. We were splitting a candy bar—one he'd bought from me—and he mentioned wanting to buy a color TV set, and did I happen to know of any at a good price? Because he knew Eddie and I were friends. I nearly said forget it, we'd all be moving soon.

That's when it hit me. I sold the Keg an unspeakably heavy TV out of Eddie's stock. Then I went on a selling spree; discounting all the heavy merchandise. All with Eddie Vermeer's approval, of course. By the week's end, Eddie's problems were solved. Almost all his inventory had been sold. Plus, I had figured out the blow-off, the hardest part of the con. For when we were told we were moving, I acted just as surprised as my peers. So none of them suspected that they had been conned. And since the goods were now theirs, well, it was their lookout how to get their stuff to their new home.

Eddie also showed me the value of reading more than newspaper funnies. It was hard work. I had learned to read on my own, picked up the basics, but I always read the easy stuff. *The Fantastic Four* was the height of my literary appreciation.

Eddie never put me down, and I never told him how inadequate I felt around him. I did want Eddie to know he'd picked the right guy as his partner. So I tried. And felt rewarded by the look on Eddie's face when I told him that when the D.C. courts shut down Junior Village, they also decided to use a private company, Caring Residential Centers, Inc., to manage Bockman's. The president of CRC was a Dr. Warren Waters. The courts felt that a private company working from a profit motive would be better able to handle problem kids like us.

Dr. Waters agreed.

At JV we had heard rumors about Bockman's—the place had a reputation, but I had heard they rewarded the kids for good behavior. The rewards were, of course, a joke. But I thought it a fine sentiment. What I didn't know was that, with the arrival of Dr. Waters, everything would change.

On the last bus ride from Junior Village, there were about forty of us. Eddie Vermeer had worked long and hard persuading our new masters to make him a trusty. Now he rode back and forth, moving his remaining inventory. Finally we reached Bockman's, in Columbia, Maryland. Only twenty minutes away by bus, but light-years away in terms of security. The Cyclone fence was topped with razor wire. As we stepped off the bus we were watched by guards in towers. I had the uneasy feeling that I was an extra in a prison movie.

We piled out of the bus and into the main entrance. The interior was large, drafty, and barren except for one painting. Looming above the entrance was a dark oil portrait of the late Leonard B. Bockman, the Maryland judge whose name graced the institution that was our new home. He had the stringent, puritanical look of his day, a stiff white face above a stiff white collar. His lips were pursed and twisted into what might have been a smile. It wasn't a very nice smile. I wondered if whoever had painted that canvas had been smart enough to collect his fee in advance.

Old Judge Bockman would have been pleased with our new

warden. *The Post* ran articles about the good Dr. Waters and his tough-love method of handling troubled youngsters. Dr. Warren E. Waters didn't hold with the new permissiveness so prevalent in youth institutions. In reporting to the D.C. courts, he told the judges that troubled children needed love, to be sure, but also a firm hand to guide them through life's troubles.

No sooner had we marveled at our new surroundings—exclamations of "what a dump!" and "garbage pit" echoed around me—than our new supervisors arrived. Looking remarkably like our old supervisors, they herded us to assemble in the large room that was also our mess hall, movie theater (they actually had movies here, too bad Angela wasn't among us), and extra barracks, for the time when our numbers increased unexpectedly.

Dr. Warren E. Waters strode to the lectern, put his hands behind his back, and took a full minute looking at us. Except for a thin, dark tonsure, he was bald. His round, rimless spectacles always seemed to reflect the lights. I couldn't see his eyes. It made me think he was stuffed with transistors and relays, not flesh and blood.

"Up until now," Dr. Waters said, "you . . . children have been coddled and cajoled. You've been pampered into good behavior and given rewards for doing the minimum of what's expected of you. In short, you've been made victims of"—and here he made quotation marks in the air—"the 'new permissiveness.'"

His head swiveled to take us in, his thin, bloodless lips a slash across his face. He dropped his hands. "That's over. The previous administration believed in a carrot-and-stick policy. The carrot was ridiculously large, the stick virtually nonexistent. From now on, there is no carrot. Now that I'm here, you'll find there's simply a much bigger stick waiting for you if you step out of line."

He took another full minute, looking us over, waiting for it to sink in. Then he nodded, once, and walked away.

Next to me, Eddie Vermeer muttered, "How to win friends and influence people."

"He's not so much," I said.

"We'll find out, won't we?"

As we filed out, a supervisor tapped me on the shoulder. Along with nine other kids, I went to Waters's office. He stood with his back to us, looking out a large bay window. It was a dark gray day and the window seemed to suck the light out of the room. He turned around.

"You little miscreants have had the run of this place for too long," Dr. Waters said.

"But I just got here," I said.

The supervisor who had led us in was a pimply-faced adult named Heintz. He gripped my elbow, his thumb hitting a nerve so that pain flashed through my arm. "Shut the fuck up, you little shit." Waters nodded his approval of Heintz, then narrowed his eyes at me.

"My job, the job the courts have entrusted to me, is to make sure Bockman's runs smoothly, without trouble or coverage from the press. That means weeding out the rotten eggs and nipping them in the bud."

Eggs had buds?

"To that end," Waters said, "I'm instituting a new policy of rapid endorsement." He sat back in his swivel chair and pressed his hands together, regarding us over his fingertips. Now I could make out his eyes for the first time. They were tiny and blue, with all the softness and warmth of ice cubes. "In the past, potential foster parents had to wait an interminable amount of time, bogged down with unnecessary background checks, merely to give you malcontents the homes you so desperately need. Now that the CRC is running Bockman's, I can accelerate that process. Starting today, all of you are leaving this facility for foster families."

He unscrewed his fountain pen to sign a form. "Dismissed."

A pimply Hispanic kid on my right crossed his arms. "And what if we don' wanna go?"

Before Heintz had a chance to smack him, Dr. Waters glanced up. "Then we'll give you a chance to change your mind." To Heintz he said, "Let's place our young friend in the penthouse. Two days, to start." He looked around at us. "Any other objections? No? Good."

Later I found out about the penthouse. The supervisor pushed us out of the room and into another bus and later that afternoon I was the proud new member of my first foster family.

The first of many.

Just then my phone started chirping. It startled me, but I was grateful for anything that interrupted my recollection of Dr. Waters. Brushing kernels of rice and shrimp tails off my shirt, I fumbled for the phone and answered it with a composed voice.

"Mr. Gidney, this is Stephanie Chilcoate, we met earlier today."

"Of course, Ms. Chilcoate. If you're calling to check on your yearbook, it's resting safely in my car."

"I'm glad to hear it. So, have you found Bobbie yet?"

"I'm good, but not that good. I think I located Bobbie's mother."

"That was quick. Was she happy to see you?"

"Yeah, when she thought I was from an art gallery. What can I do for you?"

"Just calling to see if I can send some business your way. Would it be all right if I gave your number to an associate of mine? Azalea Trace?"

"Congressman McHugh's administrative aide?"

"The same. She'll call you in a few."

We made polite sounds to each other and hung up. Three minutes later, my phone chirped again. "Hello, Mr. Gidney, this is Ayzie Trace. I hope you don't mind me calling you, I got your number from Stephanie. The congressman would like to meet with you if you have a few moments."

"When?"

"Well, this is a bit awkward, but are you by any chance near Capitol Hill just now?"

"I can see the Capitol dome from where I'm parked. Hey, is that you waving at me?"

She laughed. Her voice sounded relaxed, like she was sitting on the beach with a cool drink in her hand. "Jase is about to address a group of supporters at the Capitol Hill Hyatt, on New Jersey Avenue. If you could meet us there, we would be very grateful."

"No problem. Mind telling me what this is about?"

"It's about a job he needs done, but I think he'd prefer to tell you himself. Are you interested?"

"I was already interested, just hearing your voice."

She laughed again. "Good. We'll see you soon."

I pointed my car south. A group of supporters, she'd said. McHugh could have been inspecting the D.C. sewer system for all I cared. Ayzie Trace interested me.

I wanted to see her again.

CHAPTER 14

On the political spectrum, Jason McHugh was to the right. The far right. Compared to him, Ghengis Khan was a pantywaist liberal.

Consequently, the Capitol Hill Hyatt, which was holding his fund-raiser, was surrounded by news cameras filming left-wing protesters. There were several brand-name groups, plus a few I'd never heard of. They all wanted McHugh's head on a spit. I wondered if the size of the turnout was testimony to McHugh's chances of grabbing Broadfield's Senate seat.

Inside was McHugh's crowd—his base, I'd guess you'd call them. All of them wore big white buttons with blue and red letters that read FRIEND OF JASE. The men, for whom the Bronze Age was a recent memory, clapped their liver-spotted hands in appreciation, while their women, gowned and jeweled, smiled with blank radiance.

After touting his law-and-order credentials, and his opposition to the "mongrelization" of America, McHugh gave them a big finish, which included the words, "We shall overcome!"

While Dr. King did a 360 in his grave, I headed outside to find Ayzie Trace by one of the limos. "Jase will be so happy you could meet with him." She tilted her head toward the audience, now leaving the hotel with bovine calm. "What did you think of his speech?"

"I never knew the plural for *y'all* was *all y'all*."

Azalea Trace laughed. It sounded nicer than over the phone,

like clear water rippling over silver stones. "Sometimes his 'Loo-ziana' accent gets the best of him. He took lessons to lose it, from the same man who coached Dan Rather." Holding my arm, she steered me toward a limo.

I said, "He could do the nightly news once he gets tired of politics."

"Oh, I don't think he'll ever tire of politics. So you're a private detective," she said. "How does one get to be a detective? Is being over six feet tall a requirement?" She squeezed my arm. "Or having biceps of steel?"

She was wearing something black and slinky and shiny, with a white FRIEND OF JASE button on her chest. A nice outfit, except for the button. On her feet were small black pumps that looked like they'd be fun to take off. I thought about massaging her feet, then mentally kicked myself back to reality.

As the chauffeur trotted around to open the door, Trace released my arm to face me, her face a few inches from mine. "Jase wants to meet at The Palm. Is that all right?" The way she looked, standing there with the wind in her hair, I would've happily agreed to push the limo to Cleveland.

On the way to The Palm, Azalea Trace said, "Stephanie tells me you're locating a missing person? Bobbie Jackson, that was the name you said this afternoon, right?"

"You have a good memory, Ms. Trace."

"Call me Ayzie," she said. She grabbed the hem of her skirt and lifted it over her head.

"Well. Okay, uh, Ayzie."

She was in her bra and panties. "So, having any luck?"

"With what?"

She grinned at me. "With finding her." Now she tossed her dress onto the floor and reached for a handle coming from the back of the driver's seat. A flap opened, and she removed a neatly folded white cotton dress. Her tan was deep, broken only by pale slivers of skin that winked at me from beneath her bra straps.

"Not so far. I spoke to her mother today."

She nodded. "Stephanie told me. Will the mother help you?"

"I don't know. She denied knowing Bobbie. I left Bobbie's picture with her, maybe she'll change her mind. I'm pretty sure she was holding back."

She began slipping into her dress. "Does that happen to you often?"

"Hardly ever. Women always open right up to me." Her figure stretched the cotton fabric in interesting ways. "So you're McHugh's administrative aide. Isn't that like being second-in-command?" I thought I was doing a good job keeping my voice casual.

"Yes. It's tough work, but I like it."

"I'm figuring either you got the job through seniority, in which case you must've started when you were twelve, or you're good at what you do."

She laughed again. "Here we are."

Inside The Palm, the lights were low, and pictures of Washington's famous and forgotten covered every inch of wall space. Small tables were set apart from one another—making it a lousy place to eavesdrop—and on the tables were small candles flickering like stars in the void. At every table a few people were engaged in earnest, quiet conversation. The room had a rich and pleasant feel to it. Jason McHugh rose as we approached his table. He held Trace's hands and said, "My God, you're beautiful," then took her in his arms. Hot romance, D.C.–style. Who would break the clinch first? It was Trace. I wondered if

McHugh knew about her lack of inhibitions. Maybe stripping down in front of strangers in a moving car was a new way to relieve tension, for the stripper if not the strippee. Probably in an issue of *The Washingtonian* I had missed.

McHugh turned his tanned, rubbery face to me. He reminded me of the D.C. officials, the oversight committee, who had come to Bockman's from time to time, just to look us over. Days like that, all the problem kids were swept out of sight—troubled kids, sick kids, the desperate and confused. Gone. One big, happy, medically sedated institution, that's what we were. The oversight committee must've known what was happening. I think they were relieved to find that everything—on the surface, at least—was peachy.

McHugh gave me a two-handed clasp. Mr. Sincere. Then he invited me to sit. No sooner had McHugh told me how glad he was to meet me than the waitress—a tall, dark-skinned beauty with high cheekbones and long black hair and clear brown eyes—came to take our order. McHugh asked for a Manhattan, and Trace ordered the same.

I ordered a Makers Mark straight up. After the waitress left, McHugh leaned forward. "Mr. Gidney, I appreciate your coming here on such short notice." He fixed me with an earnest stare. "Do you know what's happening in this country right now?"

"I bet there's a party going on somewhere."

"I'm talking about the moral disintegration of our society."

"Oh, sure. That."

"Yes, Mr. Gidney. That." He eased back in his chair. "Are you familiar with how President McKinley died?"

"McKinley? Shot to death, I think at the New York World's Fair."

"'Shot to death.'" He turned to Trace. "Makes it sound like bullets riddled his body, a gangland slaying." He turned back to me. "President McKinley died from a single bullet, and not quickly. They took him to an impromptu operating room on the fairgrounds, where doctors tried to remove that bullet. If they'd been successful, President McKinley would've lived."

"Sounds reasonable."

"Yes, but did you know that in the very same room, the room where President McKinley died, there was a new device donated to the fair by Thomas Edison?" He smiled at me like a kid reciting a well-rehearsed lesson. "A fluoroscope machine, an early type of X-ray. And if any of the people there had the least idea of how to work that machine, they could've saved McKinley's life."

"I hadn't heard that."

While speaking, McHugh's shoulders and head had thrust forward again. "The point of the story is this—America has been pierced by a bullet of moral decay. Now, we have the tools to save this country, but we need the right people, with the right know-how."

"And that would be you."

He grinned. "Not just me, but that's the general idea."

"And the ethics probe?"

He waved his hand at me. "Just politics as usual, Mr. Gidney, politics as usual."

"I still don't see why I'm here."

"Let me tell him, Jase," Azalea Trace said, turning her blue eyes to me. "We need an independent investigator. I can't go into details until you accept, but it deals with the abuse of quotas to award government contracts. Multimillion-dollar contracts. We need someone experienced, like you, someone out-of-house to lead the investigative unit."

"By quotas you mean . . ."

McHugh said, "Our antiquated system of 'leveling the playing field,' which does more harm than good."

I wiped the hand he'd shaken on my pants leg. "How do you know I'm the right man for the job?"

Trace said, "Stephanie recommended you, that's good enough for us."

"I'm working on something just now."

The waitress returned. "Now, who had the bourbon?"

Trace looked at her. Her eyes had that flat look she'd given me when we first met. "You took the order five minutes ago. Try hard to remember." Her voice was a parody of concern.

The waitress grew flustered. "I'm sorry, but it's really busy tonight."

"Then I'll make it easy for you," Trace said. "This man and I ordered the same drink. *Now* can you figure it out?"

When the waitress set down their drinks, Trace muttered something I couldn't quite hear. The waitress drew in her breath, slopped my drink down on the table, and hurried away. A tense silence stretched out the moment, the only unscripted one of the evening. McHugh cleared his throat. He placed his hand on Trace's.

"Baby, you all right?" I heard concern, real concern, in his voice. It surprised me.

She seemed untroubled. "I'm fine, Jase."

Then he turned to me. "We're offering you a long-term contract, Gidney. And once this job ends, we've got other work for you. You could continue with us, if you chose."

"I've got no experience in politics, Congressman."

"Me neither, when I started. I'd never have guessed I'd wind up in Congress."

"And soon you'll be a senator?"

McHugh gave his aw-shucks grin. "That would be a remarkable turn of events. But if it happened, you'd still be part of our team. What you're doing now, when will it finish?"

"Hard to say."

"You're looking for a missing person—any progress?"

Trace said, "He spoke with the girl's mother today."

"And she's willing to help you?"

"She didn't seem that interested," I said.

"How could you tell?" McHugh asked.

I shrugged. "My keen sense of nuance. Also, she threw me out."

Trace smiled and shook her head. "Tsk-tsk, and you from the Perth Gallery, too."

"Well, finding the girl's mother sounds promising," McHugh said. "Maybe this will end quickly. Are you committed to this project?"

I said, "I'm involved, but not committed."

"What's the difference?"

"A friend once told me it's like a bacon-and-egg breakfast. The chicken is involved. The pig is committed."

"A nice distinction. But I need you to start immediately. We'll pay extra if you have to subcontract what you're doing now."

It's hard to subcontract when there's no actual fee involved, but I didn't say that. "I don't think that'll work."

McHugh waved away my objection. "I'm proposing a ten-thousand-dollar retainer now, with a guarantee of a hundred fifty thousand over the next twelve months."

Almost four times what I was making, between my own business and Shelly Russia's Polka Palace. Trying not to drool, I stood up. "Sorry, Congressman."

"But why?"

Looking at Trace, I said, "For one thing, I don't like the way she treats waitresses. And the case I'm on is for a friend. I don't see how I can subcontract that."

McHugh looked down for a second, then offered me his hand as he stood. "I'm sorry, Gidney."

It was funny, but when he said that, I almost believed him.

CHAPTER 15

I left feeling guilty about the waitress. At first I thought, hey, *I* hadn't done anything. That's when it hit me—I hadn't done anything. So I circled around to the back alley. When I came into the kitchen I saw her. "Excuse me," I said.

She looked at me, her eyes red rimmed.

"Just wanted to tell you I'm sorry."

"Not your fault," she said.

"Yes, but she said something to you, you didn't deserve it." I smiled at her. "Look, I wanted to tell you I'm sorry. I'm sorry I just sat there and let her get away with it. I was too busy being curious about her. And him. But I want you to know that next time, I won't just stand by."

She nodded, wiped away a tear. "But why did she say that? Because my skin is darker than hers? Because she has blue eyes and I don't?"

"Not much of a reason, is it?"

Outside, it was still humid but cooler with the dark of evening. I drove to the Willard, and parked near its loading dock on a short, shadowy strip of F Street that ends at the Treasury Building. It was only ten o'clock, but the streets were empty. I headed down F Street thinking about my limo ride with Trace. Was it a seduction or wasn't it? Perhaps I was an inattentive seducee. I hadn't felt inattentive.

My thoughts were broken by the ragged breath of someone hustling behind me through the shadows. I spun around to see a man swinging a baseball bat—a big one. He lashed out with a swing that would've made Reggie Jackson proud. I ducked but needn't have bothered—he wasn't targeting me—while the parking meter in front of me exploded in a shower of quarters. Then he jogged down to the next meter and killed it, too.

Then I recognized him—blue jeans, plaid shirt, brown beard, and gray eyes—Augustus, a homeless man who hung out by the Mayflower Hotel. One of the "regulars" I talked with.

A cop car came around the corner. Beacons but no siren. They pointed a beam of light and hit us square, then pulled over and got out. Two of them, a younger black guy and an older white guy, strolled toward us. There was nothing menacing in the way they walked, but their eyes never left us for a moment. Augustus backed up until he was beside me. He was breathing hard.

"How are you gentlemen tonight?" the younger cop asked as they closed the distance. He had one hand on his belt, near the butt of his Glock, and the other smoothing his mustache. The mustache looked like Shad's, without the gray.

"Just fine, Officer," I said, "and you?"

He nodded. "We've had a report about someone smashing city meters with a baseball bat. You two know anything?"

"Hey, look at that, Augustus." I pretended to notice just now. Augustus looked at me with pale, expressionless eyes. Then he nodded, his bat resting on his shoulder.

"You gentlemen see who did that?"

"We haven't seen squat. We're just meeting some friends for a drink."

"Why are you carrying a bat, sir?" he asked Augustus.

"We just won our first game and our friends are gonna sign it," I said.

"Your friend's breathing pretty hard."

"Asthma. He left his inhaler at home."

The white cop grunted and said, "He doesn't talk much."

I smiled. "I was about to say the same about you."

The black cop said, "Someone smashes a buncha meters two blocks from Lafayette Park, where a couple dozen homeless camp out, you'd think they'd be all over that. I'm seein' piles of quarters here, just layin' on the ground. Can't have been here very long."

"Oh, I don't know, Officer. A lot of homeless are honest folks. Public spirited."

The two cops shot each other a glance. The younger one shook his head in disgust and followed the older one to the cruiser. After they drove off, Augustus looked at me for a moment. I couldn't tell if he knew me or not. All I knew about him was that he was a Gulf War veteran.

Augustus nodded at me. He turned toward G street.

"Wait a second. You mind telling me why you're killing parking meters?"

He paused, thinking. Then he nodded, said, "Yes," and walked away.

CHAPTER 16

When I walked into The Cove, a small jazz club inside the Willard Hotel, I passed a line of people waiting to get in for the second show. Not bad for a weeknight. The hostess had my name on her list, and when I sat down in back, Steps was working hard. Center stage, wearing a tuxedo jacket with a white shirt open at the collar. Sweat gleamed from his forehead as his fingers worked the keys. A wave of sound rolled from his sax, sweet and urgent.

Behind Steps a young white kid played drums, lots of energy barely held in check. It was all he could do to lie back and stay with the band. I figured him for eighteen or nineteen and out to make himself a reputation. The tune had a Latin feel. The kid had built up some kind of polyrhythm with the bass player, who looked like the black deacon of a church, with a grizzled gray head and bloodshot eyes, his large hands plucking notes from the string bass. He and the kid were grinning at each other, as though they were speaking a special language within the framework of the song.

The piano player, Victor, I knew from Steps's last visit to D.C. Weighing in at about 250 pounds, Victor was from Argentina, all six foot six of him. He had a wispy black goatee and thick black hair brushed back from his forehead. While giving the audience the feel and melodic structure of the song, Victor was fueling Steps's solo with the rhythm of his piano chords. His hair kept falling into his face, his hands snatching chords from the keyboard like a kid stealing candies from the party dish.

Steps finished his solo and came back to the melody. Much too soon the song, and the set, ended. The audience was hypnotized. I counted three seconds before they realized the band had finished. Then they stood up and applauded, and kept applauding, in hopes of an encore. A voice came over the sound system, thanking the guests for coming and telling them The Cove hoped they'd come back soon. In other words, scram. There was a new group of music lovers lined up to take their places.

Steps made a helpless gesture to the crowd, whose applause finally trailed off. The guys in the band set down sax, bass, sticks, and came over to my table. "Yo, Willis," Victor boomed at me.

"Victor el Magnifico," I said, shaking hands with him. Steps introduced me to the drummer and bass player, who then drifted over to the bar, where a group of fans received them. Steps and Victor sat. "What do you think of the drummer?" Victor asked.

"An elephant tranquilizer might help."

Steps smiled and shook his head. "Kid's got energy, I'll say that. Now he needs to learn the discipline." He signaled the waiter, then said, "I told Victor you were looking for my daughter." Victor nodded. Steps said, "So tell me what you got."

"A few questions, for starters. You know anyone at the Kerberos Corporation?"

"The what? No, should I?"

"How about a congressman named Jason McHugh?"

"Fuckin' anti-Christ," Victor said, taking a sip of water. "Hope they nail him."

Steps nodded. "Can't say he's my favorite person."

"You ever had any contact with him?"

"Shit, no. What's that got to do with finding my daughter?"

"Probably nothing. Have you ever heard of Stephanie Chilcoate? Or Buford Goodwin?"

Steps shook his head. After the waiter brought their drinks, I showed Steps one of the pictures of Bobbie Jackson.

"My lord," he said.

"Have you seen her before?"

"No. But, God, for a moment I thought this was a picture of Colette. When do we meet?"

"Have to find her first. And I'm not sure she's your daughter. Remember, she told her high school buddies her father was dead."

"Lemme see." Victor leaned over to look. "All right! Not bad, man," he told Steps.

"Shut up, Victor."

Victor leered at Steps, then ambled to the bar. Steps hunched his shoulders and leaned toward me, tapping the picture with blunt fingertips. "She told this chef at Money Jungle that I was her father, right? This is her, Willis. I feel it. You close to finding her?"

"I talked to Colette today. I got the impression someone else is looking for Bobbie."

"Why?"

"Because when I told her you were trying to find Bobbie, she was surprised. Who else might be looking for her?"

"For Bobbie? Why ask me?"

I stood. "See you around, Steps. You can keep the picture." I turned to go, then felt his hand on my elbow.

"What's the matter with you, man? Where you going?"

"Out to find a client who levels with me." I saw him hesitate. "For real, Steps. I want the whole story, or I walk."

92

A white couple at the next table looked over at us. Through his teeth Steps said, "Sit down." If I hadn't looked into his eyes, I would have left right then. But while his voice was tough, his eyes were clouded with desperation and something approaching panic. He took out a handkerchief, wiped his brow. "Okay," he said. Looking down at the white tablecloth. "Okay. That last night? When I told you I didn't ask her to come away with me, well, that wasn't exactly true. See, I did ask her. And Colette, she said she would, said she'd meet me at the hotel the next night."

"What next night? You said you slept with her one time, your last night in D.C."

"Yeah, well. This is how it happened. Last three nights of my D.C. gig, we'd been together. Making love, making plans. Funny, I figured I'd have to sell her on the idea. But Colette, she didn't need to be sold. She was ready to split D.C. the first time I brought it up. Made me a little jumpy, you wanna know the truth. Like maybe I was making a mistake. But that last night—man, I knew we were in the pocket."

"Made for each other."

"Yeah. So that last night, after we fell asleep? Next thing, someone's pounding the door. Now her dad, Alvin, he didn't care for me and Colette being together. Came right out and told me so, said to leave her alone. Guess I didn't tell you that before."

I let that pass.

"Somehow Alvin finds us, and there he is, banging on the hotel door and hollering to open up, he knows she's in there. Colette, she doesn't say a word. Like she's expecting it. Now she grabs something from her purse, then over to the door. Like, if she doesn't get to that door in time, her life's over. She flings it open. All this light from the hallway spills in, I see Alvin reach for her. Her left hand goes up towards Alvin's face and he screams. Then she brings her hand down, fast. Alvin, he lets loose a roar and rushes her, knocks her down into the room and falls in on top of her, grabbing her with one hand, and making a fist with the other.

"Happens like that." He snapped his fingers. "I see Alvin make that fist and now, I don't want trouble, but I'm not watching Colette get beat on. I get around behind him and try to pull him off her. He's got his back to the door and his face is wet. Then I look at Colette and she's crying and her face is bloody.

"'I call him a son of a bitch, something like that. I pull him offa her and spin him around. His face is covered with blood. He's still grabbing her wrist, but now I see why—she's got a single-edge razor blade between her fingers. I think maybe she was trying to blind him.

"I pull him off, get him away from her, and she goes to slice him again!" He shook his head. "Never *seen* such carryins' on. I take a chance and get between 'em, try to calm 'em down, but Alvin's crazy. Won't stop hollering at Colette, then turns on me, tells me to leave her alone. Soon as he starts shouting at me, Colette, she slumps down on the floor like some kinda rag doll.

"Alvin, he gets her clothes and throws 'em at her, calls her a whore and shouts at her to get dressed. She doesn't even get her shoes on and he grabs her by the elbow and pushes her out the door, all the time calling me names, saying he'll kill me if I come near her again."

"Did you?"

"That's the last time I saw either one of them. Swear to God, Willis." While he'd been talking he had folded his handkerchief over and over, pressing it down so it stayed folded. Now he looked down at it as he said, "So, you'll stay on the case? You'll help me?"

"You thinking Alvin might be looking for Bobbie, too?"

"No. I don't know, maybe. I haven't seen Alvin since that night."

I nodded. "I'll help you, Steps."

Relief eased the tension from his face. When the other musicians came back, he forced a smile. I stayed for the next set, even though I felt tired. Steps was a pro. If he was torn up inside, you'd never know from the way he played. Hell, maybe he played better because of it.

Around midnight, I walked back to my car on F Street. I saw no pedestrians, which always amazes me. In Manhattan, people would be crowding the streets right now; on the D.C. streets, the homeless were bedding down. I was strolling past a van when my phone started chirping. Colette Andrews.

"Mr. Gidney, I—I'm sorry to be calling you so late."

"No problem, Ms. Andrews."

I let the silence stretch. Then she said, "I've been thinking about what you said today, and I've—I need to see you."

"How's first thing tomorrow?"

"No, tonight, I need to see you right away."

"Can you tell me what it is over the phone?"

"No, it's the—I need to see who I'm talking to."

I remember wanting to ask her about Alvin, and thinking how long the drive to her place would take. Just past the Willard's loading dock, maybe twelve feet from my car, I heard a hissing noise from behind.

I moved but not fast enough. Something hard and flat smashed my hand holding the phone into the side of my head. As I stumbled I caught a quick image, three or four sets of legs and shoes. For an instant I flashed on my last night at Bockman's. A bitter taste burned the back of my throat. Now I staggered in the dark and hands grabbed me and something swung up to smash my chin. I think it was the sidewalk. They grabbed hold and dragged me by the ankles toward the loading dock. I tried to twist around off my stomach. One of them said, in a kind of isn't-that-cute way, "Oh, look, he's resisting." A set of the hands loosened, and a sunburst of pain exploded behind my eyes like a star going nova. The white center reached out. I melted inside.

PART TWO

Look with your eyes and listen with your ears,
smell the incense and grasp the meaning with questions.

—RIKYU

CHAPTER 17

I'm standing frozen in the center of the maze. Buildings stretch and tower above me to form a spiral, closing in on me. Each building leaks gasoline, and on the ground tiny streams like worms coil their way toward me, the ground is level but the gas coils toward me, while the closest building erupts in flames, then the building next to it, and the one after that, like dominoes falling. I know that in a second the entire maze will ignite. Me with it, if I can't find my way out. So I run, ever so slowly, I run around corners, down long rows of blank-faced buildings, I sprint through the twists and turns like some demented rat, scratching for the way out. A moonless night, too dark to see where I'm going, all the buildings exactly the same. Then a building looms ahead, the center building, I'm back where I started, I'm running toward it, I can't stop, the heat singes my hair and screams pour out of the building ahead, in the windows the black outlines of children, it's starting all over again, the building explodes as the screams turn into something less than human, flames shoot up in twin curved columns like the horns of a bull. I scream, my voice hoarse as flaming debris lands on my back and suddenly the flames swallow me and then I heard a *click*.

A tiny finger pushed my right eyelid open.

I found myself staring at Emily, Jan and Janet's four-year-old daughter. Her round face and hazel eyes and curly brown hair were a fraction of an inch from my eye. I could have kissed her. She said, "It's lunchtime."

My heart was pounding, I was covered with sweat. I wiped my hands on the sheets.

"I made you a pee bee and jay, are you gonna eat it?" She put her hands on her hips.

Just then the door opened and Jan came in. Without a word she put her hands on Em's shoulders and steered her out the door. A moment later Jan came back with a glass of water and two white pills.

"I hope these are arsenic." I gulped them down.

She didn't smile, but smiling wasn't something Jan did a lot of. She looked as though I were one of her architecture students she'd had to flunk. "How do you feel?"

"Rotten."

"Can you tell me what happened?"

"I got beat up."

She nodded. "That's what he said, the man who brought you here."

"Which man?"

"He didn't say his name. He said you asked him to bring you here, and he left your car parked outside."

Augustus? "Older guy? Gray hair, brown beard, wears a plaid shirt?"

She nodded, her eyes so calm and serious. "Do you need anything?"

"A week in the country would be nice."

She stood. "I'm sorry Emily bothered you. Janet and I were

quite clear with her she was to leave you alone. You get all the rest you need, we're here all day."

She crossed the room and closed the door, as if I were still asleep. I wanted to sleep more, but not if it meant having that fucking dream again. I tried sitting up in bed. Big mistake. I fell back against the pillow and that hurt, too. From now on I was going to have to be more careful with my body. Maybe when I left the house I could be packed in foam peanuts.

Okay, Mr. Detective, what the hell happened last night? I got beat up. Apart from that, what happened? Let's see, I'd just heard Steps play some great music, and then I got beat up.

Oh, well, that explained everything.

My throat felt like a team of elves had been sandblasting it all night. They had laid gravel under my eyelids, too. They were full-service elves. I made it to the bathroom to inspect the damage. My face was scraped. My teeth were loose. My chest hurt, but none of the ribs seemed to be broken. Breathing was painful. So was thinking. Lucky I didn't have to do both. I stood in the shower awhile, letting the water hit me as hot as I could stand it. After a few minutes I started to feel better.

Augustus had brought me home. Had he found me on the street? Or had he interrupted whoever had decided to smack me around?

When I left the bedroom, Jan and Janet's house felt hot. I found the A/C set for seventy-eight degrees. Didn't they know it was summer? I turned it down to sixty-eight, hoping to feel the difference soon. Downstairs I found the three of them—Jan, Emily, and Janet—inside a ceremonial Japanese tea room.

What home is complete without one?

The tearoom had started life as a den, but then Jan had fixed thin shoots of bamboo around the walls and ceiling. Soft, cool light came through sliding panels covered with rice paper. From the ceiling dangled a single, plain paper lantern. There were no decorations, just a low table with a magnolia blossom, kettle, bamboo whisk, white napkin, and a bowl of tea in steaming water. The bowl was ceramic and misshapen, as though whoever had made it hadn't cared for symmetry.

What I couldn't figure out was whose idea the tea room had been—Jan, the architect, or Janet, who made her living writing verse for greeting cards. I sat beside her and she patted my hand, smiling at me. Janet had blond hair and gray eyes, a big-boned, big-hearted woman. I could understand Jan's being in love with her.

Silently Jan went through the motions of whisking the tea and offering the bowl to Janet. I said, "You got any coffee around here?"

Jan shook her head at me. Oh, we weren't supposed to talk.

"How about Coke?"

Again the head shake.

I winked at Emily. In a German accent I asked, "You haff zum Ovaltine, perhaps?"

Jan exhaled in a rush as she glared at me. I was disturbing the ceremony.

Janet patted me on the shoulder and said to Jan, "Don't get mad, honey. Remember, Willis is a few rungs below us on the evolutionary ladder."

"Thank you," I told Janet. Making a gesture that took in the room, I asked, "What do you call this?"

"The tea service is *chado*," Jan said. "The aesthetic is *Wabi-sabi*."

"Wasn't that Tonto's name for the Lone Ranger?"

"No." Jan poured the tea into the cups.

I did my Elmer Fudd voice. "Which way did they go, *Wabi-sabi?*"

Emily giggled as Jan sighed, handing the bowl of tea to Emily, who made a slight bow of her head before sipping. Jan set down the bowl and hugged herself. "It's cold in here."

I said, "Yeah, I adjusted your thermostat. It seemed a little . . ." But by then Jan was out of the room. Janet smiled and looked down, shaking her head. When Jan came back, she put my car keys and phone in front of me. She had the barest hint of a smile, so I guessed she wasn't throwing me out.

I said, "The guy who brought me, he say anything?"

"Just that you gave him our address. He put your stuff on the counter and walked away."

I didn't remember any of that. My cell phone was cracked, but the display still worked. Probably because it had smashed into something soft—my head.

Janet said, "What's the story, Willis?"

So I told them, starting with Steps's asking me to find his daughter. When I finished, Janet said, "Why are you looking for, whats-isname, Dante?"

"The kid from the Shaw house? I was thinking about the electrical outlets in that top-floor room, and the new fuse box. Then, outside McHugh's office, I saw big electrical cables going from the fuse box to the lights where they were filming." I took tiny sips of tea, a brackish green concoction. "Mmmm. Septic blend?"

"If you'd been here when we started," Jan said, looking down at the table, "you'd have something sweet in your mouth to complement the taste of the tea."

"Oh, so I got uncomplemented tea here." I turned to Janet.

"I don't know what they were doing in that house, but the electric bills were high. And they were in Bobbie's name."

"And Dante knows the answer?"

"He might."

"You said they were shooting a commercial in McHugh's office, right? Maybe Bobbie was shooting commercials," Jan said.

Janet said, "Or porn."

"Maybe," I said. "The ceiling holes in the middle room could mean something heavy had been hanging there. Maybe a grid to hold lights. And the electrical wiring to carry a heavy load, like the lights and wires I saw at McHugh's office. But why cover the windows in that room?" I told them about the discarded black trash bags. "I think someone used wide tape, like duct tape, to put garbage bags over the windows. When they pulled the trash bags down, the tape took the paint with it."

Jan said, "But wouldn't light from the window help their filming?"

"Maybe they didn't want anyone on the street to see the lights," Janet said. "Maybe they didn't want their equipment stolen."

My head was pounding. "Anyway," I said, "I thought if I could find Dante, I could find out who used the top floor and for what, and that might help me find Bobbie."

"That's why you got beat up—looking for Bobbie Jackson?" Jan asked.

"Of course," Janet told her. "Willis says those men at Kerberos knew all about him."

"It doesn't make sense," I said. "I meet with Steps yesterday morning around ten, okay? Four hours later, Varga's telling me to crawl into a hole. I can believe that one might lead to the other, but how could they follow each other so quickly?"

"And why are you important enough for them to make the effort?"

"I don't know."

"Maybe those men beat you up as a warning? To get you to stop looking for Bobbie Jackson?"

I'd been wondering that myself. Almost hoping, if you want the truth. So far, the beating was the only indication that I'd made any progress. Up to then I'd been thinking I was nowhere. Getting beat up meant *something*, if only that I'd alarmed someone. I imagined what Eddie Vermeer would tell me. I could hear his voice in my head saying, *Willis, you idiot, you're getting the shit knocked out of you for no money? Are you insane? Did you learn* nothing *from me? Quit while you're behind, kid. That's the smart move here.*

I knew what Shad would say.

I was turning the damaged phone in my hands when I saw I had gotten a message. Haggler's phone number. I used Jan and Janet's phone to call him. He wasn't at the station but had left a second number for me. It seemed familiar. When I called it, a male voice answered. I said I was returning a call from Haggler and he grunted. A few seconds later, I heard Emil's voice. "Where you at?"

"A friend's house. What's up?"

"You know a woman named Colette Andrews?"

"Why?"

"Don't fuck with me, you know her or not?"

"I met her yesterday."

"Well, I'm at her house, and she's dead today. We found your business card near the body. You'd better get over here."

He hung up. I stood, frozen, trying to process what he'd said.

I put the phone down carefully, as though it were made of eggshell.

"Is something wrong?" Jan asked me.

"I have to go."

"To find Bobbie? You're going to keep working on this?" Jan asked.

I looked at them. "Seems that way."

Janet said, "Wow, you're really committed to this."

I thought about the bacon-and-egg breakfast and sighed. "Yeah, I guess I am."

CHAPTER 18

Dr. Waters set his plan in motion—to make sure kiddie troublemakers like me were out of his hair and gone from Bockman's. I had more foster families than a dog has fleas. Except I had fleas, too, courtesy of my first foster mom and dad. They raised Dobermans, thinking they needed only telepathy to housebreak them. The smell was unbelievable.

Another family had founded their own religion, like the Amish, but not as fancy. I was their first convert. Other foster parents were car dealers, carpenters, office workers. The gray people you see every day, determined to make me into a model citizen. They bought me new clothes and shiny tight shoes. They brushed my hair and took what seemed like thousands of pictures of us all together. It made me want to toss my lunch over the fence.

Dr. Waters never got discouraged. He had taken an interest in me and would be damned if he couldn't get rid of me. I was young and white, and Dr. Waters had no trouble finding suckers—I mean, caring adults—to take me.

I had no trouble getting them to reject me. My personal best? Eighty minutes, between the time a locksmith and would-be father picked me up and dumped me back at Bockman's. I was swilling a Coke when Eddie Vermeer walked up. "What're you doing?"

"Celebrating."

"Kid, I arranged you that family." I stared at him. He rolled his eyes. "The dad's a locksmith, for crissake. Think of it as a learning opportunity."

"Eddie, you wouldn't be trying to get rid of me, would you?"

He grinned. "Good. Questions like that make me glad you're my partner."

"Just don't *forget* I'm your partner. How's business?"

Eddie flipped his hand side to side. "Waters is tough. He's big into punishment, and the only rewards he hands out are to snitches." He shrugged. "So far I haven't found much for us, but at least we're not losing money." He smiled his con man's smile.

I said, "I bet you have some promising leads."

"That I do, kid. Very promising."

My next family, the husband and wife were librarians. I must have liked this because I stayed two weeks, learning the basics of research. I discovered a lot about Bockman's and Dr. Waters's background. I discovered the hopelessly outdated D.C. policies on juveniles.

I discovered that I liked to read.

Then I was with a couple who ran a nursery, and I picked up a little about plant life and organic gardening. I enjoyed it, especially the part about using good insects to eat the bad. That really appealed to me. Then a single-woman lawyer tried to teach me the basics of our judicial system. Her name was Mary. I followed her to court one day, though it was against the rules, and who should I meet but Shad, the cop who had tagged me with my name.

"Greetings, Lieutenant Davies."

"Well, well, the baby terrorist. How you doing, son?"

"I have a new foster mom. She's a lawyer."

"You could do worse, boy. You could get me." And he smiled. He hadn't said anything that funny, but I felt like smiling back at him. He was the first cop I had ever liked.

Sometimes I think that's what killed him.

Soon after, I ditched the lady lawyer and was back at Bockman's. Whenever I figured I had learned enough from my foster parents, I pulled the plug and got returned. This is trickier than it sounds. You see, on one hand, I had to act interested in what these families where doing, so I could learn, as Eddie had said. But grown-ups tended to misinterpret that as interest in them personally, which would make disentangling myself from them all the harder. The last thing I needed was a sympathetic family willing to give me an endless number of second chances.

So I had to be a borderline pain in the ass the entire time. That part was easy. And it worked pretty well, except for a pair of real do-gooder environmentalists. I had to torch their new addition before they let me go.

Singed but happy, I returned to Bockman's only to find that Eddie was in the penthouse. Dr. Waters's policy of no carrot and a bigger stick forced him to use a block of holding cells below ground—the penthouse—as solitary confinement for stubborn boys. I asked a trusty how long Eddie had been there. Ten days.

I lifted some black spray paint from maintenance, then sprayed a message on Dr. Waters's large bay window. You know, it's hard to spray-paint letters backward, especially a cursive *f*. I sat beneath a tree nearby to await results. A few minutes and Supervisor Heintz clamped a meaty hand on my shoulder, his fingertips probing and finding the pressure points, the pain shooting down my arm. He shoved me all the way into Waters's office. Waters sat behind his desk, his face lobster red.

"Before I send you for an indefinite stay in the penthouse, I want to know just what the hell you think you're doing."

"Trying to get your attention."

"Well?"

I nodded toward Heintz. "You want the pimple king to hear what I'm going to say? I've done quite a bit of research about the CRC. And about you, Dr. Waters." His anger faltered for a moment and I saw confusion quickly pass over his features. Then he dismissed Heintz.

I nodded. "Smart move, Doc." I hopped up onto the edge of his desk and started swinging my legs. "You knew you didn't want Heintz to hear us. Shows good sense."

"I can see I've made a mistake with you, trying to help you get a normal family life."

"Trying to keep me out of here, you mean. But this is my home too, Doc."

"What are you talking about? You've got five seconds to explain yourself."

"I'm talking about twenty-three hundred and fifty dollars. According to *The Post,* that's how much D.C. gives you annually for each kid that's here. Totals over half a million. I figure, per kid, you're actually spending between six and seven hundred. What would Congress say?"

"We spend every penny of that money."

I grinned. "Sure, but on what?"

"I don't have to answer your questions."

"But isn't it better to answer me than a reporter from *The Post*? Me and Eddie have been here two years now. So I figure you owe us thirty-five hundred." I kept swinging my legs, but now I began kicking the wooden desk with the heels of my sneakers. "Each."

"Stop that," he commanded me.

I ignored him. "Also, *The Post* would ask about the penthouse."

"I'm permitted to use those cells as I see fit."

"Sure, Doc. But within reason. Your critics in Congress might take your well-meaning discipline the wrong way. They'd call it an abuse of the children you're supposed to be helping."

"You must be on something. Do you have any idea, the depth of the hole you're digging for yourself?"

"And then there's the whole problem with your accreditation."

He stared at me.

"Your title, *Doctor* Waters," I said. "How many members of Congress know you're a doctor of divinity? Where'd you get that degree, anyway? Was it advertised in the back of *Rolling Stone*?"

"Even if what you've said were true, so what? Where you're going, no one will hear this outrageous pack of lies."

I shook my head. "Bad idea. See, I wrote all this down and gave it to a friend on the outside. Every day I have to call him and let him know how I'm doing. Otherwise he'll send what I wrote to the District Department of Juvie Justice and *The Post*."

"More of your lies." His voice had spiraled from imperious to a peevish whine.

"You want to take the chance, Doc?"

We stared at each other for a moment. His eyes, watery and nearly colorless, tried to stay on mine. He lowered them.

"What do you want?"

"Eddie out of the penthouse. We go our way, you go yours. Live and let live."

His lips were pressed into a thin, bloodless line. "Is that all?"

I hopped off the desk. "For now." I went to the door and put my hand on the knob. Then I turned back. "Oh, and we want the seven grand in cash. Sorry, Doc, no checks."

He blinked at me. I slammed the door on my way out.

CHAPTER 19

On the way to Colette's house I bought a replacement phone. What I needed was a replacement brain.

Haggler's call had gotten me thinking about the timing of Colette's murder. I wondered if it coincided with my getting smacked around. If it had, it was a good bet my attackers wanted more than just to beat me up, and I'd make book that Augustus and his baseball bat had saved my life. I drove down Wisconsin Avenue, shrugging off the pain in my head and the memory of my dream, grateful once more that Emily had awakened me. I don't like the way my nightmare ends.

A chorus of car horns blasted behind me. A blond kid in a red Porsche flipped his finger at me and shouted, "You brain dead?" as he accelerated past me down Wisconsin Avenue toward Georgetown. Feeling sheepish—I'd been reminiscing and the light *had* been green for two microseconds—I put the car in gear, turning right on Reservoir Road toward Colette Andrews's house.

Traffic was heavy, but for a few blocks I could have sworn a blue van was tailing me. Last night I had seen a van parked behind the group of legs I had glimpsed as I was going down. They were wearing blue jeans. If my attackers had driven that van, they might be behind me now. I tried to remember the color of the van. But it had been too dark on the street last night and in my memory right now. Well, it was something, guys wearing jeans driving a van. That really narrowed it down. If they *were* tailing me, whoever was driving was a genius—they would lose sight of me for minutes at a time, turn off the street I was on, then magically show up several blocks later. I saw no sign of them when I turned into the Andrews place. Maybe the half-dozen cop cars parked in the driveway scared them off.

As I drove up to the house, I noticed the lambs were gone. I wondered if Emil had hauled them in for questioning. A cop guarded the door. No French maids for me. He asked me what did I want and I told him. He told me to wait. He said it in such a way as to imply that if I didn't wait, he would shoot me.

In a minute Emil showed up. After taking in my not-so-natty clothes, his eyes came to rest on my damaged face. Nothing resembling surprise or empathy touched his expression as he said, " 'Bout time. C'mon, join the party."

I walked down the familiar hallway to the study, Emil to my

left and slightly ahead of me. He's shorter than me, about five eleven, with a broad flat nose in a dark round face. His kinky hair had more gray than it'd had when he and Shad and I were running around together. The way Emil actually looked jarred with my mental picture, the one I carry in my collection of images, frozen in time—my last night at Bockman's—his eyes wide, his face shocked.

Maybe it was unfair for me to remember him that way, since it was the only time I'd ever seen his face like that. But maybe that's why it's so clear in my mind. As we walked to the study I noted his assurance and wondered what it would take to make his face contort like that today. Probably a nuclear bomb in his Weber grill. He wore a lightweight tan linen jacket with a tight checked pattern, a slightly darker pair of brown slacks, and cordovan shoes that looked too stylish to be comfortable. Emil glanced at me sideways, taking in the cuts and bruises. "So, what happened?"

"I annoyed somebody."

He grunted. "You annoy everybody."

Through the open doorway to the study I saw the forensics team, dusting for prints, vacuuming the carpet, taking pictures. Nothing looked out of place, except the corner of the room where Colette had died. They had already taken her body away. Blood and gristle had splattered across the empty wall. Then I noticed it—the little Cézanne watercolor was gone.

A man in a silk tweed jacket turned as we came to the doorway. He looked to be about five foot eight and was completely bald. His face and neck were dead white. The wattled skin around his neck made him look older than he was. I wondered how his neck had gotten that way. It looked like a deflated balloon.

"This him?" he asked Haggler.

"Yeah."

A few of the lab guys brushed past, one of them saying, "All finished here, Captain."

Heinrick watched me, dark bags under large humorless eyes. He brushed his fingertips over his bald top, the tips making a sandpaper noise over bristles of hair so short I hadn't seen them. Reaching into his jacket, he tugged out a compact cigarette case, flipped it open, and pulled out a yellow cigarette that was twisted at both ends. Homemade.

Haggler said with mock formality, "Captain, I'd like to introduce you to Willis Gidney. Willis, this is Captain Francis Heinrick."

"This way," Heinrick said. He led us farther down the hall to a study. Books lined the walls from floor to ceiling. A pleasant aroma of tobacco lingered in the dim light. On the desk was a circular rack of pipes. The pipes leaned against one another like old friends. Heinrick hit his home-rolled and blew a cloud of marijuana smoke in my face.

"You bring enough for everybody?" I asked him.

He called to one of the uniforms in the hall. A beefy young cop with red hair and a sandy complexion came to the door. "Search his car," Heinrick said.

I said, "You have a warrant, Captain?"

"No, but we can take you downtown," he said. "You can cool your heels in a cell while I get one, you want to play it out. Either way, I'm searching your car."

I looked over at Emil. His face was a mask, as though he had never seen me before. I nodded at Heinrick, and the redheaded cop left the room. Heinrick smiled without meaning, then took an ashtray out of his coat pocket. He slowly turned the joint, rubbing ash into the tray. Without looking up, he said, "You've known this man a while, Lieutenant?"

"Yeah, a while."

"Think he killed her?"

I stared at Heinrick, hoping that Emil wouldn't mention Bockman's or Shadrack Davies. To my relief, Haggler simply said no, he didn't think I had killed Colette Andrews. Heinrick nodded, he'd expected that. "Where were you last night, Gidney, between eleven and two this morning?"

"I spent the first part getting the stuffing knocked out of me. Then I was unconscious."

"Anything else?"

"The second part lasted longer than the first."

"The people who attacked you, friends of yours?"

"No, friends send hate mail. Family, too."

"Save the jokes for prison. So who attacked you?"

"They didn't give me a chance to see."

"Then how do you know they were strangers?"

I said, "Jesus," and Haggler said, "Any witnesses?"

Augustus might have seen it all, but I didn't want to drag him into this. So I shook my head. "Just the assailants."

The redheaded cop came back from my car. In one hand he held the cardboard slip with POLICE printed on it, and in the other a Ziploc bag with Dante's gun inside. I could hear him trying to keep his voice steady. "Found these, Captain."

Heinrick took the bag with the gun in one hand and a huge toke from the joint in the other. He frowned while the beefy cop shook his head, as though trying to clear it. He was gazing at Heinrick in open amazement. "How'd you know, Captain?"

"Well, well," Heinrick said, smoke drifting from his mouth and nose. He looked up from the gun to me. "You have paper for this?"

"No, I lifted it off a kid yesterday."

By now the room had filled with smoke. It drifted lazily, creating shafts of light by the windows. Everything seemed to slow down as Heinrick said, "Take him downtown."

I stared at him. "Are you serious? What for?"

"Suspicion of murder."

"What the hell are you talking about?"

He set down the ashtray and spoke as though addressing a civics class of not very bright fifth-graders. "Let's look at the evidence. You call on Ms. Andrews yesterday afternoon. She hangs up on you. Then you come out here and threaten her. The maid overhears you. You leave your card with Mrs. Andrews, it was near her when we found her. Then last night at midnight Mrs. Andrews calls you. Why? Because you scared her somehow. Then you drive over here and ice her. The medical examiner puts her death between one and three A.M. Right when you claim to have been beaten." He spoke casually, snubbing out the joint in his ashtray.

"What went wrong, Gidney? Were you blackmailing her? Did she want to change the payment terms? Try to stall you till her husband came back?"

I shook my head. "Time to retire from the Cannabis Corps, Heinrick, you're not making sense. Yes, she called and wanted to see me, but I never made it."

"That's your story." He touched his head again, his fingers *scritching* against the bristles. "Mrs. Andrews was alone last night. All the servants were out. You say you were getting beat up, but that could be self-inflicted, or you could have paid someone to do it after the murder.

"When Mrs. Andrews' maid didn't see her or hear her ring this morning, she came and found her." He turned the bag with the gun in it, light reflecting off the metal surfaces beneath the plastic. "We found a 9-mm slug this morning, dug it out of a wooden panel. And an hour ago the ME told us Colette Andrews died of a gunshot wound, fired from inside her mouth through the top of her skull. And it all points to you, Gidney."

He smiled again. "So how about that ride downtown?"

CHAPTER 20

Emil drove me in his unmarked car toward the city jail. After a few blocks I asked, "What're you carrying these days?"

His eyes on the road, he took one hand off the steering wheel, took out his gun, flipped the cylinder open so I could see it was loaded, and handed it to me butt first. A .38 Smith & Wesson. I snapped the cylinder shut and hefted it. "Lightweight."

"Titanium."

"Kind of an odd choice for the Department."

"My choice, not theirs." He looked at me. "Technically speakin', this here's a backup weapon."

"And your primary?"

"Back at the office, locked in my desk drawer."

"You know, if I'd aced Colette Andrews, I'd shoot you, too."

"Best wait till I get to a stop sign."

I handed it back to him, cylinder open. "Department wants you to carry a Glock."

He glanced at the cylinder, snapped it shut, returned the gun to its holster. "Oh yeah, big advantage to shootin' the same bullets the bad guys use. Soon's we kill the little fuckers, we scoop up their ammo and shoot some more of 'em."

I gave him a wide-eyed stare. "So you're, like, recycling bullets. A green police force."

He narrowed his eyes. "You crackin' on me, boy?"

"Never."

Looking through the windshield, he said, "Heinrick knows you didn't kill the Andrews woman."

"Strange way of showing it."

"He's a good cop with bad luck. His wife and kid died last year, auto accident."

"That some new regulation? All bereaved police captains must get stoned?"

Emil shot me a dirty look. "Two months later they diagnosed him. Pot's the only thing that's lettin' him survive the chemo." He turned back to the windshield. "The mayor's given him special dispensation, 'cause Heinrick's closed more cases than any other cop in the last fifteen years. Which by D.C. standards makes him some kinda genius."

"Arresting me is an act of genius?"

"I told him you were a part-time detective. It pissed him off. That and the stuff with Shad." He shrugged. "People make mistakes. Even Heinrick."

"Easy to be philosophical when someone else's getting shafted."

"Lemme ask you somethin'. You got any idea what you're doin'?"

"No more than usual."

Emil's jaw tightened, and when his southern drawl crept into his voice, I knew he was pissed. "What I thought. Lemme tell you somethin'—whoever capped Andrews didn't give the lady a chance. An execution, that's what I saw. Gives you an idea the kind people you're dealin' with, boy. Now, I *know* you didn't do that. The department'll test the ballistics on the nine from your car, then they'll know it, too." He glanced at me. "Won't they?"

"They will. Something else—Andrews had a watercolor in the room where she died. It's missing."

"Valuable?"

"A Cézanne."

Emil rubbed his chin. "You figure robbery as the motive."

"No."

"So why take the painting?"

"Watercolor. I don't know."

"Yeah, well, you'll have plenty of time to figure it out. And try thinkin' about what you're doin'. Just for a change."

I took a picture of Bobbie out of my pocket and handed it to him. He glanced down at it. "This who you been buggin' me about?"

"Yeah. You able to get that financial information about her?"

Emil glanced at me. "You ain't givin' up?"

"No."

He looked back at the road. "Didn't think you were."

"And that makes you angry."

He reached into his jacket pocket. "Shit, no. You're like a drunk with a bottle, Willis—didn't figure you'd let go. Damn near the only thing I admire 'bout you." He handed me a few pages of folded computer printouts. "But this is it, understand? No more favors, so don't ask me again. And I don't have to mention what I'd do to you if you told anyone where you got this."

"No problem." I scanned the list of transactions, which dated back three months. I put the list down and stared out at the road, trying to make sense of it.

"What I see here, this woman is busy—several cash deposits and withdrawals, from nine thousand to ninety-five hundred. A week or more apart." He nodded. "Also some ATMs for smaller amounts, like forty or fifty bucks."

"No transactions over ten grand."

"She's flyin' underneath IRS radar, didn't wanna give the bank no reason to report her."

I thought about the house in Shaw. Maybe I should get into the porno racket, if it paid that well. "You ever hear of a guy named Buford Goodwin?"

"Can't say that I have." He rolled into police headquarters. "But if I were you, son, I'd be thinkin' of the name of a good lawyer. Case you don't know, Vance Andrews wasn't always with the State Department. Before that he was attorney general for the state of Virginia. He's flying back right now." He turned and gave me a dead-eyed stare. "And when he gets here, Willis, he's gonna squash you like a bug."

CHAPTER 21

On that cheery note, Haggler turned me over to the finely tuned machine of the D.C. police department. Say what you will about the D.C. government's efficiency, some things they are really good at. Even though Heinrick hadn't arrested me, I got the full treatment. Maybe he thought this would break me down.

The desk sergeant had me empty my pockets. He was cataloging the items—wallet and money, cell phone, handkerchief, copies of Bobbie Jackson's photo, various pieces of paper, the printouts Emil had given me, keys, pen—when we came across a second set of keys. They weren't mine. They didn't look familiar, but then again they were just a set of keys. The clerk tucked them with everything else into an envelope with my name and three sets of numbers scrawled on the flap. The motions he used suggested he had done this thousands of times before. Nothing was wasted.

Next came the mug shots. They used a special Polaroid camera that makes four pictures on one piece of paper. They ignored my request for wallet-size copies. Then a heavyset police woman in her mid-thirties pressed the fingers of my right hand into an ink pad and started to roll them onto my print page. She held my hand in hers. Her fingers seemed all the same size and width, as though they had been squeezed from a tube and hardened. "Relax," she said.

"Could we try guided visualization? Let's pretend we're lying on a beach in St. Thomas and I'm swilling Dom Pérignon out of your shoe."

"Relax your fingers," she said through her teeth. I must have loosened up enough, because she printed my fingers and thumbs, then gave me a paper towel made from a grocery bag so I could wipe off the ink. I thought about being locked up by D.C.'s finest, and that made me think of the penthouse at Bockman's. My first and only time there.

Well, I wouldn't let the D.C. jail bother me. I'd just have to find a lawyer. If we were still married, Karla could find a lawyer for me on the Net. Maybe do a search under attorney: defense: criminal: formyidiothusband. I wiped the leftover ink on my ruined clothes while another friendly cop walked me down yet another fluorescent-lit corridor with green walls to a bank of phones. He looked at me.

"I'm thinking," I said.

I stood there, resting my hand on the phone, realizing I had no one to call.

The guard grunted. "Well?"

"I'll take a rain check."

He just looked at me for a moment, then said, "This way."

Meaning, follow me, asshole, down this long, musty green hallway that smells like piss with these sickly green fluorescent lights that flicker and strobe and into this changeless dungeon a city block long where you can breathe the same air you breathed twenty years ago and see the same faces staring at you as you walk the hallway and have the same cell you had as a kid and step to the side as the door slides open and without a word walk inside this cell because this is your cell and you know it and maybe you'll get out soon and maybe you won't but one thing for sure, the sound of the cell door closing is the loudest, most final sound you'll ever hear.

Carefully I lowered my bruised body onto the bunk bed. It was going to be a swell day from here on.

As a kid, I'd thought a stint in the slammer was the worst thing that could happen. Later I learned how portable prisons are, the kind you take with you. I remember that day I returned to Bockman's and put the screws to Waters. I'd felt happy and in control of my life once I got Waters off my ten-year-old back. I'd never tell Eddie, but I felt a twinge of sympathy for the other kids at Bockman's. In his determination to control them, Waters began to rely on punishment and ever-escalating stretches in the penthouse for offending youths. Which was any youth who offended Waters.

The result was an atmosphere very much like the D.C. jail in which I now languished—an air of anger and depression. Generally, institutions like Bockman's are no picnic. But Waters had made it something special. Break-out rumors grew in popularity, I heard them constantly. Fistfights got so frequent as to be a part of the daily routine. Supervisors just watched. Even the occasional stabbing drew fewer and fewer remarks. This had never been the case at Junior Village.

Besides the mystery food Waters supplied, we got mystery medications as well. Drugs to chill us out, like Thorazine, plus God knows what else. Supervisors were supposed to make sure we took our meds, but they had value, so it was more or less a voluntary affair. You didn't want the paper cup with the little colored pills? Supervisors would pocket them to sell later.

Before Waters, the kids had a reason to behave, they'd been given an incentive in terms of expanded privileges. Now that was gone, replaced by mistrust, tension, an us-versus-them feeling.

Only the snitches were spared. Simply by ratting out their friends, they got to live in a nice dormitory, with their own rooms and private baths and televisions. I could be wrong, but I think Waters may have actually spent the money Congress had apportioned on them. So the snitches had nice clothes and good food. And the supervisors gave them protection.

They needed it. Because our group hated the snitches more than they hated Waters. If a snitch wandered off from his supervisor, he'd suddenly become accident-prone. Very accident-prone. Often the damage was permanent.

Thanks to my heart-to-heart with Waters, Eddie and I were doing well. We had our old burglary ring operating out of Bockman's. There's no alibi like being incarcerated, so our freelance thieves were doing us proud. Eddie made sure they didn't just

hit the wealthy homes near Bockman's. He assigned them different neighborhoods far away as well. That way, there'd be no
pattern of crimes with Bockman's as a center. Just in case the
cops tried to make a connection.

One thing you need to understand—only a tiny number of
kids were part of this ring. Maybe eight at the most, hand-
picked by Eddie. We had twice as many supervisors and trusties
to keep greased, making escape and returns easy. That ate into
our profits, to be sure, but what choice did we have? The price
of doing business, Eddie said.

About a month after Waters and I had our little chat, I got
summoned to his office. The supervisor who came for me gave
me a note. It read: "I had nothing to do with this. W."

Now what?

When I opened the door I found Waters having a talk with a
cop, and the cop's name was Shadrack Davies. Not good.

"Greetings, Lieutenant," I said.

He gave me a stern look. "I'm a captain now."

"Then congratulations are in order," I said, extending my
hand.

He took my hand. To Waters he said, "This kid is something
else, isn't he?"

Waters looked a little worried, but managed a smile. I thought
his face might crack. "Yes, he is."

Captain Davies turned back to me. "I've had my eye on you,
boy."

What was that supposed to mean? I wasn't sure, but when a
cop, a captain no less, says anything like that, act dumb. Only in
this case, I wasn't acting.

"I hope I've been worthy of your attention, Captain."

"You know why I'm here, don't you?"

He knows, he knows about Eddie and me. I tried not to show it. "Collecting for the FOP?"

"Not quite. I'm your new foster father." I just stared at him. This couldn't be happening. Shad gave me an amused look. "Well, that took the wind out of your sails, didn't it?"

"Captain Davies," Waters said, "perhaps you should reconsider. I mean, this child is, well . . ."

"A royal pain, I know." Davies nodded at Waters. Then he turned and looked at me. "But there might be something there, something special."

I looked at Davies, his high, narrow forehead, those intelligent eyes. Shaking his conviction that I was a diamond in the rough wouldn't be easy.

I sat down. "Of all the orphanages in all the cities in the world, you had to walk into mine," I said.

CHAPTER 22

How much money did the District save by making the beds in jail too short? Maybe they wanted me to curl up, fetuslike, an unspoken order to return to the womb.

This thought kept me awake as I sighed and, ever so gingerly, stretched out my creaking body on the District's creakier bunk bed. My feet hung over the edge. I shifted to my side, bending my knees, so now my feet rested flat against the wall by the door. Excellent. Then I rested my head against a pillow that had the size and thickness of an after-dinner mint.

Someone had removed the light bulbs from the caged fixtures above and replaced them with compact fluorescents. More efficient, with the added benefit of keeping that certain ambience of gloom that low-intensity lighting gives you. Slightly brighter than the inside of a coffin. I wondered how much rewiring it would take to replace those lights with something else, something brighter. Then I thought about Bobbie's house in Shaw. The holes in the ceiling could have supported a grid, and from the grid you could hang lights. Still, I didn't think Bobbie was into making movies.

From the bunk above came a scraping sound, and the smell of sulfur drifted down, followed by a pungent whiff of weed. The cell was quiet for a moment, then I heard the springs above me squeak. I said, "You can show yourself, I won't bite, I promise."

A tuft of disheveled white hair inched out, followed by a pair of pink eyes behind tortoiseshell glasses. I said, "No, Counselor, I've committed no violent act."

His pink eyes blinked at that. "You know I'm a lawyer? Have we met?"

"Lucky guess."

He swung his legs over the edge and lowered himself so he was standing in front of me. He paused for a moment, then thrust his hand toward me. The one not holding the joint. "I'm Stayne Mathews."

"Willis Gidney. So, why are you here, Counselor?"

A smile flickered across his face and died. "A small misunderstanding, be out by lunchtime. You?"

"Suspicion of murder."

He edged away, pressed himself against the wall.

"I didn't do it. If it makes you feel better."

He cocked his head to the side, like a bunny catching the scent of a nearby carrot patch. "Are you telling me this to put me at ease, or are you saying you're innocent? Because either way you're entitled to legal representation." He raised the joint to his lips with a small flourish.

You have to love it, a lawyer trying to hustle his cell mate. Slowly I said, "I did not kill Colette Andrews."

He stared at me for so long that I had begun to think he hadn't heard me. He gave his head a quick shake, then another. "Whoa. Whoa," he muttered. He paced to the cell door and back. "Vance Andrews?" He was watching me from the sides of his eyes as though I were a specter he could see only with peripheral vision. "Vance Andrews, that's who we're talking about, am I right?"

"I was talking about his late wife, and how I didn't kill her."

He whistled low and shook his head. "Vance Andrews. You need some big-time help, my friend. Some big-time help."

"And you're just the lawyer to provide it."

He held up his hands. "Nooo, not me. Not me. You need some big-time help."

"I think I'm starting to get it. I need some big-time help."

"Absolutely." He nodded vigorously, then looked at his joint as though seeing it for the first time. "Forgot my manners," he said, offering me a hit.

A cop and a lawyer, and on the same day. "Very considerate, Counselor, but won't the guard mind?"

"Call me Stayne. He sold it to me. The guard."

Tempting, but I didn't hit the joint, just handed it back as the cell filled with smoke. The dim light grew hazy. Then I had an idea, about how Bobbie used the house in Shaw. "I see marijuana is making a comeback in the District."

He had just inhaled, and now spoke while trying to keep his breath in. "A comeback. Yes. Well, this has always been my favorite. That other stuff, bad news." Mathews was looking at me from his side vision again. And again with the rapid head shakes. "Bad news."

I had no idea what he meant. "I know what you mean. Bad news. So where would a fellow buy some? I mean, if there were no guards handy."

"I don't know anything about it." He exhaled an indecent amount of smoke into our tiny cell. These cells weren't the nice, airy kind with a few scant iron bars separating inmates, making for lively discussion and commerce. No, these were individual, tiny, fetid, low-ceilinged little hutches with poor ventilation. He showed me his palms. "I'm just an end user."

"You look like an end user. But where would I go if I wanted to buy in D.C.?"

"I have absolutely no idea. You could try Fifteenth, near *The Post* building. Sometimes Malcolm X Park, off Sixteenth, is good during the daytime. I wouldn't go near there at night. And there's Twentieth and H, near GW and Tower Records. But I really wouldn't know."

"Sure. But say I'm looking to buy volume, go to the source. You have a name?"

"Absolutely not. Personally, I don't know anyone who sells it or uses it. There's a guy named Griffin Blake, he's dealing quality, usually spends his evenings at this bar, the Toucantina. But I have no idea what he's doing there."

The guard came just as Mathews ground the roach beneath his tasseled loafers. The door slid open. Mathews stepped toward the opening but the guard set his hand on Mathews's chest and shoved him back.

"C'mon, Gidney."

"More pictures?"

"You're being released." I looked at the guard, wondering why I was out so fast. "You wanna stay here and think it over?" I waved bye to Mathews and stepped outside. The guard led me through a different part of the labyrinth, one I hadn't seen before. I noticed how well his complexion matched the green walls. I wondered if people were like chameleons that way, taking on the coloration of their workplaces. We walked another minute or two until I was truly lost, then came to a door and through it to where I had been parted from my possessions. The desk sergeant gave everything back to me. Everything but the photos of Bobbie.

"I came in with some pictures."

"The captain wants those."

"Why?"

" 'Cause he wants them."

Good thing I'd kept the rest in my car. While I stuffed my pockets with my possessions, I noticed three men watching me from the doorway. I'd have to get past them to leave. I signed for my things. As I approached the exit, I saw that the two younger ones had a tough, competent look to them. The eldest of the three watched me with sad, patient eyes. His tanned skin looked seasoned, like a leather suitcase with plenty of miles left in it. His hand smoothed a mane of well-tended silver hair, which made him look older than he was. I had seen his face yesterday, his features reduced into pixels at the D.C. library.

He held out his hand and I took it and he gave me the sad smile and said, "Nice to meet you, Mr. Gidney. Would you please come with me?"

"Sorry, but my mother told me never to take rides from strangers."

"Excellent advice, but we're not exactly strangers. And I've heard a great deal about you from Frank."

"Frank?"

"Frank Heinrick, the man who arrested you."

"I wasn't arrested. And don't believe everything Heinrick says."

"Mr. Gidney, if I thought you were a murderer I would not ask you to help me."

"With what, Mr. Andrews?"

His green eyes lost their sadness now. "With finding my wife's killers," he said.

CHAPTER 23

Shad's eyes were brown, not green, but he had the same intense look that Vance Andrews had. I remember looking into Shad's eyes, almost afraid of them, afraid of his ambition to make something of me. The guy was delusional, psychotic. Especially if he thought he could mold me like clay into a shape I wouldn't recognize. The prospect depressed me.

So the day Shad showed up at Bockman's to take his new foster son home, I was moving slowly. Packing my clothes, heading out yet again to a new foster family for what seemed the umpteenth time. I didn't even look up when Eddie sat on my cot. "What's the biggest problem we face, kid?"

"Inflationary pressures?" A catch phrase from *The Post*'s business section. I stuffed shirts, socks, underwear into my duffel bag.

"Cops, they're the biggest problem. You're gonna get a look on the inside, learn about their procedures. Don't you see, this will be the best training trip you've ever had."

"It's so wonderful, why don't you go?"

"I'm not the apple of the captain's eye." He clapped me on the shoulder. I shrugged off his hand. "You'll see, it won't be so bad."

"No, it'll be much, much worse."

I have to say Eddie had been right—life with Captain Shadrack Davies wasn't too bad. For one thing, he had a huge library of well-worn paperbacks. This was the first time I'd ever lived near so many books. I figured it was hands off, but no, Shad told me to help myself. Up to now all I'd read were comic books and *The Post*. I guess you'd call Shad's collection eclectic. Back then I didn't know what *eclectic* meant, all I knew was that Shad's collection amazed me. I remember the excitement of reading Jack London, the mind-bending stories of Harlan Ellison, a biography of Charlie Chaplin that had two sections of photographs that I'd pore over for days at a time. Once I stayed up all night so I could finish Alfred Bester's *The Demolished Man*.

One of things I liked about these stories were the writers' choice of words. These guys *never* said "fuck" or "shit." At first I was disappointed. Then I saw that what they were doing was much better. I tried using some of the words myself. Shad noticed. One morning we got into his big Buick and instead of heading down Georgia Avenue and into the District, he went north, past Silver Spring.

"Where we going?"

"Wheaton. Doctor's appointment."

I groaned. Since hooking up with Shad, it had been nothing but dentists and doctors. I liked that he cared about me, but I was getting tired of being a pin cushion. This doctor was different, a younger guy who had some cool toys in an office, but no exam rooms. Which meant no shots. Instead, he showed me a bunch of pictures, told me to tell him if there was something wrong with any of them. Well, there was something wrong with all of them; I got that after the second picture of a cat sitting still while mice crawled all over it.

Then he had me sit at his desk and do a couple of sheets of problems. Half the time I couldn't figure out what they were asking me or why. But I filled out the sheets.

Maybe a week later I saw an envelope addressed to Shad with the doctor's name in the upper left. Shad took the envelope into another room to read. It irked me that I couldn't read it, too. When he came back, he'd folded the letter and stuck it in his pocket. He grinned at me, looking very pleased with himself, like a guy at the track who beat the odds betting on a long shot. I asked him a few times, but he never told me what the letter said. So I quit asking and went back to ransacking his library. I'd discovered Mark Twain, and the next morning at breakfast reading *Roughing It*, I laughed so hard, Sadie Ruth told me to leave the table.

What can I tell you about Sadie Ruth? Shad's wife was a churchgoing woman with baggy nylon stockings and flat feet. Her upper lip was wrinkled from a lifetime of pursing her mouth in disapproval. She couldn't have kids, so she collected expensive porcelain dolls. Kind of like surrogate kids, only better, because they didn't talk back. She must have had thirty or forty of them, all lined up on a shelf, as though waiting for the dusting she gave them each day.

Every morning she was as nice as could be to Shad. Still, I noticed how, each morning, my breakfast milk was sour, my cereal warm and logy, and my eggs ice cold with congealed grease forming opaque lakes on them. Even my orange juice had turned.

While I struggled through this meal, she'd chide Shad with a sweet voice, say he was spending too much on this white boy, taking me to the dentist, buying me clothes and shoes when I really didn't need them.

It was funny, in a way. I mean, I didn't want to be there, either. If Sadie and I could have voted on this, I'd have been back at Bockman's by nightfall. But Shad was the boss. And I could tell he thought we were in for the long haul, just one big happy family.

Also, I might have been a bit stubborn. Her trying to get rid of me may have taken away some of the urgency I felt about getting back to Bockman's.

It was summer then, and I supposed school was out. Never having gone, I took Shad's word for it. Why not? He was an honest cop. They were getting by before I came on the scene, and I could tell because my presence was a drain on their resources. Shad never complained, but his wife sure did. Sadie Ruth made it clear that she wouldn't tolerate my hanging around the house while Shad was at work. And they couldn't afford summer camp. "White boy was your idea," she told him in dulcet tones. "He goes with you."

"The white boy agrees with Mrs. Davies," I said.

So that's how, at approximately twelve years old, I found myself riding with Shad all over Washington. He wasn't one of those police captains content to push paper around his desk, so we went to the scenes of break-ins, homicides, rock houses full of fiends banging it in. I watched Shad and his crew arrive at crime scenes, reconstruct what had happened. I saw how they used observation and deductive reasoning. And watching them was instructive, believe me. It got so interesting that I sometimes forgot they were on the wrong side of the fence. Then I'd catch myself and shoot a quick look at Shad. He'd grin at me. The man didn't miss much.

I have no idea how he cleared my presence at crime scenes with his superiors in the department. My guess would be that they didn't know. They would have given him hell if they had. They'd have said he was putting me in danger. Maybe they'd have been right. But I felt more secure with Shad than at any other time in my young life. And since Bockman's was the alternative, I'm sure I was safer with Shad.

I'd bet that Shad had it all figured out. The first time we went to a crime scene, I couldn't believe the carnage. Two men had been skull shot. They had left twin trails of blood from the backs of their heads as they'd slid down the walls. A third had been gut shot, then managed to grab the cash and the baggie of coke before tipping headfirst down a flight of stairs. We saw him on our way up, stretched out with his feet on the upper step, his mouth an upside-down rictus of surprise.

I was looking around the room, trying to keep Sadie Ruth's breakfast down, when one of the cops called Shad over. I went with him and looked into the bedroom. There was a kid my age, also head shot, lying in bed. I made it to the bathroom just in time.

Look, I'd seen dead people before. Old people who hated the shelters, homeless folks who died in the cold. Traveling with Shad, I saw a different kind of death, with different causes. I never got sick after that, which was lucky. Because it was only the beginning. Maybe it was wrong of Shad to have taken me along, but I think he wanted me to witness those scenes of crime and spent violence. I think he was making a point about my future.

His team was a loyal bunch. They ignored me when Shad was nearby and teased the hell out of me when he wasn't. The Continental Fop, Dickless Tracy—I got tagged with a few nicknames. But basically Shad's crew was pretty nice. Except for one young detective named Emil Haggler, who was a protégé of Davies. He hated me.

He bitched constantly at Shad for taking me along. Said it was a danger, not to me but to them. One day he said, "We'll be so busy protectin' this kid, we'll get our *own* selves shot, Captain."

Shad gave him a level stare. "The kid's doing fine, Haggler. But I'm a little worried about you."

Which made Haggler love me even more.

A few weeks after this, we went to a crime scene, a drug deal gone bad. Always hard to tell how things like this start, Shad said as I looked around. Did it begin as a robbery? An argument? Did the shooter steal as an afterthought? Seven bodies lay on the ground. Of the two still breathing, one had fallen back onto his arm, so that his hand was under him. It looked uncomfortable. All the others were sprawled in positions that would have been uncomfortable if they had been alive. The air was heavy with cordite, and we were staying until the photographers and ME and paramedics arrived.

A TV truck showed up outside. When Shad went to deal with the reporters, I noticed the junkie lying on his arm—his eyelids flickered. I looked around for someone to tell, hey, this guy's conscious, but they were all busy. The junkie's eyes stayed open as he sighed, and slowly began sliding his arm out from under his body. It looked like hard work. Shouldn't be that hard, unless he was holding something. None of the cops had noticed. It felt a little like a dream—I realized the danger but seemed unable to alert anyone. I drifted over to the countertop like a swimmer in waist-deep water and unplugged the clock radio. As Haggler came through the doorway, the junkie pulled his hand all the way out and in it was a little .22 automatic, which he pointed at Haggler, but didn't get a chance to shoot because I beaned him with the clock radio. The junkie fell back on the ground just as Shad walked in. He saw the gun and looked at Haggler and me.

"What's happening here?"

I said, "Nothing we can't handle, Captain." That's how Haggler and I began our rapprochement. It's still going on. For instance, I'd bet that Emil had thought he was doing me a favor—driving me from Colette Andrews's house to jail, giving me the pep talk about getting crushed by Colette Andrews's husband. Now the very same husband had bailed me out of jail.

I couldn't wait to hear why.

CHAPTER 24

I had missed two days of work without calling Shelly Russia, I'd gotten mugged, accused of murder, and thrown in jail. Compared to me, the star juggler for Ringling Bros. lived a life of mind-numbing simplicity. The only thing I was absolutely sure of was that I was *not* going to work for Vance Andrews, even if he did buy me lunch.

I pointed us to a barbecue joint on H Street. A true diplomat, Andrews had shown only mild pleasure at my suggestion. I inhaled my lunch—the tea Jan had given me that morning was all I'd had that day. Andrews didn't touch his plate. I suppose in his place I wouldn't have had much appetite, either. Or maybe he just didn't like ribs.

The problem was how to brush him off gently. Investigating Colette's murder would put me right in front of Emil's investigation. I'd rather try to stop a bull while wearing only red jockey shorts. "What makes you think there was more than one killer?" I asked between bites.

He turned his beer glass on the tabletop, tracing concentric rings. "Frank told me, they're sure there were at least two people there besides Colette when she was, when she was shot." He looked down for a second, then gave me that intense look of his. "The police are giving this case all of their resources, I have Frank's word on that. But I wanted your help as well. I thought, perhaps, you could help me find those . . . responsible. May I ask you something?"

"Go ahead."

"Was her death related to your visit yesterday?"

"I don't know."

"Why did you go to see my wife?"

I wiped my fingers, then slid a photo of Bobbie across the table. "I'm trying to find this girl, calls herself Bobbie Jackson. I think she lives in Washington and is about twenty-five years old."

"My God," he whispered. He looked up at me, the color drained from his face.

"You see the resemblance."

"Are you close? To finding her?" he asked.

"I know more than I did a day ago. When I suggested that Bobbie was her daughter, your wife denied knowing the girl in this picture. But it upset her. Have you heard of Steps Jackson, a jazz musician?"

"Well, of course I've heard of him, I may have a few recordings of his. Why?"

"It may be that Bobbie's the child of your wife and Jackson."

"I see." He studied the photo again, his face placid. I thought he'd be a tough man to beat playing poker.

"Tell me about Colette."

Andrews sat back against the padded booth, closing his eyes. "I tease her about it—I mean, I used to tease her, that I remembered more about our first meeting than she did. It was an art-gallery opening on R Street, near Dupont Circle. I was someone's guest, a man who'd been buying an artist's work as an investment. I think buying art that way is, I don't know, immoral. In any case, I had just returned from an assignment in Jakarta and was at loose ends. So I was pleased to be there.

"We arrived early, and my friend took the artist aside. That suited me, as it left me on my own to view the artwork. Suddenly this incredible flash of color streaked across the gallery, a beautiful young woman who nearly knocked me down.

"She was charging through when I stopped her—at great physical risk, I might add—to ask if I might be of assistance. There'd been some blunder with the catering, only half the food had arrived. I went to a little gourmet market and bought the remainder of what was needed. She was relieved and asked what she owed me. I must have made a good impression, for when I said the only payment I wanted was to dine with her the next night, she smiled and accepted." He looked away, out toward the street. "Two months later we married."

"Any children?"

"No. Colette had told me early on that she couldn't have children. A tubal ligation. When she was eighteen, she said. She was twenty-eight when we met."

"Did she have any family in D.C.?"

"No. Both her parents died when she was in college."

"Do you remember their names?"

"I'm sorry, but it was so many years ago."

"Does 'Alvin Middleton' sound like her father's name?"

"It's not familiar, but then she never spoke about her family. Neither of us had much family."

"Where did she go to college?"

"She was graduated from Northwestern, in Chicago. Is that important?"

"Right now I can't tell what's important and what isn't. I'm just trying to learn everything I can, in hopes that somehow it'll fit together. Did she have any enemies? Anyone who wanted to hurt her?"

"God, no, not a soul. When did you last, last speak with her?"

"Last night, just before I got mugged."

"Could it have been the same people? Who mugged you and killed my wife?"

"Could be."

"But why?"

"I may have stepped on someone's toes without knowing it."

We were silent. Outside, H Street was buzzing. The sun reflected off car windshields, sending planes of light slicing around the dark wood interior of the restaurant. Andrews was looking out the window, not seeing any of it. Then he leaned forward. "Mr. Gidney, at first I wanted your help so I could find my wife's killers. But this," he tapped his finger on Bobbie's photo, "this has made me think it's of greater importance to find this girl as soon as possible."

"Maybe you're her stepfather." He nodded as his face darkened. "But if it turns out—"

"I don't care how it turns out. Colette has been torn from me, do you understand? She was the thread running through every part my life. And she's been ripped away. The thought that her daughter is nearby and needs help is more than I can bear."

"She may not be Colette's daughter."

"She still needs help. I want you to find her."

He slid an envelope across the counter. "I haven't any idea what a detective charges for his work."

I looked into the envelope. Ten portraits of Ben Franklin looked back at me. For this much money I ought to find Bobbie and paint Andrews's house as well. "Maybe you should wait and see if I get results."

"But surely you'll have expenses—Mr. Gidney, take the damn money, I'll feel better." I put the damn money in my pocket. "Is there anything I can do to help your investigation?"

"I need some background on a congressman named Jason McHugh."

"Hart Wimple, he can answer your questions. Will a meeting today suit you?"

"Today is fine." I gave him my card.

"What will you do next?"

"Get my car from the police lot."

Andrews stood. "I'll have my driver take you." He took out a card with his name and number and the raised seal of the State Department. On the back he had handwritten another phone number. "That's my cell phone. Is there anything else I can give you?"

I eyed his untouched plate. "Just a few minutes alone."

CHAPTER 25

Driving my car back from the D.C. impound lot, I wondered what it would be like to have Vance Andrews as a father. Would I talk through clenched teeth? Just how stiff would my upper lip be?

I liked Andrews. If nothing else, I liked his wanting to help a girl who, at best, was his unknown stepdaughter. He and Colette had never had kids of their own. Seemed a shame. Have you ever noticed that the people who would make loving, interested, involved parents are usually without kids?

On the other hand, maybe they can afford to be loving, interested, involved adults because they don't have any kids to weigh them down. Would Andrews have been so quick to volunteer his help if he'd had seven or eight teeth-clenched kids of his own? Maybe not.

I pulled into a space in front of my house on Webster Street. During our almost one year of wedded bliss, I'd seen Karla leave our little brick love shack twice. Once was to check the connection to the cable modem. The other was to scream at the cable guy who'd failed to fix her connection to the cable modem.

In the bedroom, I put five hundred of Andrews's money in my sock drawer, then traded my ruined clothes for my only suit—a conservative blue pinstripe—with a white shirt and a striped tie. Then I put the other five hundred in my right shoe. I struck a pose in front of the mirror. Like the cover of *GQ*, if you ignored the scrapes and bruises.

Before my meeting with Wimple, I wanted a closer look at Jason McHugh. So I took Sixteenth south, toward downtown. When I passed V Street I spotted them in my rearview. A blue van, about three blocks behind me. I could make out the silhouettes of two men in the front. This was getting annoying.

I drove past P Street and approached Scott Circle. I slowed and the van drew closer. I was in the far right lane, the one you stay in to avoid the underpass and go around the circle to get onto Rhode Island or Massachusetts Avenues. The van was only twelve feet behind me. A white panel truck was on their left, matching their speed, heading for the underpass beneath Scott Circle.

I hit the gas just before the divider strip and pulled in front of the panel truck, whose horn blasted in angry surprise. I was now speeding under Scott Circle while my erstwhile shadows were undoubtedly stuck at a light a hundred feet behind me.

Once I zoomed out the other side, I kept south on Sixteenth, then cut right across K Street and another right up Connecticut

Avenue. I found a parking space and headless meter near the Mayflower on DeSales Street. Around the corner was the Foundation Center library.

I signed in. There were maybe twenty people huddled over terminals, prospectors gathering scraps of information about who was funding what, whose guidelines their projects fit into, how much should they request. Plus a dirty ragged guy in dirty ragged clothes asleep in front of his terminal. I slipped a twenty into his pocket.

Jason McHugh's PAC, Louisianans for a Better Tomorrow, had over thirty donors, so I concentrated on local organizations. That narrowed the number to eight. The IRS classified the groups giving money as 501(c)(3) organizations, which meant that the IRS recognized them as tax-exempt charities and required them to file form 990. The library's 990 copies told me how much each group had given and to whom.

First, the National Forum for Public Policy, or NFPP to you. They seemed to really want those folks down South to have a Better Tomorrow, to the tune of ninety thousand dollars, the only contribution they had made last year. I copied down their Alexandria address on East Mount Ida Street.

Next came the American Institute for Entrepreneurship, the Council for American Enterprise, the National Council for Policy Studies . . . you get the idea. I wrote down everything they had, not knowing what the hell I was looking for. About midway down my list I came to the Center for Domestic Issues and National Responsibility. They liked Jase, too, about forty-five thousand dollars' worth. Once again, McHugh had been the only money recipient last year. Then I saw their address. It matched the NFPP.

I got up and stretched, looked at my watch, then around the

room, then at my watch again. I'd been here fifty minutes. I did the last four in my group. The second-to-last was the National Advisory Council on Policy Issues. Was it just me, or did these guys need some help naming their organizations? They were pikers, they'd given McHugh's PAC only forty-one thousand dollars. But it was all they had given last year.

Their address matched the one for the NFPP and the CDINR Nice that they all had such close contact with one another. I wondered, when the NFPP, NACPI, and CDINR had their office Christmas party, did they use words with one another or just talk in acronyms?

Next I googled Al Broadfield and found links to other news stories about departing congressfolk. Apparently Congress was losing a record number of incumbents, at least twenty-three and possibly as many as forty.

I read. After thirty minutes I'd found some common denominators. The politicians all breathed air, and they all had received PAC contributions. In Washington, these two traits were equally vital. Also, each person who had resigned from Congress in the last two years was from the South or mid-Atlantic. All of their home districts contained areas that the EPA designated as Superfund cleanup sites. And they were all on agriculture committees and subcommittees.

I went back to the 990s for all three organizations, but none of the officers' and directors' names rang a bell. What I needed was a quick trip to East Mount Ida Street, just to check out this hotbed of charitable giving. Which meant I'd need my camera with the 300-mm lens, which I had loaned to fellow Bockman's alumnus Slip Barnett.

The Barnetts' garage was at Fourteenth and Riggs. I pulled through an alley into the back and parked. The Barnetts' Rottweilers watched me as I passed their fenced paddock. I wished they'd bark at me, rush the fence, something. Their stillness disturbed me, as though they were somehow evil, like bottled genies. As a kid, I was very lucky. In the scraps of childhood I can recall, there were few awful moments. I had managed to convince myself that evil was something you found in comic books—the Green Goblin was evil. So was Lex Luthor. Nothing like that on the streets, right? After Shad became my foster father, he changed my mind.

Once in a while Shad and I would get to a crime scene that made no sense. Like a killer who chose little kids as his victims. Shad had kept me from entering those kinds of scenes, which was okay with me. They bothered me enough just knowing about them. I mean, I could barely understand the drug deals and the shootouts and the armed robberies. That was all information I could process.

A serial killer who chose child victims? It gave me a queasy feeling as I waited in the unmarked cruiser for Shad to return. When he got back, we rode in silence. My head was crammed with thoughts bouncing like rubber balls. I finally broke the silence, asked Shad why those children had died. We were stopped at a light and he looked over at me—he never did that when the car was moving—and gave me a dead level stare. "Evil," he said.

"Huh?"

The light turned and Shad started moving, still talking to me but looking out the windshield. "You heard me. Sometimes people, they're just plain evil. Maybe they can't help it, maybe they were born that way—I don't know. There's no reason for it. But the only thing that keeps them in check, Willis, is people like us." We drove a few more blocks and he said, in a kindly voice, "You understand me, son?"

"I get you, Shad."

Now I edged past the Rottweilers and walked into the Barnetts' garage. It was the usual paint-and-body shop. A Mack truck cab had its hood up in the back, and a primered International Harvester Travelall sat patiently, its windows blinded with brown paper taped to chrome. The air had that astringent smell to it, you could get high from all the solvents.

Which could explain the Barnetts' behavior. In fact, I suspected that the Barnetts hadn't been seeing the world straight since they'd opened the place nine years ago. But it's hard to judge, their oddness always stood out. Even back at Bockman's.

On the walls was an impressive collection of calendars dating back ten years or so, gifts from the Snap-on tool company. Each calendar had a color photo of a nearly nude young woman cavorting with a Snap-on product. So what did you do all day while I was at the office, honey? Oh, housework, shopping, picking up the kids. I hardly had time to strip to my underwear and frolic with your cable cutters and micrometer set.

I was examining the printing quality from a February 1987 edition when a high voice squeaked behind me. "Jesusmaryandjoseph, it's himself come to visit."

A second voice twittered. "Sure, and dressed for a funeral."

"Maybe his, you look at that face."

"You think he's wanting to be put out of his misery?"

"Let's start with that POS he's driving."

The Barnetts. The first voice—Slip's, I guessed—laughed all the way up the scale and squeaked, "Yeah, he wants us to"—here he was nearly overcome by his own wit—"adjust the choke and then we'll throttle it to death."

The second voice—Emmet's—started laughing. "We'll ignite its ignition, grill the front grille, and cremate this clunker."

Now they were both cracking up, helpless with mirth. "Excellent!" Skip gasped. "We'll have an auto-da-fé."

"Hey, guys," I said, turning around. They were still laughing, leaning against each other, their arms on each other's shoulders for support. Their high, squeaky voices belied the fact that they were giants, with long frizzy hair and long frizzy beards. Slip's hair was prematurely gray, and Emmet's had a limp, excremental-brown quality. They wore twin green combat jackets, spotted with grease like camouflage. Their T-shirts—faded past colorlessness—stretched across beer bellies, and blue jeans sprouted toadstoollike from the tops of lusterless black boots. They looked like the chorus line from an S & M Santa Claus review.

Slip wiped tears from his eyes. "So, are you driving that in for scrap?"

"Sure, and it's worth ten dollars," Emmet said.

"Five."

I told them, "The car's fine, thanks."

Slip snatched the keys from my hand. "That's *your* story." For a big man, he was fast. Emmet, using his bulk to block my way while Slip drove my car inside, stared in apparent disbelief as it went past. "Like the flaming chariot of Helios," he said.

"Just hand over the camera so I can get out of here."

"What camera?" Slip said, starting to raise himself from the driver's seat. Suddenly we heard a *crack* and he slipped back down. "Oops."

"Now what?" Emmet asked.

"My foot went through the floor," Slip said.

I said, "Get out of the car and get the camera."

Emmet rolled to the floor to look at my car's underside. "Gidney, your floor's like an oxidation test."

Slip eased himself out, then made a big to-do of placing his hands over himself to be sure he wasn't hurt. "I think I'm unwell."

Emmet got up and hugged him. "It's okay, big guy, I'm here for you."

"I know." He started laughing. "That's what's making me sick." Then they both started in again.

I said, "Could you *please* just get the camera?"

"Always the grouch," Emmet grumbled. He pushed my car over to the lift like he was pushing an empty shopping cart.

"Sure, he's always been a pain." Slip hit the lever and raised my car to a comfortable working height. Comfortable for them— I would have needed a stepladder. They were checking out the hole in my newly ventilated floor.

"Cool. You see how it's shaped? Like Africa."

"You're crazy. It's shaped exactly like Maui. See, there's Red Beach, right there."

"And speaking of Maui . . ."

"Later, when we make out his bill."

Slip traced his finger around the hole. "We could put a plywood board over it."

"Yeah," Emmet said, "Gidney has always bored us." They started giggling again. Then they stopped laughing. Emmet said, "See that?"

"Yep."

I walked beside them. "What?"

"There." Slip pointed at something, but I couldn't see it. So Emmet grabbed something, pulled it down to show me.

It was a small electronic box, the size of, well, a small electronic box. It had an adhesive pad on one side and a small black wire on the other. "GPS," Emmet said. "A tracking unit."

So that's how they'd been tailing me. I thought back to the Kerberos cops brushing past me on K Street. They must've attached the GPS tracker to my car while I was kicking the snot out of Westy. "I'll be back."

I went out the back, headed up the alley three blocks, and cut over to Fourteenth. Only one glance down the block showed me the blue van parked pointing south, toward the Barnetts' place. Staying out of sight of their side and rear mirrors, I got close enough to catch a glance at the driver.

It was Mal. Just looking at him, my bruises started hurting all over again. The license tag was plain white with blue numbers and GOV at a diagonal of the left. Which meant that Mal was driving a government vehicle. My tax dollars at work. I copied down the tag number and went back to the garage.

One hour—which seemed like several—and countless Barnett jokes later, Slip and Emmet had repaired my floor. Then I got my camera and their bill. I was paying Emmet an outrageous sum when a hefty guy in a cap came in. Slip joined him by the Mack truck. They looked at the engine, Slip pointing out what he'd done. The man nodded and slammed the hood down.

As I walked over to the truck I saw a roll of duct tape and wrapped the GPS the Barnetts had found, sticky side out.

Emmet had raised the garage door. The man in the cap was behind the wheel now, his backup lights on and his warning beeps sounding. I hefted myself up onto the running board so I was level with the truck's passenger window, and asked where the man was headed.

"Savannah."

Perfect. "Have a nice trip."

"That's my plan."

I wedged the ball of tape with the GPS into a corner of the cab's backside. Then I climbed into my car, waving my thanks at the boys. They both smiled and gave me the finger as I drove out behind the truck. It was a convoy, with the Mack in the lead and the blue van fifty yards behind me. We headed down Fourteenth Street, past the Jefferson Memorial, across the Potomac River, then onto 395 south. Past the Beltway, traffic thinned and the van dropped way back, until it was just a blue speck in my rearview. Well, with a GPS to help them, they didn't need constant visual contact, did they? I kept close behind the Mack.

Once we reached Quantico, the highway began to get hilly. At a crest, where Mal could see me, I put on my left blinker, signaling that I was about to pass the Mack. I wanted Mal to think I was just in front of the truck. As I reached the bottom I sped up, then at the top of the next hill I floored it as I dropped out of my pursuers' visual range. When I reached the next trough I was doing ninety. I veered off to the right at an exit, out of sight of the van. I screeched to a halt and waited. Less than a minute later, Mal sped by.

I hoped he had plenty of gas.

CHAPTER 26

East Mount Ida Street is a cozy little stretch of low-income housing, safely nestled between the railroad tracks and the flight pattern for Washington National Airport. Ideal, really, if you like the sounds of screeching jet engines mixed with the low rumble of freight trains.

The address from the 990 forms pointed to a gray clapboard house that had been divided into apartments. I checked the names on the mailbox. All three organizations were listed, but, from the plastic toys on the porch and rusted cars surrounding it, I guessed the address was just a mail drop.

Parking across the street and half a block back from the drop, I switched on the camera, rested the end of the 300-mm lens on the steering wheel, and waited. And waited. I could feel my hair grow. The glamour of investigation. Problem was, the Barnetts and Mal had burned up most of my afternoon. I'd run out of time. Hart Wimple was expecting me in twenty minutes.

So I popped the trunk and took out a toy I had made. A little webcam with a tiny SD card recorder. I set it to capture a frame every second for the next twenty-four hours. The street seemed to be empty. Good. I set the webcam/recorder in a clump of bushes with the lens trained on the doorway. Smile, you're on Gidneycam.

In near-total darkness, Hart Wimple thumbed an intercom switch and said, "Run the sixth spot, and then let's hear from the Ax Murderer." I sat beside Wimple at a long table, watching twelve people on the other side of a one-way mirror react to TV commercials that Wimple had produced. There were ten commercials in all. The first five had been testimonial in nature, with big close-ups of everyday folks talking about Wimple's candidate as though he were the Second Coming. As commercials go, they had all the excitement and drive of a stubbed toe.

All the focus-group members had a box with a dial they could turn to a positive number when they saw something they liked, or a negative number for the parts they hated. Using these techniques, consultants like Wimple could pepper their candidates' speeches with catchy phrases like *a thousand points of light*, instead of annoying facts or positions of their own.

The Ax Murderer was an outspoken part of this focus group paid to watch political commercials. Since Wimple had never seen these folks before, and probably would never again, he and his assistant quickly gave them nicknames—the Ax Murderer, the Pedophile, Leona Helmsley, the House Frau, Dr. Demento—well, you get the idea.

"Watch this," Wimple said to me, as though performing a sleight of hand. The next spot had nothing to do with Wimple's man. It attacked his opponent, Congressman Smoot. The spot began with a ground-level, wide-angle shot of bloodhounds sniffing along the ground, their wet, black noses inches from the lens. A bunch of good ol' boys with big bellies and mirrored shades were in the background, holding the ends of the leashes.

Then a voice-of-God narrator told us that Smoot had the worst attendance record of anyone in Congress. If he wasn't doing his job in Congress, just where the hell was he, anyway? The focus group loved it. Especially the Ax Murderer.

"They say they hate negative ads, but they all respond to

them." Wimple shook his head and grinned. He looked to be a healthy sixty-five, with blond hair turning white and a ruddy, outdoors face. He wore a pink shirt with button-down collar and a white cable sweater over it. Prescription glasses hanging from the center of his sweater's neckline. His hands were large, with fingers puffy and twisted by arthritis. He wore pleated khaki slacks and, of course, the regulation tasseled loafers.

The phone beside him rang and as he picked it up he said, "So you're Gidney. What happened to your face?"

"Acupuncture-encounter group."

He nodded at me absently while his assistant switched off the TV sound. Now I could no longer hear the commercials, just see them. The new spot had the camera moving toward a melting ice cream cone with Congressman Smoot's face in the white center. I tried guessing what it was about. Smoot was soft on crime?

Then the door opened. A short, blocky man entered. "Let's get started." He looked to be about sixty, but not a young sixty. His craggy face was set beneath a mass of curly graying hair. Long arms and a long torso, and short legs that barely reached the floor. He looked as though he'd spent a lifetime speaking down to people he'd had to look up to.

"Gidney, this is—"

"Senator Alfonse Broadfield," I said.

"Former senator," he said as he took my hand.

Wimple said, "Have a seat, Gidney. You, too, you miserable cocksucker." We sat.

"You two been friends a long time?" I asked.

"What do you care?" Broadfield asked me.

"Just making conversation."

"Why don't you try making quiet and let the grown-ups talk?"

"Jesus, Al, don't scare him off till we know if we can use him." Wimple sat on the edge of the table, carefully crossing his ankles and his arms. "How can we help you, Gidney?"

"I need to know about Jason McHugh."

Wimple smiled. "To know him is to love him."

Broadfield said, "He's a slimy piece of shit."

"Don't equivocate, Al," Wimple said.

Broadfield snorted in derision. "He forced me out of office, him and that little bitch, Trace. Now they've got an instant campaign to take my seat. Instant campaign funds, too."

"You read the papers, Gidney?" Wimple asked.

"Just the weather report and 'Zippy.' "

"Maybe you saw where a number of congressmen are leaving office?"

"Possibly as many as forty. All married, with one exception." I looked over at Broadfield.

"I'm the only gay member to leave office, far as I know." He sighed and looked at us. "Christ, it feels funny to just come right out and say that, after hiding it for three terms. But it doesn't matter anymore. A gay congressman in a liberal district is one thing. But McHugh and I are from the South. My constituents liked my record okay, but . . ."

Meanwhile, the TV next door was showing black stretch limos pulling up to the Capitol, and identical men in identical suits with identical briefcases getting out. Smoot as a tool of special interests? "So McHugh forced you out?" I asked.

"Not him personally. He's got a group of cutthroats doing his dirty work. Those other people leaving, I know for a fact that only two had their own good reasons."

"You've all been forced out of office? Why haven't you gone public?"

"Damage control. I can leave quietly and still have some kind of career in my home state. Or I can go public and watch it all blow up in my face. Besides, what am I supposed to have said? 'I'm a gay man, I didn't want you all to know, please let me stay'?"

"Why are they forcing you out?"

Broadfield looked at Wimple, who took a cigar from a humidor on the credenza, then sat behind the long table and arranged his feet on top of it, tilting back in his chair. "Gidney, have you ever heard of a corporation called Chirr AG?"

"They're a big company."

"Like the QE2 is a big ship. Chirr is multinational. Mining, munitions, communications, agriculture. All on a global scale. Back in the seventies they took controlling interest in a leading tobacco company. So it's no coincidence that so many departing congressmen have ties to agriculture. Chirr's been suborning members of Congress for the past two years. California legislature, too."

"Same group that approached you?" I asked Broadfield. He nodded. "Why?"

"Because of this vote coming up before the Senate Subcommittee on Agriculture. Chirr's got inside information; they've used their tame congressmen to schedule that vote so it turns a profit. Over the past two years they've been stacking the deck with friendly congressmen. If a congressman won't roll over, he gets blackmailed and a forced retirement. They've approached every member of the agriculture committees. Over forty people. Either they stay on and work for Chirr, or take the heat and leave office."

Wimple said, "That's what's happened to Al."

"Who are these guys?" I asked

Broadfield smiled without humor. "They didn't show their credentials."

Wimple said, "It doesn't matter. If a congressman gets smeared, it kills any chance for a lobbying or consulting job afterwards. Shit, that's why most of them are congressmen in the first place. Lobbying's where the money is."

"I'd think it'd be hard to blackmail so many people," I said.

Wimple said, "Sorry to disillusion you, Gidney, but Congress isn't filled with the brightest people in the world. It's not hard to take photos of some poor jerk who thinks he's God's gift to the ladies." Wimple made a deferential gesture to Broadfield. "Or the men." Broadfield nodded, his expression sour.

"Pictures?"

Broadfield said, "Video. They approached me eight months ago, lobbying hard to change my position. But they didn't spring the tape on me till the weekend."

"Okay," I said. "So what does Chirr get out of this? Does the agriculture angle help their tobacco companies?"

Wimple shook his head while Broadfield told me, "Big tobacco's dead in the States. Leaves Chirr with a problem. And they have a huge agricultural apparatus in place with nothing profitable to grow. They need a new market."

"So what will they grow?"

"Hemp."

"You mean pot?" I thought of Heinrick and Mathews, the cop and the cell mate.

Wimple shook his head. "We're talking industrial hemp, Gidney. The THC content is something like three percent. It's grown overseas for rope, paper, clothing, canvas. Even beer. But not in America."

"Why not?"

"Because it contains *some* THC. Not enough for anyone to get high on, but having *any* THC makes it illegal to grow in the U.S."

"That doesn't keep it from being grown," I said.

Broadfield said, "We're talking about agribusiness. The scale is different. Like comparing your aunt Ruby's tomato garden with Kraft and Del Monte. You have any idea how much money's involved? And what kind of return they're expecting? Anyone gets in the way, they'll get squashed." He looked down. "They made that very clear to me."

I nodded. "So Chirr controls the agriculture committees, gets them to change the existing law to allow the growing and selling of industrial hemp."

"Changing a law takes time and usually more than one vote. But the vote coming up in the next few weeks is crucial. They're spending a fortune, juggling members of Congress. And what they're spending is nothing compared with what they'll make," Broadfield said.

Wimple said, "Just why are you interested in Jason McHugh?"

I said, "I think he may be more than just a bent politician. I think he and his aide, Azalea Trace, are more than just willing subornees. They're more involved. And somehow, I don't know why, I keep crossing paths with them while I'm looking for a girl."

"You have anything on McHugh?" Wimple's eyes took on a spark of interest.

"No."

Wimple leaned back in his chair and rolled his cigar between his fingers. "That's too bad. Because if someone got McHugh out of our hair, the Democratic National Committee would be appreciative."

"How appreciative?" I asked.

"Oh, I don't know." Wimple spoke like a man used to spending other people's money. "Twenty thousand, something like that."

Twenty thousand. That was how much profit Eddie and I had cleared at Bockman's, right at the end. Too bad that twenty thousand now could in no way change the way things had worked out then. Wimple turned to look through the glass to the room next door. "Any campaign in America today, the candidate gets to present the public with two messages. Three at the most. The first message is the candidate's name."

"Of which McHugh's constituents are well aware, thanks to the media," Broadfield said.

Wimple said, "And the second, in McHugh's case, is this racist 'America for Americans' campaign that seems to play so well down South."

Broadfield snorted. "What Wimple's not saying is that we're running around with crossbows and McHugh's got all the arrows. He's also the best fund-raiser they've got. If he makes it to the Senate, he'll take a shot at the White House. Putting him out of business now would be better for the Democrats than a million bucks' worth of political ads."

"Good luck," I said as I stood. I headed for the door, then turned. "One last thing. Senator, what do you know about the Superfund site designations in your state?"

"Just some EPA bullshit. Forget about it. The important thing is McHugh."

I was waiting for the elevator when my phone started chirping. "Hello?"

"This Willis Gidney?" A woman's voice.

"Yes. Who is this?"

"Listen, you gotta stop what you're doing."

"Who is this?"

"You don't know what you're stirring up. Just leave me alone."

"Miss, I annoy hundreds of people a day. I can't help you if you won't tell me your name."

"I'm Bobbie Jackson. And I'm telling you to leave me alone, stop looking for me."

"Are you in trouble?"

"Just the trouble you're making."

"Do you know about Colette?"

"I—I know about Colette. You have to stop now, you're stirring up things you don't understand."

"I understand the same people who killed your mother may be looking for you right now. Where are you, Bobbie?"

"Goddammit, did you hear me? Leave me alone!"

CHAPTER 27

Bobbie's phone call rattled me, both what she'd said and how she'd sounded. I walked down Seventh Street, back to my car, hearing her voice sound brittle as porcelain. Like the heads of Sadie's broken dolls. I shook my head, clearing it of the image and angry with myself for dwelling on the past. Try to think about what had happened.

First I had met with Steps, gone to Money Jungle, then to Vital Records. I had overpaid a D.C. employee to do a computer search of birth certificates, then I'd met Chilcoate and Trace on the Hill, gone to Pencil's Neck, and gotten a call from Varga. I felt sure that Varga and Mal were responsible for clobbering me last night. There had to be a link somewhere.

I still had Bobbie's voice in my ears when I stopped at Jan and Janet's house. Now that I'd had a chance for a second look, I realized that the mystery key set was theirs. Then I remembered seeing Emily running through their dining room waving the keys over her head. She must have slipped them into my pocket. When I handed the keys over to Jan, she wrapped her arms around my neck and called me her hero. Take a hike, Galahad.

Next stop, Pencil's Neck. Inside, I asked if the same young woman was there, the one with the dreads who smelled of sandalwood. A few minutes later she came over, looking at me and smiling. She had dimples when she smiled, I hadn't noticed them before. What kind of hawkshaw was I, missing an important detail like that?

When she saw my bruises, her smile faded. "My God, Val Lewton. Did you get, like, cursed by the Cat People?"

"Something like that. Look, I have a computer question and, for some obscure reason I can't explain, I thought of you."

"Intuitive reasoning, I've heard of that." She smiled again. "Okay, an espresso drink and my break time's yours."

One latte later, we were surfing the Net. We were at forty gigs, she told me. I gathered that was fast. We started investigating Jason McHugh, and she zipped from one site to the next like a pinball hitting the bumpers. Now she was explaining to me how to access McHugh's tax records through some Washington watchdog organization, and I was pretending I understood her.

What I learned was that, while not poor, McHugh was far from a multimillionaire. Which meant the instant campaign funds

Broadfield had groused about had come from outside McHugh's personal holdings. We couldn't find out where.

When Bobbie had called, her number had displayed on my phone. Now the woman with the dreads did a reverse search, matching the number to a location. We found it was a pay phone at Eighteenth and Columbia Road in D.C. I wrote the address in my notebook. Next we looked up Chirr and its holdings. Among them was the Kerberos Corporation. Which meant that the pirates suborning Congress could very well include Varga and his little buddy Mal.

Finally we did a search on the word *hemp* and got twelve million matches. "Is there weed in cyberspace?"

"Let's, like, narrow the search," she said.

So we tried *industrial hemp* along with *ideal growing conditions*, which slashed the number of matches down two million. "Better," she said. "How 'bout *ideal growing conditions in the United States?*" We tried that and found only twelve thousand matches. We started reviewing them and found that industrial hemp likes an arid environment, plenty of heat, and occasional rain.

When we looked up what constitutes an EPA Superfund cleanup-site designation, we found that these were toxic dumps like Love Canal. The only things that grew out of these dumps were class-action suits. I hid my disappointment with masterful self-control. She leaned back in her chair and smiled at me. I still couldn't figure out the shade of blue of her eyes. Periwinkle?

"Okay," she said. "We start with a right-wing ideologue, then a multinational conglomerate, and now we're, like, on to hemp and the EPA. I hope you don't mind me asking, but a girl gets a little curious. Just what the hell is going on?"

"I wish I knew." I took a sip of coffee, letting my thoughts percolate. "Okay, here's what I have so far. A friend of mine hires me to find a girl that may or may not be his daughter. I search an abandoned building, one of her old addresses. One room has holes in the ceiling, and I'm guessing someone taped black trash bags over the windows. And it may have been the same someone who upgraded the electrical system for that part of the building. Up to now, I thought they were using the house for filming."

"Not anymore?"

"Now I'm thinking they were maybe using the lights to grow something."

"Like industrial hemp?" she asked.

"Like some really potent weed."

"I've read about using like, high-intensity lights, harvesting lots of dope from a tiny area."

"A few ounces?"

"A few kilos. Sea of green, it's called. So they sell the weed for five, six hundred an ounce, that like, pays for the hardware. The rest is profit."

I did the math in my head. "I'm in the wrong business," I concluded.

"Okay, so you like, find a house set up for pot growing. Then what?"

"Then comes the part I can't figure." I thought about how little time had passed between my starting to look for Bobbie and meeting up with Varga and his goons. "Let me ask you—could someone who really knows computer programming—"

She moved her head so the dreads swayed back from her face. "Someone brilliant with a pleasant disposition?"

"Yeah, someone like that, could she write a kind of reminder program?"

"I don't understand."

"Sorry, I'm not being very clear. Look, yesterday I went to Vital Records."

She nodded. "Over on Maine Avenue."

"Right. And I paid for a computer search for a birth record. Now, let's say that someone wanted to know if anyone was looking for them. Could they, uh . . ."

"Embed a program within the search program?"

"Yeah, that's it. A program that would let them know if anyone was looking for them."

Her eyes got a merry look to them. "You are *so* full of it."

"Excuse me?"

She waved her hand at me. "You had me like, going there, I admit it." She looked at me closely. "You're kidding, right?"

I looked past her. Through the front door came Mal and another man. I took her elbow, got her up from her chair.

"What's up?" She looked at my hand on her elbow.

"Let's get out of here." They hadn't seen us yet. I tried steering her toward the rear of the store.

She yanked her elbow free. "What's your problem?" Her voice conveyed that she was ready to scream and make me regret it.

Mal turned and saw us. He smiled at me and waved. The son of a bitch was actually happy to see me. I spotted the rear exit. "Look, I'm sorry. I don't know a clever way of saying this—but we have to get out of here. I'll explain later, just come with me, okay?" I kept my voice down, hoping she'd do the same. I shouldered open the exit door. "Please?"

She stood still, then followed me. The door led to an alley. A garbage truck was backing up, *bleep-bleep-bleep*ing, about to block our way. I steered her around it as Mal burst through the door. She turned her head, too late to see him past the truck. Now we were on Seventh. Mal was blocked by the truck, and my car was just ahead. She pulled away to face me. "I should get back."

I looked her in the eyes. "I swear I'm not trying to hurt you. But that guy behind us is a killer, and you're in danger." I opened the passenger door for her. She stood still, looking at me, trying to decide. Her eyes held mine. Then she shook her head and got in. I slammed her door as Mal and his buddy ran out onto Seventh, the new guy crossing the street toward the same god-damn blue van while Mal scanned the sidewalk for us.

I got in on the driver's side. For a change, my car started the first time. I floored it down Seventh. In my rearview I saw the van U-turn and follow, fast. I had lost these guys twice today, they weren't going to let me outdrive them.

I hung a right onto Pennsylvania and saw a sea of green lights. Goddammit, where was a red light when you needed one? I slowed to a crawl and edged up to the crosswalk at Fourteenth as the light went red. In the rearview I saw Mal right behind me. I inched my car forward. "Seat belt," I said.

"What? Why?"

"Please, just do it."

She buckled herself in. The light was still red. No traffic on Fourteenth. I inched forward a little more. The van stayed in place, they weren't worried. Good. Forward a little more. Now I had about five feet between us. I hoped it was enough.

I kept my foot on the brake and shifted into neutral. Just as the adjacent light turned yellow, I stomped on the gas pedal and slammed the shift into reverse. The gear box screamed as my car jumped back and slammed into the front of the van. Amid the crunching noise I heard a wonderful double *pop* sound and saw in my rearview the dual airbags explode in their faces.

I shifted into first and peeled away from there.

She turned to look back as we pulled away. Then she gazed at me. "You knew that would happen?"

"I hoped it would."

She gave me a look, probably thought I was an escaped lunatic. "Well, you sure know how to show a girl a good time."

PART THREE

*There are many names for the various kinds of hot
water kettles, but we still call them kettles.*

—RIKYU

CHAPTER 28

A fact of life: when you're a kid, twenty thousand dollars is a hell of a lot. Even when you split it with your best friend and partner. Our various enterprises—Eddie's and mine—had netted us that much when I went to live with police Captain Shadrack Davis and his wife, Sadie Ruth. The year I spent as Shad's foster son, I'd kept track of the doings at Bockman's. I still had a stake in what happened there—I was still Eddie's partner—and I wanted my share.

Plus, I felt guilty about living with Shad.

I mean, the guy was trying to reform me, and here I was pretending to go along. Thinking it would aid my life of crime when I finally got out of Bockman's. The guilt really put a damper on things, and Shad did things for me you wouldn't believe. Not just clothes and shoes, but swimming lessons, medical checkups. The dentist too. I remember lying in bed in my jammies with Shad's dark face hovering above me, the taste of soap from his just-washed fingers as he flossed my rear molars. At this rate I could've easily stayed with Shad, even though his wife hated me. What changed my mind was *The Post*.

Someone had gotten out word about Waters's use of solitary

confinement. The penthouse was an abuse of the children Waters had been sent to protect, that's what a congressman had told reporters. The next day the paper ran editorials about Bockman's and Dr. Waters. I didn't think it was possible, but conditions at Bockman's had actually deteriorated since I'd left. Some kids had set fire to one of the barracks and, while no one had been hurt, the smoke signals had made *The Post*'s front pages. Now was the time to retrieve the twenty thousand, at least get it off the grounds.

Relax, I told myself. Eddie and I had a good hiding place, a place Waters would never think of looking. But I couldn't relax—the papers were carrying stories about Bockman's every day. Apparently some bright congressmen had had the idea to look more closely into Waters's qualifications, as I'd done months ago. There was also the matter of accounting. Just how much was the good doctor spending on his charges?

I had to get back there. That's what I kept telling myself, my final week with Shad.

The atmosphere at Bockman's had never been sunny. But the day Shad took me back, in the central yard by the main entrance, I sensed a brewing shitstorm of biblical proportions. None of the kids said hello to me, or to anyone else. No one looked at anyone else. The exercise yard was full of kids, but it was completely silent. If anyone threw a glance my way, it held fear and hatred. Part of it may have been me, feeling lousy about the way I'd left Shad.

I hadn't done anything to him. Not directly. But I *had* to get back to Bockman's. And I didn't want to hurt Shad. Sadie Ruth, however, was fair game. So that morning I'd smashed all of Sadie Ruth's pretty little porcelain dolls—her surrogate children. A long line of them, broken arms, heads smashed, their empty eyes staring. Now there was no longer a place for me in their home.

That wasn't why I felt lousy. I didn't care about Sadie Ruth or her dolls. It was because Shad knew what I was doing, knew I wanted to be back at Bockman's. We both knew that he wouldn't just let me go. So I simply acted as I had in the past. Shad was too angry to speak, and I could think of nothing to say. Not a word passed between us on the way to Bockman's. Words couldn't help us now.

Through the windshield I saw my peers scuffling around the dusty, fenced-in yard of Bockman's. Predators kept in check by whatever the drug of choice was that week. Stoners, losers, addicts, mental cases—kids destined to grow up in America's jails, kids who would always answer questions with a "sir" or "ma'am" attached, kids who would always eat their food too fast, their fork hand a blur while their other arm curled protectively around their plates.

I got out of the car. I just stood there, smelling the dust in the air, how it mingled with the fear, hearing footsteps but no conversation, no laughter, nothing that sounded like children. I took a last look at Shad's profile through the open window. For a moment he just sat there. Then he turned and looked at me and I felt the despair washing over me, and I knew then that he had tried his best with me and failed and I had been the architect of that failure.

Before I could turn away, he said, "Willis." He seemed so tired, as though all the strength had drained out of him. "Get back in the car, son. You don't belong here." He had spent his money on me, his time, he had risked his marriage.

I couldn't let him go on this way, with a no-win proposition like me. I looked him in the eyes. I wanted him to know that

I believed, really believed, what I was about to say. "Yes, I do, Shad. I belong here." A few seconds passed. Then Shad faced front and drove away.

When I walked into the main building, someone grabbed my elbow. I felt a thumb press into a nerve and my arm go numb. I looked up and saw Supervisor Heintz's pockmarked face grinning at me. That made everything perfect. "Well, the little blackmailer is back," he said.

CHAPTER 29

The woman with the black-and-tan dreads said, "Now that you, like, kidnaped me, you want to tell me your real name?"

We were driving to Adams Morgan, the point from which Bobbie had phoned me. "Willis Gidney." I held out my hand.

She took it. Her hand felt warm. "Lillian McClellan. You can call me Lilly. So you weren't bullshitting me back there?"

"Why would I bullshit you?"

" 'Cause yesterday you said you were like Val Lewton? Which means you were how old when you directed *The Leopard Man*? Minus thirty years?"

"Sorry, I get a little playful every now and then."

"Don't apologize, I liked it. But I figured you were kidding me about the computer program, 'cause I wrote a program, just like the one you described, and embedded it into the computer search program at Vital Records."

I pulled over. The car behind me—a yellow Porche, this

time—blasted its horn while its driver, a redheaded lad, gave me the finger as he sped by. Too much testosterone. I turned my attention back to Lilly.

"When was this?"

"I don't know, maybe two years ago, I suppose. A woman hired me."

"You remember her name?"

"Of course. Roberta Jackson. What's wrong?"

"That's who I'm looking for. Why didn't you say something yesterday, when I told you her name?"

"It didn't register—you said you were, like, looking for someone named Bobbie, I thought it was a guy's name. Plus, I write software all the time. Bobbie's was like an old job, I only remembered it because you mentioned Vital Records, then described my program."

"And Bobbie Jackson paid you to write that program? What does it do?"

"Sends her an e-mail anytime someone accesses the birth certificates using her name in the search criteria. In case a relative was like trying to find her, she said."

That explained how Varga had gotten onto me so quickly. Thanks to Lilly's program, Bobbie had gotten an e-mail when Vital Records ran a search for her, then she'd put Varga on my trail. Hardly the way to treat well-wishers trying to find you. Except that Bobbie wasn't on the lookout for well-wishers. The pieces started to fit. I didn't like it much. "You have her e-mail address?"

"I never did. See, she wanted that, like, private. When I wrote the program, I let her input whatever e-mail address she wanted. I never saw it."

I waited for Lilly to tell me more, and she waited while

I waited. Then I eased my car into the stream of traffic on Columbia Road. A few minutes later, Lilly and I were walking south on Eighteenth Street in Adams Morgan. I knew I wouldn't find Bobbie in front of the pay phone Lilly had traced, but I had hoped that the neighborhood might tell me something.

Adams Morgan used to be a funky old D.C. neighborhood of working-class people living together relatively peaceably. Some good restaurants, too. Now, with each passing second, developers were cloning Eighteenth Street into the next Georgetown. As we passed the Gap, Wendy's, Banana Republic, McDonald's, Starbuck's, Bank of America, and McDonald's, I discovered that the neighborhood was indeed telling me something, just not about Bobbie.

"You haven't told me why you're, like, looking for her," Lilly said.

"That's right." I was walking and scanning the faces in the crowd. Nothing.

"So tell me."

"I was hired to find her. And I think she's in trouble. The guys that came after us are after her, too. I think they killed her mother, Colette."

"Jesus, are you sure? Why?"

"Don't know. Colette wasn't surprised to find I was looking for Bobbie, but she was surprised when I told her Steps hired me to find her. Which means someone else is looking for Bobbie, too, someone Colette was afraid of. She called me last night, wanted me to drive over so she could tell me something, but I didn't get a chance to hear what."

"Right, you said that in the car. No, I mean, like, why you? What do you care if Bobbie's in trouble?"

I looked at her. There was nothing judgmental in her voice, she wasn't criticizing me. She looked interested. Perhaps a bit amused. Still, her question irritated me. "Why? Because she needs help."

We were halfway down Eighteenth, and none of the young faces drifting past belonged to Bobbie. From somewhere came the smell of marijuana and I wondered if Griffin Blake had supplied it. Too bad Heintz wasn't around anymore; tie him and the Bockman's crowd with Blake and you'd have something.

Lilly said, "So, you see yourself as some kind of Sir Galahad? Saving the weaker sex?"

"Give me a break, okay? You get paid to write software, I get paid to find people. Let it go at that."

"But this is fun."

I didn't know if she meant looking for Bobbie or needling me. "Look," I said, "the main thing right now is, get her out of harm's way."

"And raise your batting average, saving two damsels in one afternoon."

Christ. I looked over at her and she was smiling at me. The dimples, the merry look in those blue eyes of hers. Maybe they were a bluish lavender?

Her face was kind of nice, especially with the smile. Funny that I hadn't noticed before. Her smile almost compensated for the dreads, the silver ring in her nose, the baggy shapeless clothing, and the annoying personality. Almost, but not quite.

She'd removed the rubber band from her ponytail and, as she walked beside me, her dreads were floating free, like some cloud of black and light brown. I couldn't help but look at her, yet I noticed that no one else seemed to see her. This didn't appear to trouble her. It would have bothered the hell out of Karla, assuming she'd ever left our house.

Thunder rumbled as we reached Florida Avenue. No Bobbie, of course. I could have walked back. Or I could have stopped everyone who walked past me and asked them where Bobbie was. Or found a rooftop and screamed Bobbie's name. The first fat raindrops smacked my head as I took Lilly into Manuelo's, a Salvadoran restaurant I frequent, and ordered some taquitos—beef for me, veggie for her. I pulled out the printouts Emil had given me.

"And those are?"

"A list of ATM transactions Bobbie made on her account."

Manny, the owner, came by, looking busy and prosperous. "Ah, Willis, good to see you, man." He looked at Lilly, his hand smoothing his black mustache, his dark eyes sparkling. "And with a lady."

I said, "Hey, Manny. Got that rodent problem licked yet?"

He sighed and said to Lilly, "Guy sees a mouse here one time, just once, years ago, and he never lets up." He turned to me. "So what're you up to, cowboy?"

"Slumming. You got a D.C. map I could look at?"

"Yeah, so long as you promise to come back soon. And you bring this exquisite lady with you." Lilly inclined her head slightly and made a small wave at him. I had seen a similar gesture the last time Queen Elizabeth had motorcaded down Pennsylvania Avenue. Instead of going away, Manny took her hand in his. Then he actually bowed and kissed it, the show-off. Could he have seen her beauty outright, when I had needed an extra day? No way, I decided. Guy was a born hand kisser, that's all.

Manny brought back the map, which I spread over the table. While we munched our food I ran down the printout and marked xs on the spots where Bobbie had made her ATM transactions. These machines are everywhere, so I wasn't surprised to find that she had used one near the pay phone at Eighteenth and Columbia.

But taken as a pattern, they seemed to center farther east, around Thirteenth and T Streets. At that time, Fourteenth Street marked the DMZ—all streets to the west had been gentrified. Bobbie seemed to live in that part of D.C. that had stubbornly refused to let yuppies make it into a cute, faceless place to live. Thirteenth and T was not a great neighborhood but was worlds better than Bobbie's Shaw address. I put away the map and pushed my empty plate aside. As I pulled out my phone, I noticed that Lilly had one veggie taquito left.

Once I got the toll-free number for Bobbie's bank, I called the customer service center. A recorded voice gave me a number of options. I ignored them. After a minute, a real live person came on the line, her voice strident with vile pertness. "Thank you for calling Ameribank where we care about *you* this is customer service representative Denise speaking how may I help you," she sang at me.

Whatever do they pump through the air ducts there? "Hey, Denise, this is customer service recipient Bob Jackson speaking, and I've lost my ATM card. Can you send me a replacement?" Lilly looked at me in disbelief. I didn't know if they had Bobbie down as a "Ms." Jackson or not, but life's a gamble.

"Do you have your ATM card number handy, Mr. Jackson?" As far as Ameribank was concerned, one Jackson was as good as another. I read her the number off the statement, eyeing Lilly's last taquito and attempting to lift it off her plate via telekinesis.

"And may I have your mother's maiden name as verification for security purposes."

"Middleton," I said. As I said it, some kind of warning bell sounded way off in my consciousness.

"One moment."

Lilly grinned at me, then pushed her plate toward me. Apparently she had some redeeming characteristics after all. Outside, the rain came down in waves. It was kind of cozy in the restaurant. I had just stuffed the last taquito into my mouth when Denise chimed in, "Yes, I have your account information here." She sounded extraordinarily pleased with herself.

"Great," I said around my mouthful of food. "I guess I need a new card number, huh?"

"Oh, yes. We can assign you a new number, and you'll get the card in seven to ten working days. Do you want this card sent to your home?"

"Yeah, but I've moved and I don't want the card to go to my old address. I sent in a change of address card to you two weeks ago, but you may not have received it yet. My old address is 427 Seventh Street Northeast, Washington." Which happened to be the house in Shaw where I had taken Dante's gun from him.

"The address I have for you is 1347 T Street Northwest, 20009."

I scribbled down the address in my notebook. "That's it. Thanks, Denise."

"Oh, my pleasure, Mr. Jackson. Is there anything else I can help you with?"

"Well." I made it sound like I really didn't want to trouble her. "I'm just a little concerned that someone tried to use my card since I lost it. Have there been any transactions on it since yesterday?"

"One moment." I waited while I heard the clicking of computer keys. Lilly smiled and shook her head. "Mr. Jackson, I see one withdrawal for two hundred and fifty dollars, placed at our ATM at Twelfth and P Streets yesterday evening, around eleven thirty." That fit in with pattern I had seen, but the amount was quite a bit larger. Most of Bobbie's withdrawals had been for thirty or forty bucks, tops.

"Yes, that was mine. And nothing since then?"

"No, that's the most recent transaction I'm seeing."

"Good. Thanks again."

"You're welcome, Mr. Jackson. And have a *nice* day."

"Sorry, I've made other plans." I put the phone away.

Lilly turned the notebook around and read the address. "Is that our next stop?"

"My next stop. After we find a safe place for you."

"Like, my home?"

"Like, bad idea."

"Hey, those two guys were after you, not me."

"They didn't follow me to Pencil's Neck." I was certain of that. I folded my napkin and placed it on the table, wondering how to tell her. I was pretty sure that now was not the time for Shad's lecture about evil and keeping it in check. My voice soft, I said, "Lilly, these guys are on cleanup detail, taking care of loose ends. You're one of them. That's why they showed up at your job."

She folded her arms. "Why would they do that?"

"Because you wrote that program, you're a link to Bobbie. Something's going down, I don't know what, but until I can clear it up, would you humor me a little? Please?"

"It's ridiculous." Her voice lacked conviction.

"Of course, but let's play it safe. I'll get you a room somewhere.

This is all going to blow over in a day." I tried to sound confident.

"You're not just, like, hitting on me, are you? This whole thing about getting a room somewhere? I mean, you're nice but—"

"It's not a come-on, Lilly." Christ, as if. What I wanted more than anything was simply to get away from this woman. Why should *I* care if Bobbie was in trouble? Jesus Christ. I sat back in my chair while one of Manny's nephews cleared our plates. After he walked away, I said, "If the people chasing us are the same ones who killed Colette yesterday, well, I want to be sure you're safe. Worst-case scenario, I'm wrong and you spend a pleasant night enjoying room service."

"Well. I guess one night would be cool."

"Good. I'll drop you. Then I'm going to track down Bobbie."

"Wait a sec'." A smile played across her lips. "If I'm, like, in danger, I'm sticking with you."

I shook my head. "You'll be safe at a hotel."

"After we find Bobbie. She'll need protection, too, right? We'll all go together." She smiled at me again. Yeah, kind of a nice face, with a personality like a week-old flounder.

But I was the boss here—important to establish that here and now. "Absolutely not. If I say you're going to the hotel, you're going. Got it?"

CHAPTER 30

Lilly said, "I see a space, up ahead on the left."

She didn't have to sound so damn cheerful. I yanked the steering wheel to the left.

"You know, it's like bad for your teeth to grind them that way."

I grunted and switched off the engine. I sat for a moment, just looking through the windshield at the row houses on T Street. The rain had let up when we left the restaurant. Now I could feel the humidity, like breathing though cotton. "I'm going to check this out. Alone. You wait here."

"I'll go with you."

I turned to her. "Hey, you got a vacuum between your ears? This could be dangerous. You'll be safer in the car, and I'll be right back. Okay?"

She shook her head, her dreads swaying. "No, I'm like, much too scared for that. You've got me freaked out, so I have to go with you." Her eyes had that look, this was a big joke to her.

Maybe she was right.

We walked over to 1347, a broken-down house in a row of broken-down houses. Somewhere, a baby cried. A gray picket fence that had once been white sagged across the front yard, with a gap like missing teeth where its gate had been. We walked through. The push-button doorbell had been jammed in all the way. I knocked, we waited.

No answer. I thought the baby's cry was louder. Coming from inside?

We walked through an alley and, once behind the house, stepped around rusted auto carcasses, TV housings with no tubes, an engine block, an empty film canister, and broken plastic toys with their bright blues and reds and yellows somehow alien in this place. A plastic doll's head with Caucasian features and dark brown color stared up at me, mutely asking if I'd seen its body. I thought of Sadie Ruth, her porcelain dolls in pieces on the floor. Stairs led to a screened wooden porch, where scraps of green paint had peeled from the dead gray wood underneath. The baby's cry *was* coming from inside. I rapped my knuckles against the screen door. The baby's crying stopped—just for a moment— then began again with new desperation. I heard the baby's panic grow, its screams too much like the screams in my nightmares.

I raced past the screen door to the second door, wooden with glass panels and a dirty gray towel hanging on the inside for privacy. Cordite fumes worked their way through. That, and another odor. I felt sick as I rattled the knob. The baby screamed, now more animal than human. I kicked out a glass panel. The glass tinkled to the floor and I heard a kind of thud and abruptly the crying stopped. I glanced at Lilly in the sudden silence. Her face had gone pale. I reached in past the jagged glass and unlocked the door.

Blood had splattered across the kitchen walls. The baby, a little black girl in pink with a pink-and-white bib, had been strapped into a high chair, and in her fright seemed to have rocked the chair to the floor. She lay unconscious in a pool of blood.

It wasn't hers. It belonged to the remains of a white woman sitting in a chair by the table. Her head was gone. An explosion of blood and gray matter had smeared the wall behind and slightly above her. The body was slumped in a chair, looking almost relaxed. Pale hands rested on knees, palms up. At her feet lay a rack for holding pots and pans. Inside some of the pots were small drops of blood. Like a cooking class taught by the Marquis de Sade.

Behind me Lilly took a sharp breath. Undoing the plastic catch that kept the baby strapped to the high chair, I carefully picked her up in my arms. The pulse in her throat was strong and steady. We walked to the porch, then I handed the baby to Lilly, the blood from the baby's clothes sticking to mine.

"Wait here," I said. She nodded.

I went through the kitchen, careful not to step in the blood. I did a quick search. I found no more bodies, which was good. A room on the top floor had holes drilled into the ceiling, like the house in Shaw. Some kind of scent I couldn't place floated around me.

Back downstairs I checked the breaker box in the front hallway. The wiring looked new, recently converted to carry high electrical loads. Also, like the house in Shaw. I wondered if Dante had been through this house as well.

On our way out, something in that trash heap caught my eye, a gray plastic film canister. It stood empty with its open end up. Inside, it looked dry. I took out a plastic bag from my pocket and placed the canister in it, careful not to leave my prints. Then we took the baby to my car. No one shouted, no one called the cops, no one noticed us. We could have detonated a small nuclear device in that neighborhood and no one would have noticed us. We drove away with the baby unconscious on Lilly's lap and nobody stopped us.

CHAPTER 31

I drove to Jan and Janet's house. No one tailed us. Was the dead woman the baby's mother? Except the baby's skin was a very dark brown and the dead woman's pale white. Though that didn't necessarily mean anything. How long had the baby been there, anyway? With a headless woman as company. I'm no expert, but I would've guessed from the warmth of the woman's skin that she had been dead for an hour, tops. Maybe less.

Whoever had killed her had placed the business end of the weapon in her mouth. Mal's handiwork? Before he went to Pencil's Neck, to collect Lilly? I didn't know why he would kill the woman in the kitchen, why he'd spare the baby. I was just glad that the baby was alive.

I held on to that thought, it helped keep some of the rising fear at bay.

Maybe, because of the holes in the ceiling and the beefed-up electricity, the woman was tied into this whole mess and Mal was tidying up. Maybe he'd thought that killing her was the right thing to do. Or he could have killed her for no reason at all. Maybe he simply enjoyed it.

Janet opened her door, looked at the blood-smeared baby sleeping in Lilly's arms, and let us in without a word. She left the room, then brought Jan back with her, Emily trailing behind.

"Everyone, meet Lilly and the, uh, baby," I said.

Janet took a look at Lilly and me, then began feeling the baby's head and neck. "What's happened to her?"

"She took a fall."

"She's covered with blood, Willis."

"It's not hers."

Janet shot me a quick look, then took the baby carefully from my arms and went upstairs. Jan asked us to sit down. Lilly sat while I went and washed my hands. When I came back, Lilly was alone, pacing the floor of the living room. She was hugging herself as she walked.

"Janet's the one with the blond hair? She took Emily to a neighbor's."

"I need to call the cops. I'll be right back." Which was only partly true. What I really needed was a few minutes alone. I found being with Lilly exhausting.

At the door I heard a sob. I turned and saw her, standing still, hugging herself, the tears rolling out of her eyes and down her cheeks. I hadn't seen anyone cry in a long time. Years. My ex, Karla, had never cried.

I just stood there for a moment, looking at Lilly, not knowing what to do. Then I could almost feel Shad behind me, pushing me across the room, guiding my arms around her. I patted her on the back, told her it was all right, she should cry, just let it out. I smelled the sandalwood in her hair. Her sobbing slowed, then stopped. She moved away from me and, to my surprise, I found I didn't want to let her go.

She looked at me, her eyes red and face wet. "I'm okay."

"You sure?"

She nodded and sniffed.

"All right. I'll be back in a second." I went to my car, then drove to Wisconsin Avenue and called from a supermarket pay phone. I told the desk sergeant that there was a dead woman at 1347 T Street Northwest. When he asked my name, I hung up. I sat in my car for a moment. The image of the woman in the kitchen was hard to shake.

When I opened the door to Jan and Janet's, Lilly and Jan were sitting on the couch, Lilly with a cup of tea in her hands. She gave me a weak smile. "How's our patient?" I asked.

Janet came down the stairs with a tray. "I gave her a bath and now she's sleeping." On the tray were cubes of soft cheese, slices of peeled apple, and an empty little cup with two handles and a top. Emily's baby cup. She set down the tray. "You want to tell us what happened?"

I told them. I finished by asking if the baby could stay with them, I didn't know where to take her. Janet had listened with her arms crossed, her face red. "Willis, you're taking that child to the hospital."

"You said she's all right."

"I said she was resting. She may have a fracture from the fall, she needs an X-ray."

"How does she seem to you?"

"Goddammit, Willis, either you take her or I will."

"The hospital will want insurance information, they'll want proof I'm her father."

She looked at me for a moment. "You want to raise her your-self?"

"Me? Are you nuts?"

"That's the alterative, right?"

"Look, I'll take the little spud to Juvie Services first chance I get, okay? I just need to park her with you while I sort out this case."

"She needs an exam. Now."

Lilly cleared her throat. We looked at her.

"Uh, I know a place we could like, take her."

CHAPTER 32

The Washington Free Clinic has six examination rooms the size of phone booths connected to a bigger phone-booth-size room on the second floor of a church off Sixteenth Street. Folding chairs lined the walls of the bigger room, and in the chairs were people. Almost a perfect cross section of race and class. Some of them seemed impossibly young; I saw a kid barely into his teens get up and walk into an exam room. Lilly said a lot of people came here for HIV testing—without their parents or insurance companies knowing the results.

An old wooden desk fronted an older receptionist, a woman with steel-gray hair and steel-rimmed glasses who looked at least ninety. She looked at us with gray eyes that seemed to have seen all the trouble the world had to offer. After she'd asked me to write down my initials and birthdate, she told us to take a seat.

We sat. The baby burbled happily on my lap. I wondered how old she was, which led me to wonder when her birthday was and who would celebrate it. Maybe no one. *Well, kid, join the club. I'm sure you'll find the Juvie Justice system as much fun as I did.*

Right now she didn't seem to care where she'd end up—she was more interested in trying to make the gray-haired woman smile. Behind the woman stood an old-fashioned glass-door cabinet, locked and full of drugs. A much younger woman with a stethoscope draped around her neck came over, unlocked the cabinet, and took out a few small packages, samples the drug companies give away.

Back at Bockman's, Dr. Waters gave away truckloads of drugs, but it didn't help him. The drugs were part of the Bockman's recipe for a riot: start with three hundred kids in a space designed for ninety. Separate from parents and guardians. Remove any incentive to cooperate. Convince them with punishment that they have nothing to lose. Add more drugs, then stir them together so their ideas intermix. What you end up with is not a crime-prevention system—it's a crime-generating system. I think Waters saw it coming, even while Congress investigated him.

He cracked down on the supervisors who were reselling the downers we were supposed to be taking. Did I mention that these supervisors were not the cream of the public-servant crop? They were also without any medical training or background. I mean, how much medical training do you expect from a person who earns minimum wage? Yet, supervisors were handing out prescription pills like candy corn on Halloween.

I was amazed that so many kids actually took this crap. Maybe they were depressed to start with, figured they couldn't be any worse off. And of course, some were taking drugs anyway. The little blue pills and orange pills they popped were just more spice in the stew.

A place like Bockman's, kids escaped. Escapes happened the

whole time I was there. Kids were still busting out after Waters took over, but not a huge number of them. Nobody outside noticed. A week before the riot, kids broke out every day. The cops brought them back, a day or two later, but the escapes made the local papers. And that made more heat for Waters.

The supervisors felt the heat, too. Waters must've leaned on them pretty hard, because they pressured the kids for information, threatening them with the penthouse. Or worse. One night the supervisors made a gauntlet in the hallway of dorm B, the disciplinary house. They grabbed some kids out of their beds and made them run naked down the hall and whacked them with wooden ax handles. They weren't acting on their own. Waters was desperate to know what was happening in the very facility he had been hired to control. But the supervisors couldn't gather the intelligence Waters needed to keep the lid on.

Some kids were so freaked out, they went to Waters for protection. Waters told them he'd help them if they gave up information—snitched on their friends. Problem was, there was no longer any core group of kids, so there was no intelligence information to gather or repeat.

Under this pressure, our dear Dr. Waters did not bear up well. At the best of times he was no Saint Nick. So I could guess how spiteful, enraged, and trapped Waters must have felt. I might've even felt sorry for him, if he hadn't thrown Eddie and me into the penthouse. That's where I was when I heard the first gunshot.

A hand touched my shoulder, and though the touch felt gentle, I jumped.

"Wow," Lilly said, "quite the startle reflex."

"Thanks."

She just looked at me. I hate that. "You okay?" she asked.

"Sure."

"I think they just called your name," she said.

Well, not my name actually. The steel-rimmed glasses called out again, "Double u gee, seven four seventy-five." That was me—my initials, plus the birthdate the District had assigned me. We stood. Lilly and I argued about what to call the baby—I liked the name Sarah while Lilly preferred Claire or Clara—then out came the doctor. He looked to be about seventeen. At least he was older than the baby.

We followed him to an exam room, where he gave her a good going over, weighed her, measured her height, and didn't ask a lot of foolish questions—like were we the baby's parents, had she been immunized, all that stuff. He only blinked when we said we wanted a full range of tests, including HIV. He did ask for the baby's name and I blurted out Clara just as Lilly said Sarah.

The doctor looked from Lilly to me. "Sarah Clara?" We nodded. "Or Clara Sarah?"

"Sarah Clara," I said.

"How nice." He said it the way a stranger might tell you a tree just fell on your car.

Sarah Clara took a liking to him, she was cooing and laughing while he tickled her, the tickling covering up most of his examination. He took a blood sample from her heel. She squawked, but not too much. As the doctor carried the sample out of the room, I took Sarah Clara in my arms, patted her back, and said there, there. I have no idea why I said that. When I glanced at Lilly, she was smiling. "Something?" I asked.

"No, nothing."

"You look amused," I said.

"Just thinking about damsels and your batting average," she said.

I had to dump this woman before I killed her.

The doctor came back, said Sarah Clara had no broken bones, that the blood-test results would be ready in two days, and showed the good sense not to ask why we wanted them. He did ask if we had any favorite books on child care. That was cute. I said no, we didn't, and he recommended a few. After we strapped Sarah Clara into Emily's old car seat, I took Columbia Road to the Calvert Street Bridge, back to Jan and Janet's house.

"So, this has been fun," Lilly said. "What's next?"

"Next we drop off the baby, then put you in a hotel room." And out of my life for good.

"What are *you* doing next?"

"Well, now we know it was no coincidence, me getting beat up after I started searching for Bobbie."

"Thanks to my programming skills."

"Right. What's bothering me is a different coincidence."

"Sure, the fact that all these ex-congressmen have, like, Superfund sites in their districts."

I looked at her. Apparently I wasn't the only one who'd noticed. "Yeah, well, I need to take a look at one of those sites."

"Jim Dandy to the rescue. What're you looking for?"

Jim Dandy my ass. "I don't know. But the trail on Bobbie is cold and I have to do something. She's involved in this, maybe it will lead me to her."

"Cool. I can like, look up the nearest site once we stop at my place to get my laptop."

I shook my head. "Too dangerous."

"Hey, I have a life, you know? I'm working on like four different software contracts. I gotta get some work done or I'll have four pissed-off ex-clients and no cash."

Ooh, she was getting steamed. Good. Why should I be the

only one? But I was tired, tired of arguing. And being around Lilly was wearing me down. "Look," I said, "you have to know the difference between what you want and what you need, okay? I know where we can get you a laptop."

She shook her head. "I need mine. All my work is stored there."

"Try to make do for one night, okay?"

"One night? And then this'll all be over?"

"Absolutely," I assured her.

CHAPTER 33

I parked a block away from my brick house on Webster Street, then sneaked through the alley in back. With Lilly in tow, of course. It was only seven o'clock or so, but, beneath the dense mulberry trees that lined the alley, there was little light. A wind was stirring, causing tree branches to whisper about the rain that might be coming soon.

"Why are we here?"

"You want a laptop, you get a laptop."

We passed a row of trash cans.

"Something stinks here."

"You could have stayed in the car," I reminded her.

"Oh, right, and let *you* pick out a computer for me. Besides, I wanna see where you live."

Great. As I approached my house, our next-door neighbor's dog, Max, a big black Labrador, began barking at me through the fence as though I were the doggy Antichrist. He flashed his teeth and growled with the sound of pure menace. At least Mal hadn't staked anyone out in back. Thank you, Max. I leaned down by the fence, proffering my hand. Advancing with many warning growls, he lowered his head, sniffed, then started thumping his tail. In the near dark I could see his pink tongue flapping.

"Good boy, Maxie. Are you all alone out here? Anything happening?" I let him lick my hand through the fence. We walked past him to my backyard. Lilly stayed close as we went up the back stairs. The rear door was bolted shut from the inside since my ex, Karla, had lost the key. But a trained eye might notice some bricks a different color than the rest. I started taking them out of the side of the house.

"What's that?" Lilly whispered.

"Milk chute." I removed the last brick, revealing a 36"×24" rectangular piece of wood hinged to the inside of the house. Left over from a different time, when men in white jackets drove horse-drawn milk wagons at dawn. Not even Karla had known about this. The milk chute, I mean. I think she knew about dawn. I swung the little door open, revealing the shelf where full bottles would've replaced the empties so long ago. The corresponding door on the inside was hidden behind a poster mounted on lightweight foam core. It barely made a sound as I pushed it onto the floor. I clambered inside, then offered my hand to Lilly. "Welcome to the inner sanctum."

The living room was a disaster—books littered the floor, couches were overturned and pillows slit open, foam-rubber cushions lay like huge yellow anthills. Karla's family portraits on the wall next to the stairs had the glass smashed out of them. The big mirror at the bottom of the stairs showed the room again, making two messes instead of one. A little visit from Mal.

Lilly crossed her arms. "You married to Martha Stewart?"

"Not anymore. C'mon upstairs, you can borrow a laptop."

On the second floor, Lilly fired up the computer, then smiled at me. "I think we can make this work."

"Great, let's get out of here." Suddenly I couldn't wait to leave this place.

We'd started downstairs when I saw them, two of them at the bottom. They had been quiet coming in. The bigger one looked up and charged at us. I gripped the banister and snapped a roundhouse kick to his head, sending him over the railing and down. Outside Max started barking, he was missing all the fun. The second one shoved his hand in his coat. I snatched a framed portrait off the wall and threw it at him. He dodged it but it gave me a second. I jumped down at him, slamming him against the wall, my left hand pinning his arm inside his jacket. He was too busy getting his gun out, he didn't watch my right. I swung an uppercut that snapped his head back into the mirror, the mirror cracked in a starburst as I jerked my arm back, my elbow smashing his jaw. He tumbled forward.

I didn't bother catching him.

Once he hit the floor, I bent over him and fished out his gun. Another 9-mm; they really were the caliber of choice these days. A Beretta, made nearby in Maryland. Shoot globally, shop locally. I looked for a wallet but found nothing. I searched his buddy, with the same results—no hotel-room keys, no matchbooks with scribbled phone numbers, no written deal memos outlining their responsibilities as bad guys. The bigger one had a scar running across the bridge of his nose, and a gun identical to his buddy's. I wasn't in the market for more guns, so I ejected their clips and took them with me. "We're outta here."

I looked around. Lilly was frozen at the top of the stairs,

clutching the gray laptop to her chest. "Lilly?" I said. I held out my hand.

She came down the stairs tentatively, like a beauty queen accepting an award she isn't sure she wants. She couldn't take her eyes off the two hoods on the floor. When she reached the bottom I took her hand, leading her around their bodies and toward the back. I realized that I enjoyed holding her hand and let go. She looked behind her. "Who are those guys?"

"Hired guns. Working with the men I saw today at Pencil's Neck. The big ugly spud with the scar was outside Jason McHugh's office yesterday, wearing a Targus Security uniform. Kerberos owns Targus, and Chirr owns Kerberos."

She took one more look behind her as I ushered her out, then stared at me. "Where'd you learn to fight like that?"

"I got beat up a lot as a kid."

CHAPTER 34

Lilly said, "Cool, it's got four G Wimax."

"I love that kind of talk," I said.

We were speeding out of D.C. and into Virginia on Interstate 66, past Rosslyn and through an orange-lit tunnel that seemed garish in the dusk, then past Falls Church and Vienna. *Moodsville*, an old Tommy Flanagan disc, came out of the stereo while Lilly played with the laptop. She seemed pleased. Apparently my lack of understanding didn't dampen her enthusiasm one bit.

"For those of us who don't understand," she said, "I can access the Net from just about anywhere. Even this ratty old car, for instance."

"How nice for you."

She shook her head. "What's the license number for that van, the one whose airbags you popped?"

I fished the scrap of paper out of my pocket.

She took it and started typing away. A few minutes later she said, "Well, well."

I kept driving.

Then she said, "How 'bout that."

I was silent.

She said, "I bet you'd like to know what I just found out."

I shrugged. "If you want to tell me."

"You know, you're a real bastard sometimes."

"Nice that you notice."

"Not that you like, deserve this kind of information, but that van is a government vehicle—"

"I knew that."

"—Registered to the EPA."

"Ah."

"That means?"

"It bears out something Wimple and Broadfield said—that Chirr is buying their way into some kind of new agribusiness. Where's the van supposed to be stationed?"

She typed some more. The warm night air blended with her smell of sandalwood. I glanced at her profile. This sounds weird, I know, but with the golden sunlight on her she looked almost human. She caught me looking at her. I turned back to the road.

Soon we were nearing Front Royal. In the rearview mirror I could see a good distance behind me. No one tailed us. We passed collections of shopping malls and gas stations and fast food plazas, one after the other, bathed in the unearthly glow of white-blue lights set high on metal stalks. America, the beautiful.

"Looks like that van is garaged at a toxic-cleanup facility outside Morgantown."

"Just where I happen to be driving," I said.

"I figured you were, like, going someplace."

"Now, if you were to cross-check your list of Superfund areas—"

"Way ahead of you. It's on the list, all right."

Smart. I nodded at her. "Which means the van Mal used to tail me was an EPA-registered vehicle that should have been at the Morgantown Superfund site."

She asked, "Why was Mal using a government-tagged van?"

"Let's find out."

We settled back for the drive. Halfway there, we stopped for gas at one of those trucker stops that has showers, a game room, and a store. I had a voice mail from Emil. When I called back he asked, "Where you at, Willis?"

"About a hundred forty miles west of D.C. What's up?"

"What's up?" He didn't sound happy. "Lemme ask you something—where were you this afternoon, around five?"

"Doing errands. Why?"

"Because we got a call, someone tipped us to a homicide in a row house at Thirteenth and T. Any of this sound familiar?"

"Should it?"

"Well, I heard the voice of the tipster, the one who phoned it in. You know we tape those calls, right? Now, I could take your voice print, but I don't think I need to, do I?"

"No."

"Yeah. And the house is owned by a lady in Florida and managed by a D.C. firm who told us a Miss Bobbie Jackson is rentin' it. But that lady who lost her head, that wasn't Bobbie, was it?"

"I don't know who it was, but I'd bet the same people who killed her and Colette smacked me around yesterday and broke into my home this evening." I told him about the little to-do at my house.

"Uh-huh. Back to T Street, Willis. You happen to notice a high chair on the floor? Knocked over, but no baby there?"

"Yeah, I saw that. Pretty weird, you ask me."

There was a momentary pause. "Where's the kid, Willis?"

"How should I know?"

"Heinrick says Andrews is pressurin' him, says I should give you a wide berth. So I'm tryin' to be a team player here. But you need to come in and talk to us."

"Fine. Tomorrow morning, soon as I get back. Okay?" He grunted. "Hey, now that we're pals again, I need a favor."

"Told you the bank-account stuff was the end, Willis."

"But that was before I received Heinrick's blessing. Anyway, it's such a small favor, I hate to ask it."

"Then don't."

"But you're so good at this stuff. And how am I gonna learn without your example before me?"

He sighed. "You want a favor, you best be explainin' why you want it."

"I found holes in the ceiling of the T Street house, just like the house in Shaw."

"So what you want?" When Emil got pissed off, his voice got that southern drawl, what he called his 'Bama roots.

"For you to go through the Pepco bills for D.C., see if the

T Street house matched the kind of usage the Shaw house had. Maybe there's a way to cover the D.C. area, see how many residences had huge electrical bills for the same time period." Lilly came back and sat in the car.

"Sure thing, boy. We all just sittin' around here waitin' for some private badge to phone us an' tell us what to do."

"Is that a 'no'?"

He hung up on me. A lot of people had been doing that lately.

"What's wrong?" Lilly asked.

I told her my theory. She said, "So all you need's someone to check the Pepco accounts in D.C. for a few months."

I nodded. "Be right back." I went in to pay for the gas. The truck stop had a nice collection of guns, knives, camo shirts, Dixie flags—everything for today's trucker. Also a nice hardware section. I paid for the gas and a few extra items.

It was twilight when we reached the toxic waste site. I parked a quarter mile away. A chain link fence, placed on an embankment six feet tall, surrounded the place. I couldn't see in without climbing the embankment. No Trespassing signs every twenty feet along the fence warned me that this was an official EPA cleanup site. More signs warned of hazardous waste. The fence was twelve feet high and topped with razor wire.

When the EPA is protecting the public, they mean it.

I was climbing the embankment for a better look when a patrol car slid to a stop in a cloud of dust. Two white guys got out of the car, a lanky one who was the driver, and a short chunky one. Their uniforms had the lightning emblem of Targus security. Coincidence?

"Are you lost, sir?" the lanky one asked.

I gave him a sunny smile. "I'm looking for the Mahatma Ghandi Memorial Barbecue."

"Sir, this is a toxic-waste site. I'm going to have to ask you to leave."

"I'm sure this is the place, I think it's just over that hill. Could you fellas unlock the gate for me?" I jerked my thumb toward the land beyond the fence.

The short cop extended his hand so that his fingertips touched my chest and pushed me back against the embankment. "Maybe you don't hear so good, sir." He had a snarl in his voice and a hand on his nightstick as he took a step closer. "Maybe you need help to unclog your ears." Just then Lilly pulled up in my car.

"Boo-boo," she called, "are these nice policemen helping you?"

The guards looked at each other uncertainly. Beating me up was one thing. But in front of a witness, well, that was something else. "They're saying the picnic's moved," I shouted back.

She looked smug. "See? If you'd stopped and asked directions when I said to, we wouldn't be lost."

I edged past the guards toward my car, making a "what can you do?" gesture. "Women," I said, "one's not enough and twelve's too many." I got in the car. Lilly drove as I raised my eyebrows at her. "Boo-boo?"

She grinned at me. "Hope you have nice lodgings in mind for us."

"You'll love it," I told her.

Four miles and fifteen minutes later, we checked into the Capri Motel on Route 7. The sputtering neon motel sign boasted of a swimming pool—which looked more like an algae farm—and cable TV. I paid for two adjoining rooms. Lilly followed me into the first room and took a look. Fake wood paneling on the walls, a pine dresser missing half its knobs, and a lamp without a shade on the bedside table.

"Chic," she said.

"Rustic charm," I said.

From the rafters swayed a vertical strip of sticky yellow fly-paper, nearly black with victims. Lilly gestured to it like a model on a game show. "This is your idea of like, kicking back and enjoying a pleasant night of room service?"

There was a little box near the bed. I dropped in a quarter and the bed started vibrating across the floor. "Hey, Magic Fingers. Now there's something you don't see every day."

"Thank goodness."

She dropped the plastic bag on the bed. At the truck stop I had bought toothpaste, floss, and a few other essentials. I opened the adjoining door to the second room, went in, turned on the lights. It was the mirror opposite of the first, down to the creaky bed with cigarette burns in the sheets.

I turned to Lilly. "I'm going out now, look at the wonders of nature."

"The toxic site."

"Yeah."

"In the dark."

"Uh-huh."

She took a step toward me. "Too dangerous. You could, like, fall into a pool of carbon-tetrachloride-laced sewage."

I gave her my valley-girl voice. "Eww, no way, I promised myself I'd never do *that* again."

"Wait until morning."

"Now's better."

"And what am I supposed to do?" Her voice had grown very small.

"Do the work you said you needed to do." I pointed at the laptop. "Remember? Your clients?" I placed my hands on her shoulders and felt her body tremble, though it was warm inside the room.

She nodded, glancing away. "Yeah, like I'm really gonna concentrate on that now." She looked up at me. "Look, I'm a little scared, okay? I'd like it better if you stayed." She rested her hands on my chest.

My throat went dry, like the first time I'd met her. Maybe I was allergic to sandalwood. "Look," I said, "the whole idea of driving out here was so I could take a look at this site, see if it's for real."

She moved closer. "When will you come back?"

"When I'm finished." I looked into her eyes. In this light they were a blue purple, lovely and deep without end. I leaned forward and kissed her. She pressed against me and kissed me back. I put my arms around her and she rested her head on my shoulder. I liked the way her body felt next to mine.

"And if you don't come back?" she asked.

I ran my hand through her hair. "You can keep the laptop."

CHAPTER 35

I followed the perimeter of the fence. It formed a rectangle, about 100 yards by 40, completely enclosed. The signs, the razor wire—it seemed like a lot of security for a fenced-in site, toxic or not. The only gate into the area fronted the main road. I felt exposed getting in that way. If a fellow had had the foresight to purchase wire clippers when he'd stopped for gas, he'd be able to simply clip his way through.

I was such a fellow.

The crickets stopped while I climbed the six-foot embankment and snipped a hole and crawled through, sliding down the other side. I got up, and soon felt my feet sink into muck. One cricket started again, then the others picked up the chorus. No moon tonight the and though stars were bright I didn't see the stand of vegetation until I tripped over it. So I picked myself up, brushed myself off, started all over again. Thank you, Jerome Kern.

I tried to avoid tromping through whatever was growing here. What kind of plant thrived on hazardous waste? Nothing smelled toxic. The air had a kind of rancid sweetness. I made my way to the opposite fence, then turned back.

I looked for and eventually found the hole I'd made, which was lucky since I had lost my clippers while stumbling around. Back in my car, muddy and tired, I sat for just a moment, thinking about toxic waste, which was not very enjoyable. Then I thought about kissing Lilly—much better. Was I taking advantage of her? She'd just been through a terrible experience, she was scared, vulnerable. Best to keep her at arm's length. Treat her like a kid sister.

That's when the light hit me in the face.

"Well, well. Look who's back."

"Put your hands up, sir, and get outta the car."

They were on foot, this time—I hadn't heard any car drive up. I shielded my eyes from the beam and got out. The lanky one held the flash, while the short, fat one grabbed my arm and threw me against the car. We went through the drill. When he frisked me, I was glad I'd lost the clippers.

"You don't take advice too good, do you, sir?" the one with

the flashlight said. Amazing how much *sir* sounded like *asshole* when he said it.

"Yeah," the short, fat one said, snarling at me. "Don't you know there's toxic waste here?"

"Sure," I said. "I've just never seen it up and walking around before."

The fat cop grunted and swung the gun barrel at my head. I'd seen it coming and stepped away, driving my knee into his side about where his kidneys were. He gasped and fell over. I looked up just in time to see the lanky cop swing the flashlight. I heard the lens crack, and then I heard nothing at all.

CHAPTER 36

Heintz shoved me in front of Waters's desk. Waters paced back and forth. He gave Heintz a distracted nod, who glared at me before closing the door. Waters stopped pacing. There was something in his eyes I didn't like. *Bluff it out, kid.* I perched on his desktop and started swinging my legs, smacking my heels into the sides. "I've told you not to do that," he said. His heart wasn't in it now. He had other concerns.

I gave him a big smile. "What's up, Doc?"

After a few more laps behind his desk, he said, "I have a problem."

"More than one, according to *The Post*. But I'd guess your chief problem is money, and how you've spent it."

He pressed his bloodless lips together.

"*The Post* says there'll be a congressional investigation into your company, CRC, and your accounting practices. And they'll look pretty closely at you, of course. Whaddya think, Doc? Been on TV before? Got the name of a good makeup lady?"

He turned at me, his voice a snarl. "You little mercenary. I know you and Vermeer have been making fistfuls of money over the past two years, and neither of you have bank accounts—I'd know if you did—so here's my proposition—"

I waved him away. "Not interested."

"Oh, I think you will be," he said. "You and Vermeer will turn over all of your funds to me. Today."

He paused. I looked at him and laughed. "That's it? That's your offer?"

His smile was thin and bloodless. For a moment I saw the old Dr. Waters before me. "Tell me, who do the boys hate more than me?"

"Nobody."

He nodded. "Exactly. I'm the most powerful, and thus the most hated. I control their miserable lives, hand out the punishments, and get them to snitch on each other."

"So? What's this got to do with me and Eddie?"

"And the snitches, in turn, get dorm C. Our deluxe accommodations. Plus extra supervisors for protection."

"They need 'em."

"Certainly. Among the . . . children, the snitches are the most hated, wouldn't you say?"

"Sure." I didn't like where this was going.

"Imagine a snitch without protection."

"Wouldn't be fun."

"True. But one of your fellow cutthroats would soon end the snitch's misery, don't you think?"

"Any of this have a point, Doc? I'm feeling my fingernails growing here."

"That's the second part of my proposal. You and Vermeer turn over your cash, all of it, to me today. And I won't place you in dorm C, with the snitches."

"With the—? But we haven't ratted on anybody."

"You and I know that, but no one else does, do they? All they'll know is that you and Vermeer are in dorm C." He shrugged. "You couldn't blame them if they jumped to the wrong conclusion." I stared at him. "Oh, there is one small problem. The extra supervisors assigned to the snitches. I'm afraid we won't be able to provide protection to you or Vermeer."

"We wouldn't last a day."

"I'm afraid not." His voice was a savage parody of concern.

I shook my head. "You're crazy, Doc. The paper says you embezzled about a million and a half. Even if we did turn over our cash, it wouldn't be nearly enough to bail you out."

"Oh, every little bit helps. And I'd consider it a vote of confidence in my abilities."

I looked down at my sneakers. They were new Keds, Shad had bought them. They were no longer beating a rhythm against his desk. "What does Eddie say?"

"Vermeer refuses to grasp how serious this is." He picked up the phone, said something into it, then hung up. As Heintz came through the door, Waters said, "I'm relying on you to convince him." To Heintz he said, "Place our friend in the penthouse, next to Vermeer."

The smell of rancid decay was even stronger in the rain. I came to on my stomach, soaked and sputtering into the puddle that formed beneath my nose. I rolled onto my back. Fat drops stung my face like hornets.

I wanted to rest, but the rain wouldn't let me. I turned on my side, then tried to get on my hands and knees. They refused to cooperate. After all, they had helped me so far, and what had it gotten them? As far as they were concerned, I could lie in the mud. I pleaded with them, promising a warm bath back at the motel. Nothing doing. I felt nauseated, and swallowed to keep the bile down. My head had a cavernous feel to it. My skull felt heavy.

Come on, Gidney. You can do it, just roll over and get up. I groaned and reached and grabbed the door handle, used it to pull myself halfway up. *All right, high fives all around. Now go the rest of the way, into the car.* I felt myself starting to slide down. Be a shame to waste all that effort. I took a breath, got all the way up, then leaned against the car until the dizziness stopped.

Finally I got in. I closed my eyes for a moment, hearing the raindrops plunk off the metal roof above me. Suddenly I jerked my head back—I had fallen asleep in my car. The wind and rain sounded almost like children shouting. I wiped the rain off my face, found my keys, started the car, and drove away from there.

By two in the morning I was back at the motel. Lilly's room was dark. I unlocked the room next door, then turned on the bath and peeled off my muddy clothes. What a mess. While the water was running I looked in the mirror. An angry red line of dried blood cut across my left temple where the flashlight had struck me. I used soap and a washcloth. It didn't look too bad.

I switched off the light and had just snuggled into bed when I heard a click. Lilly stood there in a cotton T-shirt, silhouetted in the doorway, the light behind her outlining her body. Quite a nice body. Part of me, the tiny part that could still string two thoughts together, wondered why she chose to hide a body like that under baggy shapeless clothes.

"Willis?"

"Everything's fine, Lilly. Go back to sleep." That's right, treat her like a kid sister. A lovely, voluptuous kid sister.

"I want you to hold me," she said.

"Sure." I sighed. "At breakfast, okay?"

"Now," she said, advancing into the room and drawing back the covers.

There's no stopping some people.

CHAPTER 37

When I woke up the next morning, Lilly was gone and so was my car.

I sat up, rubbing my eyes. I didn't feel too bad. In fact, as I walked to the bathroom, I realized that I felt better than I had in months. As though I were getting away with something, like spending the night drinking and then waking without a hangover. I stepped around my shoes and what used to be my best suit, still lying in a heap on the bathroom floor, plastered with mud and local flora.

Maybe I should have been worried about Lilly's leaving. I let the shower get hot while I unwrapped a bar of hotel soap the size of a matchbook, then stepped in. In a moment I was singing "Lush Life," my voice bouncing against the tiles and sounding just like Johnny Hartman's. That's when it hit me—no nightmare. For the first time in I don't know how long, I'd slept through the night.

When I stepped out of the bathroom I saw Lilly typing away on the laptop. She stood and, keeping her eyes on the computer screen, walked toward me until we stood toe-to-toe. Then she looked up and smiled. Her smile jolted me, like sticking a fork into a hot toaster. She put her arms around me. "Time to get dressed?" she asked, brushing her lips against mine.

I held her close and kissed her. "Later." Then, as the bed's gravitational field pulled us in, I asked her, oh so tenderly, "Would you mind taking that goddamn ring out of your nose?"

She pushed me down on the bed. "Yes," she said.

As I lay in bed, I thought I wasn't getting much accomplished today. Except keeping out of Emil's way. I wondered if he would've appreciated the sacrifice I was making.

As if reading my mind, Lilly gave me a final smooch, then rolled away. I sat up and watched her get dressed. She really had a lovely body, but you'd never know it to see her in those clothes. "If this programming thing doesn't work out for you, you could always work as a model."

"Been there, done that, got the wet T-shirt," she said.

"Really." She could've used a few extra pounds, but at least she didn't have that half-starved, caved-in look that grips models like a case of TB.

"Yeah, my mom's idea, a way to make some money. She was like a cheerleader in high school, real rah-rah type, you know?"

"Today we call that bipolar."

She grinned. "Exactly. Well, she got herself knocked up when she was like, a senior. So she raised me herself. I was a cute kid, believe it or not, so for extra cash she had me, like, doing commercials when I was a baby, and modeling clothes at around five, and lingerie starting at about, oh, eighteen or so."

"You wouldn't happen to have any of those later pictures lying around, would you?"

She sat on the edge of the bed. "Pervert."

"I'm a detective, there might be hidden clues."

"Keep dreaming." She kissed me and got up.

"So what happened to modeling?"

"It sucked. A bunch of vapid people with cameras, hanging around you all day, treating you like shit. And it's not healthy—the pills, the cigarettes. The eating disorders. Neuroses, I saw 'em spring up like mushrooms on cow shit. Plus some other stuff."

"Like what?"

She pulled on her baggy pants. "Like, they scan a photo of some woman into a computer and put it on the cover, like here's what 'beautiful' is, and we should all get upset if we don't measure up. Or that love and happiness is just hitting the right combination of makeup, deodorant, toothpaste—you know."

"Still, a person can make a lot of money."

"'It's no trick to make a lot of money, if all you wanna do is make a lot of money.'"

"I admire a woman who can quote lines from *Citizen Kane*," I said. I watched her move, the unconscious grace she gave to all her getting-dressed actions. *Jesus, chill out, Gidney.* In my all-business voice I said, "So you take steps to hide your looks. I mean, I have to admit, I didn't notice when we first met that you were, uh, somewhat decent-looking."

"It's not my fault you're in love with me. You know, there's like four or five straight guys at Pencil's, and not one of them has thought to hit on me." She nodded, her black-and-tan dreadlocks swaying. "And when I'm online, my looks don't matter. People accept me for who I am. I enjoy programming, I'm good at it, and I'm starting to make money."

"You're running your own business."

"And my own life. Shouldn't you like, start getting dressed?"

"Just don't try to run *my* life," I said. I looked down at the heap on the floor. She saw me, and padded into her room, then came back with a white plastic bag with the Walmart logo on its side.

"Here, I bought these while you were zonked out."

Inside were underwear, slacks, and a polo shirt. I looked up at her. "Walmart?"

She gestured at our rooms. "You brought me to Middle America, so I'm, like, bringing Middle America to you."

I tried on the clothes. They were new and uncomfortable. "Thanks. Guess I can make do with the shoes." I picked them up, saw that the folded hundreds Vance had given me were still there, and started brushing the mud off the soles.

"Willis." I glanced at her. "Look," she said, pointing at my shoes.

I looked down. Along with the dried mud were spiked green leaves. I had tumbled through a field of them last night, in the dark.

"Holy shit," I said.

CHAPTER 38

I drove Lilly back to D.C. and its attendant layer of summer smog. On the way, we listened to an Orioles' game and after a few miles Lilly asked who they were playing. "No idea," I said.

"And when did they start games before noon?"

"It's on CD, I've got a bunch."

She gave me a look. "You're listening to an old game and you don't, like, know who they're playing? Do you know who wins?"

"I'm sure someone does."

"Then why listen?"

I shrugged. "I like it. The sound of the announcer speaking and pausing and speaking. The crowd chattering in the background. The occasional sound of ball and bat connecting, the announcer getting excited. The crowd shouting. It's like listening to a kind of music that's timeless and faraway."

She shook her head. "You are *so* strange." A few more miles rolled beneath us, then Lilly, looking up from the laptop, said, "Listen, I've been thinking about last night . . ."

Here it comes, I thought. *The guilt, the remorse, the recriminations. It's All My Fault.*

". . . And I've changed my mind about the Magic Fingers. For a quarter it's like the best deal in town."

"Run away with me," I said. She smiled at her screen. I looked over at her. "How's your work coming?"

"Oh, I've made a list of fourteen locations from Pepco—"

"Huh?"

"—That correspond with Bobbie's high electricity bills."

"You did that?"

"Well, you said your friend Emil wasn't planning to."

"You hacked into the Pepco computer? You can do that?"

Lilly shot me a cold stare. Then her body relaxed. "You don't know much about computers, so I'll assume you weren't, like, trying to insult me. But for your information, the Pentagon is hard. Pepco is easy."

"A genius with attitude, that's what you are. You have the D.C. map we marked up yesterday?"

"With Bobbie's ATM transactions?" She got it from the backseat.

"So. How do those locations fit in with the list from Pepco?"

We rode along in silence. A few minutes later she said, "Well, not all of them match, but eight or nine of the ATMs match the Pepco locations."

"And each location has an unusually high electric bill, even in winter."

"People use electricity for other things. Like baseboard heaters."

"True, but this is all I have to go on. Are all these Pepco accounts open?"

I heard her tapping away and a pause. Then she said, "They're all closed, except for one, at 1105 Q Street Northwest."

"And they all closed on May twelfth."

She looked over at me. "That's right. How'd you guess?"

In my Howard Duff voice I said, "That's no guess, sweetheart."

"Wow, was that Howard Duff?"

A woman who knows Howard Duff is more precious than

rubies. "May twelfth," I said, "a day that will live in infamy, the same date Bobbie's house in Shaw had its juice turned off. Okay, so a number of houses were part of this. Maybe they were all being used for growing pot, like the house in Shaw. Maybe Bobbie had help, maybe she was involved in all of them somehow."

"You mean they had people growing pot all over D.C.? Like a franchise?"

"Works for McDonald's." I took us past Alexandria's Old Town and onto East Mount Ida Street. The Gidneycam was still in place. I cabled it into the laptop, then scrolled through the pictures. Sometimes you get lucky. The camera had caught a frame near sundown yesterday. A tall thin black man with a wool cap.

She leaned in close. "What?"

"I've seen this guy before." I told her about Bobbie's old house and my run-in with Dante.

"So he's tied in with McHugh?"

"With someone who's funneling money to McHugh."

Lilly sat back. "You're saying Jason McHugh is running a campaign using money from the sale of drugs?"

I shrugged. "Is it so different from the CIA selling coke to fund the Contras?"

We headed back to D.C. I turned down Thirty-fifth Place and parked in front of Jan and Janet's house. Inside, Jan was seated on the living room couch, holding Sarah Clara, who was giggling as Emily danced around the room. "May I borrow two envelopes?" I asked.

Jan she pointed to her desk. As I got the envelopes, smiled a rare smile at me. "We're enjoying each other's company."

"Good, because I'm hoping she can stay one more day."

"One more day, one more day," Emily shouted.

"Inside voices, sweetheart," Jan said absently. Her smile faded. "That's fine, but what about this child's future? She needs a home."

"And her real name. We can't like keep calling her Sarah Clara," Lilly said.

"I'm open to suggestions," I said.

"I suppose we can wait one more day, we'll get her test results then. But what if she needs medical attention?" Jan said. "If she has no parents, we have to take her to the proper authorities."

"You make it sound like she's committed a crime."

"Willis, we're the ones committing the crime." Her voice was quiet.

"Tomorrow, okay? I'll take her in tomorrow, I promise."

Jan nodded. Lilly had sat on the couch beside her, and now she held out her hands. Jan gave her the baby. Lilly started bouncing Sarah Clara on her knee and Emily began jumping in tandem.

"Lilly, I'll come back for you after I talk with Emil. We'll grab a bite and see what's what."

She looked up at me. "Wait a sec', I'm not, like, spending the rest of my life in these clothes. You said this'd all be finished to-day."

I headed for the door. "Today's not over yet."

"You're a real bastard," she called after me.

"Keep telling me and I'll start to believe it."

Outside police headquarters on Indiana Avenue, I tried to get my story straight. I was still trying when I walked into Hein-rick's office. Heinrick was behind his desk, with his feet up, a joint burning in his hand. Emil was sitting on the edge of the desk, looking sour. In the corner stood a man with a thin, pale face. He wore a blue pinstriped vest and matching pants.

"Morning, Captain, Emil." I looked at the thin man.

"This is Elliott Spear, he's DOJ. Sit down, Gidney," Heinrick said.

I sat. "You know, you can take THC in pill form, too."

"Where's the fun in that?"

He ground out the roach in his ashtray, put the ashtray in his desk drawer while the pale man regarded him with distaste. "I'm too busy for this shit," Spear said. "You charging him or what?"

"Let's hear what he has to say, first," Heinrick said. He turned to me. "Tell me about yesterday."

I gave them a fairly complete account, getting a call from a woman who said she was Bobbie, getting the address for the T Street house from the bank, and what I'd found there. I left out the part about Lilly being with me. And taking the baby. Heinrick nodded when I finished. "Cute, calling the bank. Sure you didn't impersonate an officer to get that address?"

"Being a good consumer works just fine," I said.

"That's 'cause we live in a service society, Gidney," Heinrick told me. "All of us, the cops, the dealers, the DOJ, the smart-ass sleuths who are a constant pain in my ass. Even the people who blew the head off that woman on T Street, they're providing a service, too."

"I don't think the vic would've agreed," Emil said quietly.

"Murder method's the same as the Andrews woman, according to the ME. Both women took a gunshot to the head. So what's the connection, Gidney?"

"I have no idea," I said.

"For once I believe you."

Spear said, "The call you made, the *anonymous* tip, came from a pay phone in Northwest, upper Georgetown. Why didn't you make the call from T Street?" He crossed his ankles. The guy's feet were long and thin, too.

I said, "I didn't want to touch the phone, leave prints on it and disturb the crime scene. Plus, I had to get out of there before I lost my lunch."

Emil said, "You was always the sensitive type."

"That still doesn't explain why you didn't ID yourself when you called," Spear said.

"Here's why," I said.

I took out one of the envelopes I'd borrowed from Jan and tossed it across Heinrick's desk. Heinrick opened it, then fanned out the spiked marijuana leaves that were inside. "A present? For me? How considerate."

"When I spoke to Emil last night, I was out in West Virginia. If I had waited at the crime scene, I wouldn't have found that."

"So you were in West Virginia and found a handful of pot?" Heinrick asked.

"A field of it."

Heinrick looked mildly interested. He passed the envelope over to Spear. Spear took a look and said, "Waste of time, even if it's true. So someone's growing pot out in trailer land, so what?"

I said, "It's not growing in a trailer park. I found a field of marijuana in a fenced-off area, a Superfund cleanup site. There're EPA signs everywhere. But it's guarded by private cops—who work for Kerberos. They seemed unhappy to see me." I looked at Emil. "Is that possible?"

"You're saying the EPA is growing pot?" Heinrick asked.

"I'm saying somebody is."

"Any proof?"

"Just what you see there. And this fresh cut on my head."

"Anyone could have done that," Heinrick said. "I can think of several who'd like to."

Spear shook his head. "I've heard enough." He started out of the office.

Heinrick, his feet on his desk, folded his arms and looked up at the ceiling. "Probably you're blowing smoke, Gidney. Still, be a hell of a thing. If you're right, I mean. Can you imagine the press coverage?" He held up his hands, framing the headline. "'EPA Site Used for Growing Pot.' Poor bastard who broke the story, he'd never get his name out of the papers."

Spear hesitated, his hand on the doorknob. Quietly he said, "Maybe a few discreet inquiries would be in order."

Heinrick nodded. "You're just the man to make them, El-liott." Spear closed the door behind him. The smile dropping from his face, Heinrick turned to me, making a shooing motion with his hand. "Goodbye, Gidney."

I took out the Ziploc bag with the film canister, placed it on Heinrick's desk.

"Now what?"

I said, "The house with the dead woman? I found this out-side."

"So?"

"It stopped raining about ten or fifteen minutes before I got there. This was in the yard, faceup. The inside was dry."

Heinrick took his feet off his desk. "So, being the clever boots you are, you figured the killer or killers left it there in between the time they aced the woman and you showed up, that it?"

"Yeah. Thought you might like to run it for prints."

"Since Andrews is an interested party, okay. We get anything, Haggler will call you." Heinrick scribbled a note on his pad, then looked at me. "Fuck off, Gidney, I'm tired of looking at you. And next time you phone in a dead body, it better be yours."

CHAPTER 39

My last night at Bockman's.

Also my last night in solitary. Stretched out on the bunk, pissed off at being there, thinking up ways to get back at Waters and Heintz, feeling the silence, not meaning to sleep. But I was so tired. When I thought back to smashing Sadie Ruth's dolls, I had to remind myself that this had happened just this morning, not weeks or months ago. Finally I must have drifted off, because the first gunshot woke me.

I was terrified, out of the bunk and on the floor as if *I* had been shot out of gun.

"Willis." Eddie's voice, from across the hall.

"Here," I said.

I strained to hear what was happening outside. The silence following that shot was so long and so deep, it felt like the pressure on your eardrums when you're under water. Then I heard more shots, and a burst of automatic fire. The guards, shooting back. I heard a key turn in the lock and then Eddie opened my door, motioning me to get out quick. Leave it to him to have his own set of keys.

"You don't believe in due process?" I asked him.

"Not here, not tonight."

We sprinted down the hallway. "Where're the guards?"

"Running scared of the kids, who're running scared of them."

"And where are *we* running?"

"Away. Soon as we get the stash."

Of course. The money. At the time, it made perfect sense to me.

We burst out of the basement stairs and into the courtyard, bathed in flickering light. Acrid smoke drifted lazily through the spaces between the buildings. Across the yard, kids with gas cans were outside the snitch house, they had blocked the doors and set the fire, and in the orange glow I could hear the kids trapped inside, they were screaming.

I stopped.

"What?" Eddie said.

"We gotta help them." The screams changed into something no longer human.

He grabbed my arm. In the firelight his face was cold. "Kid, they're toast. We gotta help ourselves." This was a side of Eddie I'd never seen before.

"How?"

"The cash."

"Later—that could be us in there."

"And I'm saying the snitch house is just the first house that'll burn tonight."

"How do you know? Sell 'em the gas?"

He shook his head. "We *earned* that money. You wanna give it up, fine. I'll be happy to take your share."

He knew exactly how I'd react. And I knew that he knew, he was saying that so I'd come along with him. He was conning me. Second nature for him, I guess. Easier than saying "please." By now the only sounds from the snitch house were the flames crackling and climbing skyward.

The kids were silent, but I could still hear their screams. Years later, I can still hear their screams, over and over. Every night.

CHAPTER 40

The ATM closest to Bobbie's house, at Eleventh and Q Street, was inside a little convenience store at Twelfth and P. According to Ameribank customer-service representative Denise—who cares about *me*, I might add—this was the machine Bobbie had last used. Inside, I bought some coffee, stale crackers, and processed cheese of an orange color that doesn't exist in nature.

Across the street, I relaxed in my car. I was hoping Bobbie would use the ATM again, so that I could meet up with her, reason with her. Failing that, I would charm and persuade her. I was also prepared to knock her down and drag her to safety.

I had a lot of time on my hands, waiting in the car. Some of it I spent wondering how Bobbie had the money to pay Lilly to write the computer program. Then I wondered how Shelly Russia was doing, so I called him. He said I was fired. I could tell that made him happy. I called Emil, but he was gone. I called the time lady, who informed me that I had been sitting on my butt for about a thousand years. At least she didn't hang up on me.

Through the windshield I saw a young black woman approach.

She looked like Bobbie. The strain on her face, the ridges above her eyes, made her look older than she was. Even from across the street she looked haggard. She didn't move like a twenty-something. More like a Medicare recipient.

She went into the convenience store. From my vantage point I could see her slip a card into the ATM and punch in her number. No money came out, of course. I had canceled her card yesterday. She tried a few more times, then left the store. She barely had the strength to push open the door. As though she were sleep-walking.

I followed in my car. She didn't notice me. I could have driven on the tree lawn next to her and she wouldn't have noticed me. I figured to let her reach the house on Q Street, then talk with her. Too chancy on the street, she might make a scene or try to run for it, though she didn't look like she had the energy to run. Around her were barefoot girls riding bikes, shirtless boys in shorts chasing one another, and kids with bright green water guns the size of bazookas. She paid them no mind. She led me right to the house at 1105 Q Street, the house Lilly had located through her search. She dragged herself up the steps, unlocked the front door, and closed it behind her. I was halfway across the street when I heard a flat, loud *clap*, like a tire blowout. I ran up the stairs and through the front door. The woman who looked like Bobbie just stood there, a startled expression stretching her face tight. A few feet into the room stood Mal, with an automatic in his hand and two new friends beside him. "Well, well. Look who's joined the party," he said.

"Varga is very upset with you, Gidney," Mal said. "You know what he told me after you left his office?" If he'd really expected me to answer him, he should've taken the tape off my mouth. "'A waste of oxygen,' that's what he said. But I don't see it that way." Mal took out his 9-mm and placed it on the floor. He hadn't shot the Bobbie look-alike, just put a bullet in the ceiling to get me into the house. Apparently she had been making hourly trips to that ATM in hopes of drawing me out. After I'd chased her inside, Mal gave her some cash. She left, then they took me upstairs and tied my hands and feet to a chair.

Now I was in a room like the one I had seen in the house in Shaw, except that high-intensity lights hung from a grid anchored to the ceiling. Black cables coiled their way down to GFI outlets in the walls. The grow tables were gone, but there was a smell to this room, a sweet rancid smell of decay. I tasted bile in the back of my throat and swallowed hard to get it back down.

"Want to know how I see you, Willis? Hmm?" He began to walk around me, out of my field of vision. While he walked he made these little noises, humming noises like a tiny motor boat. "A blank canvas, that's what I see."

I thought about Colette and the woman in the kitchen. *Don't act scared, don't act scared.* My new mantra. I gestured and made sounds so that he'd take the tape off my mouth. He peeled it back. I said, "What happened to the Cézanne?"

He gave me a blank look.

"The little watercolor hanging in Colette Andrews's house?"

"Oh, that was a Cézanne?" He shrugged. "I tossed it."

"Why?"

This amused him. He smiled, the skin around his eyes and mouth puffy and purple with chemical burn. Probably came from the propellant for airbags. Did it hurt as bad as it looked? I certainly hoped so. "Because it was hack work. Part of the corrupt art establishment. We'd all be better off if we took the contents of every art museum and burned them. Can you imagine the type of fire that would make?"

"Expensive." I tried twisting my wrists loose from the ropes that held them. No luck.

"Oh, sure, the collectors would all cry. The fat cats, the critics. But it would be a boon to every working artist in the world."

"Why?" Maybe if I twisted and pulled.

"Because the art you see in museums is irrelevant. Art today isn't made with brushes and canvas. I mean, shit, we're in the twenty-first century. There's a new sensibility. That means a whole new way of making art, new canvases, new materials." He came closer. His breath smelled like burned plastic. "You want to know how we make art today? What kind of materials we use now? Instead of paints and canvas?"

I swallowed. "People."

He smiled. His green no-blink eyes had a serpent's gleam. "Varga underestimated how smart you were." He let the tense of that last sentence sink in, then asked, "You haven't told me what you thought of my picture."

"What picture?"

"Here." He reached into his jacket and took out a stack of photos, quickly thumbed through them until he found the ones he wanted. "Take a look."

Mal had photographed the wall behind Colette, the pattern of spattered blood from his gun and her brains. "Isn't that amazing? Who would've thought some old spade could have had anything so beautiful locked inside of her? Here, look at this one." A different shot, closer, of the same pattern of blood and brains. "You need an artist, to bring out the real beauty in people. That's why I shoot only film—no digital. It's all about the look. And when the material dries out, it's like—" he paused, groping for the words, "like you can see the art evolving, changing. Interacting with the environment." He showed me a third photo of the wall from farther back. "Let's see Cézanne do that."

I felt a drop of sweat crawl down my back.

"You know what I'd like? I'd like to do a video installation with four or five people. Somehow synchronize the gunshots so we get five patterns on the wall, then film time-lapse over the next eight hours and see what happens to the patterns as the blood dries. Wouldn't that be fantastic? Incredible? I think the Whitney would love it."

"Definitely." Sweat soaked my shirt. "So you tossed the Cézanne to make room for your own, uh, artwork. And that other woman, the one in the kitchen with the baby. I noticed you took down the pots and pans behind her."

"Well, of course, *some* things don't change. You still need a blank space to maximize the effect. Think of it this way—those two bitches'd die someday anyway, right? And what would it mean? Nothing. But I've given them something, a chance at immortality through the artwork. I'm sure they'd thank me if they could."

"The baby, she wasn't the right size."

He nodded. "Kind of like fishing. You know, catch and release." He looked around the room, then at me.

"How much?" I asked.

"Huh?"

I swallowed. "How much are they paying you?"

"Oh, I get two hundred fifty flat per day plus expenses."

"But that's—"

"Peanuts, I know. Why? Thinking of offering me double? And

are we talking money or canvases? 'Cause you should know that's why I'm into this." He grinned at me. "Now it's my turn to ask 'how much?' "

"Do I get paid?"

"No, how much do you weigh?"

I puffed up my chest. "A lot. Two fifty at the very least."

He looked disappointed. "Shit. I should've had Varga's guys position you before they left." He placed the photos on the floor by the gun.

"Your film canister? The plastic one you left behind on Q Street? It had your prints all over it. The cops've got it. Be smart and get out now."

"My prints aren't on file, not anywhere." He grabbed the back of the chair, trying to drag me closer to the blank wall.

That's when the door burst open and Dante walked in, pointing a MAC-11 at Mal's chest. Mal reached for his gun and Dante said,

"Purple spots will die

Before he touches his piece.

No skin off my nose."

Slowly, Mal put his hands in the air. Dante swung the MAC in an arc, connecting to Mal's temple. Dante was fast, and Mal had no time to react. He collapsed.

Dante looked at me. "He gon' kill you?"

I nodded.

He smiled. "Tha's my job."

CHAPTER 41

"Before I cap your enormous white ass, gimme back the piece."

I shook my head, making a show of feeling sorry for him. "Not that way, Dante."

He seemed affronted. I knew he wanted to shoot me, and that if I acted scared, he would. But one thing I learned at Bockman's was that you never acted scared, particularly if you were. So I pretended I wasn't bound to a chair looking down the barrel of his gun, which, by the way, seemed larger than the Harbor Tunnel.

"I mean, where's the incentive, Dante? What's in it for me to give you back your gun?"

"Shit, man, take a look." He waggled the MAC-11 in front of me. The MAC is an ugly piece, metal wrapped around metal with no thought to design or aesthetics. "So do like I say."

"But you said you were gonna cap me anyway. See? If you're gonna kill me either way, I've got no incentive. Now, if you had said, give me back the piece *or* I'll cap you, that would be different. See, that way, you could always shoot me *after* you got the gun back."

He sighed. "Fuck the gun." He pointed the MAC.

"You kill his new partner, Mr. Blake is going to be angry." Just a guess, but I hoped a good one.

He touched the barrel to my head. "Shit, you say anything just about now."

"Why do you think I spent all that time looking for you? Just to give you your gun back? Because I'm a nice guy? I have a proposition for Griffin Blake that he wants to hear, and I want you to take me to him."

"Fuck that."

"Dante, use your brain. Think of all those houses closing down, all over D.C. What, something like fourteen houses? All that pot growing, kaput. That's gotta hurt Mr. Blake, right? But I've got a way for Blake to make it all back and then some." I was overloading him with information. *Keep it simple, Gidney.* "Look—you can be the guy that brings the boss good news, meaning me. Blake'll love you for it. Or you can shoot me and Blake will be angry and have you killed. Your choice."

Dante rubbed his chin with his free hand. "Most likely you're fuckin' with me so's I don't cap you." He paused, his eyebrows down. He was thinking. I smiled encouragingly. "I suppose I could always take you to him, then cap you later."

"See? I knew we could come together."

He frowned. "Course, Mr. Blake won't like it, you knowin' where he be at."

"We'll work something out."

Let's take a moment for a quick lesson in economics. In D.C., an ounce of superb hydro costs six hundred dollars. Yeah, I know, when you were a kid pot came in nickel bags. Great. I'm talking about this century, okay? So a pound fetches just under ten thousand.

Now let's say the equipment Bobbie used may have cost as much as a thousand dollars, tops. Maybe there was another five hundred or so I didn't know about, so let's say you're in the pot-growing business for fifteen hundred dollars. If it takes a plant three months to grow and get harvested, you'd get a dividend of 540 percent. Do it four times in a year, you're around 2,160 percent. Compare *that* to your semiconductor fund. So I had no trouble understanding why Dante had placed me in a room in a chair with my hands tied behind me. Hell, at this point I was getting used to it.

I wasn't used to the ski mask Dante had shoved over my head. He'd spun the mask around so I couldn't see. Through the scratchy wool I heard a voice approach. Now the voice said, "Screw Asia. Keep buying 500's of Global Growth, and hedge with puts on the S & P for August." It was a nice voice, male and cultured as all get-out. Even words like "screw" came out pleasant. It was a voice you could get to love, a voice you could listen to all day.

Except I didn't have all day. I made a deferential cough. The cultured voice—which undoubtedly belonged to the man calling himself Griffin Blake—said, "Gotta go, George." I heard him cradle the phone, then he said, "And what can I do for you?"

"For starters, you can take this mask off my head."

"A risky idea, friend."

"I like taking risks. Sometimes I even drink D.C. water right from the tap." Blake must've given Dante some sign, because he pulled the mask off my face. Behind the desk sat the owner of the voice. I'd seen his face before, except now a crop of blond hair had been blow-dried off his forehead. No glasses, no acne, no buck teeth or worried expression on his face. His eyes still had that strange aspect, the left eye looking at me, the right one staring at something above my right shoulder. As though part of him were there with me, and part of him could see ahead to the next several moves on the chessboard.

He smiled. Confident, almost defiant. As though nothing I could say would shake him. Using his name from Stephanie Chilcoate's yearbook, I said, "Well howdy, Buford."

The smile fell off his face. In sections, like a scaffolding brought down by a single loose screw. "I think you have me confused with someone else, Mister . . ." he picked up my wallet from his cluttered desk and glanced inside, "Gidney."

"Buford Goodwin, graduated from Cardozo High School, with interests in biology and chemistry. Good specialties for a marijuana designer. And you studied debate. Should we debate what happens next?"

"I doubt there's any need, friend. We'll just let Dante tend to you, shall we?"

A truck rumbled past the bay windows behind him. Goodwin tapped his fingertips on the wooden desk between us, the type of desk an eighth-grader might have in his room—cluttered with magazines, papers, yellow legal pads. Someone had used the pads to sketch a series of molecular chains. A little wooden cylinder with a green diode on its side was glowing near Goodwin's tapping fingers. Waste baskets full of loose papers sprouted like mushrooms around the room.

I laughed. "You're in deep shit, Buford." He didn't like my laughing at him, but who does? "Not just your operation, you personally."

"What operation?"

"Your little franchise business, growing pot all over D.C. How did you arrange it? The operator paid a fee up front for the license? Then you supplied the hardware?"

230

He looked at me for a moment. "This reminds me of the movies where the bad guy tells the good guy everything he wants to know. Still, I never could see just why the hell the bad guy does that, considering he's going to kill him anyway. Of course, in this case, I'm the good guy." He put his hand on the cylinder and turned it, making the diode wink on and off. Maybe it was some kind of air freshener.

I said, "The killers tracking Bobbie Jackson are looking for you, too."

He stared at me with his left eye for about thirty seconds, while his right eye was seeing something else. Then he asked Dante, "This gentleman wired?"

"Nope," Dante said.

Goodwin turned back to me. "Why are you so interested in my business?"

"I'm helping a friend find Bobbie. A house on Seventh in Shaw had utilities under her name. The bills were high, but I suppose the grow lights you're using suck up a lot of electricity. That's why the power had been upgraded. And you didn't want anyone on the street to see what you were up to, so you blocked off the windows with trash bags. When I ran into Dante, I thought he was selling crack to a kid. But that was wrong, wasn't it? He was keeping the kid from selling crack in your territory."

Goodwin didn't answer, but he was letting me continue.

I said, "I've seen a couple of your pot-growing houses. Security must be a bitch. But I guess, with a partner like McHugh you thought you had all the protection you needed."

At the mention of McHugh's name, Goodwin's face puckered. He looked down at his messy desk. "Never trust a politician."

"Well, let's not condemn them all. I'm sure quite a few stay bought. So McHugh, under the pretext of searching for—what did Trace call it?—economically feasible buildings to renovate, was actually supplying you with locations for growing cannabis."

"Indigo." He corrected me without looking up. "No one's growing cannabis anymore." He extracted what looked like a wooden ballpoint pen from the center of the cylinder.

"Whatever. In return, you donate money to him through your three tax-exempt charities." I rubbed my chin. "You know, I think that's called money laundering. And what was Bobbie's job? She recruit the franchise owners?"

"She distributed clones of the plants, and the software. See, it's computer controlled, the light intensity, distance between light and plant, cycles for the lights, irrigation." He'd warmed up while he talked about this part, and his left eye twinkled at me. He was into it.

"Smart. A person wouldn't have to make but a few visits to the site."

"Two visits, actually, if you do it right. One visit to set it up and another to harvest."

"And you split the profits with McHugh."

McHugh's name soured Goodwin's enthusiasm. "Bobbie and I had a deal with McHugh, we worked a sliding scale. It worked out pretty well."

Which would account for the instant campaign funds Broadfield had mentioned. "What's special about the clones?"

He reached into his desk drawer and pulled out a plastic bag of grass, packed a tiny amount in the end of the wooden pen, then picked up the fat cylinder off its base. The green diode went out and I saw three brass contacts on the bottom. He put the wooden end of the pen into his mouth, with the marijuana load pointing down, then touched it to the fat cylinder. I couldn't see anything ignite, but a moment later he sent a plume of smoke into the air.

"You see, friend, the biggest problem I have is rip-off artists. Pot is a tempting target. And security, as you say, is a bitch. So I've designed a plant that, on its own, wouldn't get you high. Simple hemp. No one wants to steal it. But after it's harvested, the plants get my special treatment. Brings them up to snuff, and unleashes a really wicked THC content."

Made sense. "So whoever grew pot for you had to have you process it. So you'd know how much they've grown, and what your cut should be. What's special about the treatment?"

He smiled. "That's really my business, isn't it? Coke doesn't tell Pepsi, do they, friend?"

I said, "Coke's owners aren't being hunted by gunmen, friend."

He fidgeted in his chair. "Well, I suppose I could safely say that I use an enzyme bath to align the THC molecules into a pattern I find pleasing." He tapped the end of the wooden pen on his blotter. The marijuana spilled out. It looked unsmoked to me, but he brushed it onto the floor. He looked back at me and giggled. "Very pleasing. Even delightful."

I pulled out my second envelope, the one containing the rest of the pot I had found the night before, and tossed it to him. He opened it and pulled out the two remaining marijuana leaves. He looked up at me. "This is mine. Where did you get it?"

"I found them growing in a so-called toxic-waste site yesterday. Heavy security." He just looked at me. "Don't you get it? Next week Congress will start the legislative process to make growing industrial hemp legal. But, unofficially, at least one tobacco company has already started."

"No one's going to smoke it," he said. "The THC level—"

"Is nonexistent, right." I sat back in my chair. "I'll tell you what I think happened. Let's say a congressman, one you trusted, was approached by a multinational corporation, one that offered cash for McHugh's vote on a bill legalizing industrial hemp. McHugh wants Broadfield's Senate seat, so he makes them a counteroffer—their support in exchange for your formula. Think back, Buford. Did McHugh ever have access to your formula?"

After a deep breath, he put his hands together and rested his chin on his fingertips. "You're implying that legalizing hemp growing is only a first step. Once the crops are in place . . ."

"They're already in place, and out of sight in phony Superfund sites. In a year all these bought congressmen will press for the legalization of smokable marijuana."

He smirked at me. "Like that'll happen."

"Don't you read? Right now in California pot is virtually legal. State budgets are hurting. If tobacco sales keep sliding, it *could* happen. And who's in a position to benefit?"

He got a worried look on his face. Finally. "I see where you're going."

"And I can see where your business is going—up in smoke. McHugh's new friends don't need to legalize pot to get you out of their way, Buford. All it takes is a bullet."

"All right, all right." He waved his hands at me. "What do you want?"

"Untie my hands and I'll tell you." He nodded to Dante, who undid the ropes. I rubbed my wrists to get back the circulation. "I want Bobbie someplace safe."

"I haven't seen her in weeks." He looked at me. "That's the truth, friend."

"I heard from her yesterday. She's scared, which shows she's got more sense than you." I waited a beat, then asked, "You think she's hiding out with her father?"

"No, he died long ago."

That was the answer I'd expected. "I talked with Bobbie's bank. They asked me her mother's maiden name, and it made me wonder if Bobbie's grandfather, Alvin, might still be alive?"

He shook his head; this had nothing to do with him. "Anything else?"

"Yeah. I want the goods on Jason McHugh."

"Why ask me?"

"I was kind of hoping you'd supply me with incriminating evidence."

"And incriminate myself at the same time? Now who's being stupid? You think we had a written contract?" He shot me a pitying look. "McHugh wouldn't hand me that kind of leverage. Listen, friend, you'd have to be a lot bigger and tougher to nail McHugh."

At this point, Goodwin was small potatoes compared to McHugh. But, if I was right about McHugh's connection to Chirr, there had to be something incriminating, some evidence that would tell me where to find Bobbie. And I had an idea where to find it.

I said, "Don't worry, I'll nail him."

He took another drag, exhaled an enormous plume of smoke. He said, "Sure you will, Gidney." Smoke spread out into nothingness.

CHAPTER 42

Augustus was taking a break from smashing parking meters when I found him on Desales Street. He kept close to the narrow strip of shadow the Mayflower Hotel cast on the hot noon sidewalk. He didn't look like a homeless person, more like a general contractor waiting for a delivery of lumber. He watched me coming, his pale gray eyes expressionless.

"I never did thank you for saving my life the other day," I said as I approached him. He didn't react very much. Which is to say not at all. So I plunged ahead. "So thank you. You really saved my ass." He watched me the way a bear at the zoo watches humans. Maybe I'd do something interesting, maybe not. "Look," I said, "if you're gonna go all gushy on me, just forget about it."

More watching. He was smart enough to know that I wanted something, but he wasn't going to help me ask for it. "So, I wonder if you'd be interested in helping me with a little B-and-E?"

When he didn't answer, I said, "It's this place in Georgetown? Called Kerberos? Maybe you've heard of them?" He nodded. "Well, I have to go inside. And I need help. You interested in that?" I needed leverage against McHugh, Goodwin had been right about that. I figured there had to be some kind of documentation on Jason McHugh and Kerberos. If I could find a link, I could use it to stop the killers from chasing Bobbie and Lilly. And me.

He stared at me for a moment, as if we were playing a chess game and I had made a move so stupid that he thought I was setting a trap. His face stayed masklike as he said, "Buy me a mocha and we'll discuss it."

Discuss it? Jesus, it was like meeting with a CEO. We went into the Mayflower. Over our coffees and the hostile looks from the staff, I said, "I need a distraction, long enough for me to get in the building, and then another so I can get out."

He sipped his mocha, skim milk with no whipped cream. "It'll cost."

"Fine." I slipped him two of the hundred-dollar bills Andrews had given me. He kept staring at me until I slipped him a third, then he tucked them into his shirt pocket.

"You planning to do this all by yourself?" I asked.

"Don't worry. You've got friends in low places."

"Okay. Problem is, the place is very tight, tough to get into."

He nodded. "Tomorrow. Meet me under the Whitehurst at nine."

"I figure the hard part will be getting into the building." I sipped coffee. "Wish there were a way to make myself, I don't know, invisible."

For the first time since I'd known him, he smiled at me. "That part's easy," he said.

My run-ins with Mal and Dante had ruined my Walmart clothes. Next to having sex with Lilly, this was the best thing that had happened to me that day. I liberated a Franklin from my shoe and scored some thrift-shop clothes on the way back to Jan and Janet's house. The front door was unlocked.

I felt a quick stab of panic—had Mal and his buddies been here? These were my friends—had I put them at risk? Wishing I had Dante's gun back, I stepped inside. A creak on the staircase, and I saw Lilly coming down. She was barefoot, wearing faded blue denim bib overalls over a sleeveless black top. Her hair was back in a thick ponytail, which bounced as she stepped down. She wasn't smiling. But at least she was safe. I realized I'd been holding my breath, and exhaled in a rush of relief.

"Hey," she said, "you were supposed to be here like hours ago."

"Sorry."

She fingered my shirt. "I see one of us has new threads."

"For a person who's forsaken the fashion business, you seem to care a lot about clothes."

"Well, shit, Willis. I just spent like an hour rummaging through Jan and Janet's stuff, and I look like a farmer's wife."

"Oh, I don't know, you've got a kind of *American Gothic* thing happening."

She drew near and I noticed how the faded blue of the denim overalls matched her eyes. Looking into those lovely eyes, I felt something new. New feelings scare me. Things were complicated already. The very last thing I wanted was to get involved with Lilly. I thought about what Steps had said about love. I had to agree—as I grew older, the only thing I was sure of was that I had no idea what love was about.

She moved closer. I noted how her black top stretched across her body. I'm nothing if not observant. Even in this get-up, she was gorgeous. But with that face and that figure, she'd have looked great dressed in brown paper bags.

"American Gothic?" she asked.

"Sure. You just need to accessorize."

"Like, with a pitchfork? Wanna guess where I'd stick it?"

The woman simply never let up.

"Today," she said. "You promised I'd go home today."

Not with Mal on the loose. I said, "And you will, my sweet, but I need your help finding Alvin Middleton." Home was dangerous for her, but maybe I could distract her with the investigation. So I told Lilly how I'd been thinking about Alvin since I had given Bobbie's mother's maiden name to Bobbie's bank. I should have thought of Alvin a long time ago. If Colette had lied to Vance about Alvin's death, maybe Alvin could help me find Bobbie.

Lilly said, "No more help until I get out of these ridiculous clothes and into my apartment. I've done as much as I can with that laptop, I need my own stuff."

"Oh. This is about your stuff." I put my arms around her, but she pulled back, kept her distance. "Look," I said, "I don't care a bit if you go back there right now and get your head blown off, but I happen to know Jan loves those overalls."

"You're such a bastard."

"But kind to animals. And fun at parties."

A trace of a smile curved her lips. I felt her body relax as she leaned forward. "Can I ask you a personal question?" she asked. Her dreads brushed my face.

"Um."

"When we're in bed, what do you fantasize?"

"A bottle of maple syrup and a guitar strap figure prominently. And that's all I'm prepared to say without my lawyer present."

She rubbed her cheek against mine. Her skin was so soft. She sighed and I smelled her hair. "So. The house is empty. What do you wanna do?"

"Find Alvin Middleton." It was all I could do to get the words out.

She nodded, as if this were the answer she'd expected. She

broke away from me and said, "You're lucky I like to be with you." I opened the yellow pages and began calling nursing homes. She came back with the laptop and started typing. Ten minutes later, she said, "I can't find him."

Even if Alvin was still alive, I had no reason to think he'd be living in D.C. or Maryland or Virginia. He might have moved to be with family in Georgia or California or Borneo. But at least I was doing something, which was better than doing nothing. It would've been nice if Alvin lived in a place that started with an *A* or a *B*. Two hours later I was calling someplace called Tranquil Terrace, and yes, they had an Alvin Middleton there. They made it sound as if I were looking for a spare part for a car Detroit had stopped making decades ago.

Tranquil Terrace—I wondered how much Prozac went into the creation of *that* name—was near the Eastern Market, on Pennsylvania Avenue. I told them I'd like to come out and they said visiting hours ended at five. I hung up and Lilly said, "Great. You can take me to Capazello."

"Let me guess, it's a clothing store."

She grinned. Then the front door opened. Janet came in with Emily and Sarah Clara. Emily hugged Lilly, while Janet said, "Oh, good. Willis, I've got the address you wanted." She held a slip of paper with the address of D.C. Child Services and the name of a caseworker. "She's expecting you."

"Now? I thought we said tomorrow?"

"No, you said tomorrow. Jan and I agree, it's best for the baby—and for you—to do this as soon as possible. What if her family is trying to find her? You can't just keep her, Willis."

"I don't plan to."

She pushed the paper at me. "Take the appointment."

I nodded, put the paper in my jacket pocket, and placed the

jacket on a chair. Emily reached in and took the paper out. She winked at me. I winked back, but Janet took the paper from her and handed it back to me. "Don't forget, you promised," Janet said.

Lilly said, "Oh, he never forgets a promise, do you, Willis?"

CHAPTER 43

You know how dogs and cats always sense when you're about to take them to the vet? Sarah, who loved riding in the car, hollered as I strapped her into the baby seat. Go figure.

With Lilly double-parked outside, I carried Sarah across the portal of D.C. Child Services. I felt her little body stiffen, her arms tighten around my neck. Yet, here we were, just as I had promised. I stepped to the back of a long line in a room that smelled of diapers and exhaustion and hopelessness. There were no windows, no pictures on the wall, only the regulation TV tuned to a soap opera that gave the adults something to take their minds off the kids. The kids were everywhere, running through the room like packs of wolves. They ran past and stole a look at Sarah, as though it might be fun to torment her for an hour or two. A real feral look they gave her. I remembered that look from my childhood.

A few decades later, the line inched forward. The women behind the counter seemed hapless, overworked. One of them— an elderly black lady with a puckered, disapproving mouth and baggy stockings—moved past me quickly. Her name tag read

WALTERS. In her arms were a stack of case folders, must've been at least thirty. And each folder held the life and welfare of a little kid. None of these people was cruel or vindictive or indifferent—they didn't need to be, the system took care of that for them.

First, they'd take Sarah away from me. Then they'd put a plastic strap on her wrist so that they could keep track of her, so many children here. They'd take her to a barracks-style room that Hermann Goering would have loved, and then they'd leave her in a crib. She could sleep or not, but eventually, after lots of crying, she'd sleep. And she'd wake up different, a little colder, a little bit hardened to survive what she was about to go through. If she was lucky, she'd survive it.

There must be some other way, there had to be. The thought of Sarah going through what I'd gone through, and maybe turning out like me—or worse—was more than I could take.

I carried her back to my car. Lilly gave us the once-over. I said, "They said to come back tomorrow, it's too close to the end of the day to process her. Next stop, Capazello?"

Lilly glanced at the outside of D.C. Child Services, then back at me. She knew I was lying. I knew she knew this, and she knew that I knew. I braced myself, ready for the hard time she was about to give me. Instead, she gave me a small smile—the type you'd give a kid who'd dropped his ice cream on the sidewalk. She brushed the hair off my forehead and kissed me. I liked that.

Forty minutes later we were parked outside Capazello. Sarah perched in my lap, her hands on the steering wheel. Her tiny hands tightened and turned the wheel, and little motoring sounds came out of her mouth. Pack your bags, Dale Jarrett. Lilly came out in her baggy new clothes, which seemed quite a bit like her baggy old clothes. She gave me a co-conspirator's grin.

Then we drove to see Alvin Middleton. Lilly took Sarah's

hand as we toddled our way into Tranquil Terrace. The builders had used only the finest cinder blocks, eight floors of them, painted gray, surrounded by a broken-asphalt parking lot enclosed by a twelve-foot Cyclone fence. The fence kept anyone from actually parking there. All the doors and first- and second-floor windows had black bars across them. Kids had tagged their street names all the way around. Inside, they made you go through a bulletproof door, then pass through a metal detector.

On the other side sat a heavyset white guy in a blue rent-a-cop uniform. A roll of fat bulged over his belt and seemed to be pulling him to the floor. He asked us why we were there, shifting his bulk on a padded stool. He seemed bored, but maybe he was just tranquil. So far, he was the only tranquil thing about the place.

I gave him the name of Mrs. Ross, the woman I'd spoken to. While we waited, Sarah grew fascinated by the flickering fluorescents inside the Coke machine. Lilly concentrated on not brushing against any surfaces with her new clothes. Ten minutes later, an elderly black woman with a kind expression and lots of gray in her hair came to see us. "You're here to visit Mr. Middleton?"

"Yes, I'm Willis Gidney."

She took my hand in hers. "Annie Ross. And who's this?" she said, kneeling down to place herself at Sarah's eye level. "A granddaughter?" Sarah gave her a mistrustful look.

"No, we're just friends of the family," I said.

She stood up, still smiling at Sarah. "Well, that's fine, he'll be glad for the company. Follow me, please." She led us around a corner, past a big room with bare walls. Inside were a dozen elderly folks, asleep in front of a TV. With the lights in the ceiling casting a uniformly green shade to the room, the old folks looked like fossilized fish in some forgotten aquarium.

"How do you know Mr. Middleton?" she asked as she pushed the Up button on the elevator.

"We're friends with his daughter."

"Oh? Which one?" she asked as the doors slid open.

Lilly and I exchanged confused looks. "Colette," I said. Maybe it was called Tranquil Terrace because everyone here was tranked out. "How long has this been a rest home?" I asked as the elevator chugged us up to the sixth floor.

"Well, it began ten years ago. This building was put up as public housing, but we're slowly converting it into a retirement community, one tenant at a time. Mr. Middleton's a senior member, he's been here from the start."

Probably made him top dog on the shuffleboard court. The elevator doors slid open. We went down a dark, musty hallway that smelled of age and meals cooked long ago. Tiny white fluorescents in the ceiling only added to the overall gloom. I noticed several doors ajar. Maybe it was easier for the staff that way. Privacy didn't seem to be a concern.

We stopped at the door to 613, which was also partly open, and Ross gave two sharp knocks before pushing it in. The room was long and narrow. The only light came from a four-by-six-foot window at the opposite end. To the right of the door was a small kitchen alcove, which looked unused, and halfway down on the right was a second door, which led to the bedroom and bathroom. I could see an unmade bed through the door and a nightstand covered with bottles of pills. To the right of the window was a TV, the picture hazy and red. To the left was a couch, and on it, presumably, sat Alvin Middleton.

He didn't seem to know we were there. When Ross cleared her throat and said he had guests, he turned and looked at us. His face was crisscrossed with thin white lines—scars from when

244

Colette had cut him with a razor in Steps Jackson's hotel room. Not for the first time, I wondered what could make a daughter hate her father so much.

His eyes had a wide-open quality to them, as though he'd once received a terrible shock and never recovered. His gaze drifted to me first, then to Lilly. But when he saw Sarah his eyes grew wider. At first I thought he was making a funny face to amuse her. Then I recognized his expression—he was terrified.

I stepped between them, blocking his view. "Mr. Middleton? I'm Willis Gidney. May I speak with you for a moment?" I don't think he heard me. He twisted on the couch, looking around me; he couldn't take his eyes off Sarah. "I need to talk with you about your granddaughter. Mr. Middleton?"

His breathing had been regular when we walked in, but now it grew ragged. Drops of sweat beaded his skin, which tightened across his face. The scars appeared to grow paler. Lilly said, "Oh my God." Middleton's eyes rolled back into his head and his eyelids flickered and folded down and he pitched back, limp, across the couch.

I felt for his pulse. "Call 911."

Ninety minutes later, we were sitting in the emergency waiting room of DC General, inhaling the smells of medicine and antiseptic and decomposition that seem to be part of hospitals everywhere, when a short, black-haired woman doctor in a white coat asked if we were Mr. Middleton's family. She spoke quickly and her Pakistani accent made her hard to understand. "We're family friends," I said. "May I speak with him?"

"He's had a mild stroke." She paused thoughtfully, the way

245

doctors do. "I suppose it's all right, provided you keep your conversation brief."

Alvin lay crumpled in a large white bed. He looked defenseless, almost childlike, the size of the bed making his frail body seem smaller than it was. His eyes shifted up as I walked in. "Mr. Middleton, are you all right? I'm sorry if we caused you any trouble. May I speak with you a moment?"

He stared at me.

"It's about Bobbie, Mr. Middleton. Have you seen her?"

He shook his head slowly, his eyes staying locked onto mine.

"Have you spoken to her or been in touch with her?"

His look grew wary.

"I'm not from the police, Mr. Middleton. I think Bobbie may be in trouble."

He tried clearing his throat. When he spoke, it was so soft that I couldn't hear him. I came closer, saying, "Pardon me?"

He pointed at the water glass and, after taking a sip, whispered, "I never laid a finger on that child."

I thought he meant Sarah, which made no sense at all. "Which child is that, sir? The one we brought with us?" He just looked at me, eyes sunk deep in his head, his brow hooding them from the light.

Then I got it. In the elevator, Ross had asked me which daughter. I leaned against the wall. My insides flipped over. I had to get out of there. "Mr. Middleton," I said, staring at him. His face showing nothing. I had to ask but I didn't want to hear the answer. "The child, the one you never touched." I swallowed, my throat felt stuffed with cotton, I could barely force the words out into the tiny room. Jesus, how could anybody breathe in here? "Do you mean you never touched Bobbie? Or Colette?"

Tears welled in his eyes.

"You're saying you never laid a finger on Colette?" I watched the bottom lid of his eye well up until a tear spilled over the edge and ran down his scarred cheek. I thought about Colette having her tubes tied when she was eighteen. And about Bobbie, in high school, saying her father was dead. And then later claiming she was Steps's daughter. I rested my head against the wall, eyes shut.

"They're both your daughters, aren't they, Mr. Middleton? Colette and Bobbie?" My throat clogged, I could barely talk. I saw Alvin's tears coming faster now, racing to get out.

"Was Colette already pregnant when she slept with Steps?"

The doctor came in, saw Alvin crying, his body shaking. She turned to me. "You'll have to go now."

I found my way to the hallway, where Lilly was watching Sarah fool with the elevator buttons. As I walked toward them, I couldn't hear my footsteps. Lilly looked up at me. Something changed in her face. She put her arms around me.

"It's all right," she said.

I touched something wet on my face. Tears. They were mine. Strange, I couldn't connect the tears with anything I was feeling, yet there they were. I wiped them away, took a deep breath.

"Bad news?" she asked.

"Yeah. For Bobbie. And Steps." *Shit,* I thought, *it would've been better if she'd been his daughter after all.* We stayed that way for a moment, hugging each other, then Sarah saw us and started pushing her way between our knees.

"Maybe you should answer it," Lilly said.

"Answer what?"

She reached into my pocket, pulled out my phone and a small, blue plastic Cookie Monster figure. She gave me the phone. I didn't know where the Cookie Monster had come from. Probably Emily. I stuck it back into my pocket as I put the phone to my ear.

"Mr. Gidney? This is Vance Andrews. Something, something's come up. I've—I've just received a call from the kidnapers."

"Bobbie's been kidnaped?"

"Yes. They want two hundred fifty thousand dollars for her. And they specified they want the two of us—they want you to come with me tonight when they, when they make the switch. Yes, those were their words." His voice had a loose, hopeless sound.

"It sounds like a setup."

"A what?"

"What are the odds, Mr. Vance, that Bobbie would just happen to be kidnaped now?"

"You're saying they're not kidnapers?"

"I don't think they are, and I don't think they're interested in ransoming her. If they have her and she's still alive, it's to use her as bait."

"I see."

"Have they offered any proof to you that she's alive?"

"Yes, I spoke with her on the phone. Briefly."

"How do you know it was her? You've never spoken with her before, have you?"

"No, that's true."

I looked at my watch, it was five thirty. "Can you get the money in time?"

"I told them it would be no problem. But the truth is, I can't. Not even if they'd given me a full day."

"I wouldn't worry about the money, Mr. Andrews. I'm sure they're planning to kill us no matter what we do."

"Well," he said, "that's a relief, isn't it?"

CHAPTER 44

"How do you do, Lieutenant? Won't you please sit down?"

Emil grunted and took a seat next to me on the couch in Andrews's study, the book-lined room where Heinrick had blown smoke at me the day before. The room was dark now, just a few lamps burning. Even though it was nearly summer, the room was cool and smelled of wood fires from winters past. I'm sure Lilly would've liked it—liked it a lot more than my depositing her and the baby back at Jan and Janet's house.

"Any more calls, Mr. Andrews?" Emil didn't say from whom, but we knew what he meant.

"No. They're supposed to call soon. With instructions."

Emil nodded. "That's what Willis told me when he phoned."

"Yes, I agreed with his suggestion to contact you."

Andrews didn't know I'd suggested it only after Lilly, Jan, Janet, and even Emily had made it clear they'd make my life hell on earth if I didn't. If Sarah could've talked, I'm sure she would have joined in. Nothing like having four or five women gang up on you. The only bright side was, they were so busy beleaguering me about getting the cops, they'd neglected to badger me about not having left Sarah at D.C. Child Services.

Emil shot a glance at me. "First smart thing you done, callin' a professional."

"A shame there were none available," I said.

Emil shook his head, then said to Andrews, "When did they

call you?" Emil took out his small black notepad and started writing.

"Around five fifteen. Would either of you gentlemen care for a drink?"

"And they demanded the money at that time? No, thanks."

"Yes, that's when they said they'd trade Bobbie, Ms. Jackson, for the two hundred fifty thousand."

Emil looked at me, then said to Andrews, "Did they say how they want it?"

"How they—oh, the cash, you mean. No. I think I might have a drop of brandy. Mr. Gidney?"

"No, thanks." I turned to Emil. "What do you think?"

He pulled out his cell phone and punched in a number. "I think it stinks."

Vance sat in an ancient wingback chair, resting a snifter on his knee. "Why does it stink, Lieutenant?"

Emil was talking into his phone. I said, "Because real kidnapers would've given you time to get the ransom money. They wouldn't call you after the banks were closed. And they would've been particular about what kind of cash to bring—unmarked bills, used, no sequential serial numbers. Things like that."

"They'd tell you 'no cops,'" Emil said, the phone to his ear.

"So this means . . ."

"It means they're either dumb as a box of rocks," Emil said, "or it's their way of gettin' you and Willis in the open." Whomever Emil had called answered, and Emil started speaking.

Andrews sipped his brandy. "Why get us in the open?"

I said, "Bobbie and her high school friend, who calls himself Griffin Blake, had a deal going with Jason McHugh. Blake's developed a formula, he called it an enzyme bath, that turns industrial hemp into potent, smokable weed. There's a multinational company called Chirr, which is planning to grow acres of hemp, sooner rather than later. So McHugh stole a copy of Blake's formula to buy his way into Chirr's good graces. Now, with Chirr behind him, McHugh's poised for the big time. The little people have served their purpose. Chirr's using heavies from a subsidiary, Kerberos, to tie up loose ends."

"Like Colette."

"I don't know that Colette was actually involved. But if Colette called Bobbie after my visit, Bobbie set off an alarm somewhere. So they've been trying to kill her. And me."

Andrews stared at me. His phone started ringing and Emil said, "Here it comes," into his phone. Andrews blinked, breaking the stare, took a deep breath, and picked up the handset. I had the extension to my ear. Maybe they'd decided to forget the whole thing and were sending Bobbie home in a cab.

"This Andrews?"

"Yes."

"Gidney there?"

There was some kind of electronic distortion on the voice, but I took a guess. "I'm here, Mal," I said into the extension.

The voice made a weird scraping noise, which I guessed was Mal chuckling. "Never heard of him. Bring the money to Gravelly Point, north of the airport. You know where that is?"

"We know it. When?"

"Eleven thirty tonight. Just you and Andrews."

"Does Varga know you're moonlighting?"

"Just be there, Gidney."

"How do we know Bobbie's all right?"

There was a pause, a click, then the distortion went away. A frightened woman's voice said, "This is Bobbie. Please, please do what—" Then they broke the connection.

Emil looked at me. "Well?"

"Sounds like the same woman who called me yesterday afternoon."

"Don't mean it's her," Emil said.

"No. Does it matter?"

He shook his head. "At this point, no." We all rose to go. I took another look around. It was a nice room. It seemed a shame to leave it.

CHAPTER 45

It was 11:37. I stood near my car with Andrews. And, according to Emil, twenty cops were hunkered down over Gravelly Point like rocks in a quarry. I couldn't see them. All air traffic into National had been curfewed over an hour earlier, and the park had officially closed. I was kind of hoping the Park Service cops would come by and chase us all away. There was no sign of the kidnapers.

"I forgot to mention, we had the West Virginia Staties check out that toxic site," Emil said. "The one you told Heinrick and Spear about?"

"And you found?"

"Just a field, Willis. An empty field."

"They cleaned it up fast."

"Funny thing, Spear was curious enough to start checking other new Superfund sites, and guess what he found?"

"Jimmy Hoffa?"

"More fields, recently plowed, surrounded with high fences and razor wire."

"And the EPA?"

"They don't know a thing 'bout it."

"Spear sounds okay."

"He's a publicity hound and an asshole but, yeah, he's a good investigator." Emil gave me a level stare. "Maybe he can even find out where that baby disappeared to, the one whose high chair you found."

As if on cue, my phone rang. Mal's distorted voice said, "Here's the drill. Lose the cavalry, then drive to Silver Spring, the intersection of Colesville and East-West Highway. There's a Starbucks by the Metro. You stay in the car, Gidney, and Andrews makes the drop. Oh, yes, if you bring the cops, Bobbie dies."

After Mal hung up, I repeated his instructions to Emil and Andrews. Emil wiped a large, meaty hand across his forehead. "Well, at least now they actin' like kidnapers. I guess that's somethin'." He got on his walkie-talkie and called Crane.

Crane was a scrawny plainclothes guy, all elbows and knees, who'd handled lots of kidnapings. The department's expert. Emil deferred to him. Crane said he'd planned for this and would dispatch a team of five to the scene.

"Our men will penetrate the perimeter undetected and be activated for response prior to the arrival of yourself and Andrews. Then, when the perpetrators strike, we counterstrike with extreme force." Crane looked around. "Any questions?"

"Could you say that in English?" I asked. It was warm out. I was shivering.

Emil said, "Shut up, Willis." He turned to Crane. "Why does Andrews have to come? We could dress one of your guys to look like him."

He shook his head. "Negatory. They may have telescopic abilities and ascertain it's not the real Mr. Andrews. In these cases it's always best to comply with their demands insofar as possibleness allows. Neither Vance nor Gidney will be exposed to potential lethalities."

Whatever that meant. Emil wiped the sweat off his face, his eyes on me. I turned to Vance and said, "Mr. Andrews, this is gonna be dangerous, no matter what Ichabod says."

Crane glared at me while Andrews shook his head. "I understand your, your caution in this matter, Mr. Gidney. And I thank you for your consideration. But this young woman's life is at stake. I'm obliged to help her."

"How 'bout you, Willis?" Emil asked. "You comin' along for the ride?"

I felt sick. "Yeah."

Emil said, "Shit," stretching out the word.

We had caravanned across the Fourteenth Street Bridge and turned onto North Capitol Street when I swallowed down some bile and said, "I'm afraid." Emil edged his foot off the gas, the big sedan slowing as he glanced at me. "I'm scared shitless," I said. "I'm afraid of dying, of headless bodies with stiff fingers reaching for me. I've never met Bobbie, never seen her. I don't want to lose my life in a trap Mal set."

"What *do* you want?"

"To run away."

"Makes sense."

Right, finally—that's what he meant. But it was too late for me to do anything sensible. Mal had seen to that. When I thought about the way he had killed those two women, and why, I could see Shad's face, those intelligent brown eyes. The crime scenes he'd taken me to. My last night at Bockman's, my nightmares every night since, always running. How much longer? How much longer could I keep running?

I'm no hero, okay? Mal scared me, I had no problem admitting that, and I didn't want him using me as raw materials for his artwork. But I had to take a stand, and this moment, right now, was all I had.

And Lilly—what if Mal killed her? Would she become part of my nightmares, every night? Christ, she was hard enough to take in real life.

Plus, Andrews had paid me to protect Bobbie.

Emil said, "You lookin' a little green, that's a fact. Want me to pull over?"

"Yeah. But keep driving."

Emil watched me, then relaxed and chuckled. "Shit, boy, that's some shout out you give yourself."

The midnight train was pulling out of the Silver Spring Metro station when we arrived. Six hours before the next one. I hoped I'd be around to see it. I couldn't see Crane's guys anywhere, though he'd assured me that they would be "assuming tactical attitudes." Which sounded like they were posing in front of mirrors.

Starbucks had a few tables and chairs they left chained outside at night on a dark, raised platform four feet above the sidewalk. A stack of wooden six-by-sixes formed the platform's supporting wall. There was an iron railing at the edge, then the sidewalk, and a row of bushes between the sidewalk and the street. Colesville Road was eight lanes wide here. On the other side of the street was a nine-story building. As I pulled up in front of it, Andrews said, "Look there," and I looked and saw her, a young woman sitting in a chair. Something silver reflected near her wrists. Handcuffs, pinning her in place. I pulled to the side. There was a stillness all around us. No crickets, no one walking by, no passing cars blasting out music. It seemed as though the rest of the world had ceased to exist and all of reality was draining out of this tiny patch of concrete where people were going to live or die.

Andrews picked up a small briefcase from the backseat. Emil had agreed with me, the ransom demand had been an afterthought. So we figured the kidnapers wouldn't mind a copy of the D.C. white pages instead of a quarter million. Emil and Crane were a block away, presumably engaged in their own telescopic activities, as Crane would say. I hoped they were in contact with their team. Andrews cleared his throat, murmured something I couldn't hear, and was about to get out of the car when I heard myself say, "Let me take the money."

He looked confused. "But they said—"

"I know what they said. But you're completely exposed out there." I shifted in the seat to face him. "Mr. Andrews, the technical term for this is 'a bad scene.' My car offers some protection. Take it. I'll run the briefcase over."

"I want to do what's best for Bobbie."

"It'll be harder to look after her if you're injured." *Or dead.*

He nodded. "All right. Thank you, Mr. Gidney."

I took the briefcase and started across the street. My mouth felt completely dry. One or two cars hushed past, then it was quiet again. The kind of quiet in those Westerns when they're expecting an Indian attack and some geek says it's real quiet out there and another says yeah, too quiet, and then the arrows come raining down. Except tonight I didn't think they'd use arrows.

"Bobbie?" I crossed the street, close enough for a good look. Even in the dark I could see it was her. She turned toward me. I came close and saw the gag in her mouth. She wore sandals and blue jeans and a white shirt. Her shirt was stained with sweat. Her eyes were wild. I bent down to remove the gag and saw a tiny red dot flick onto her forehead. I tried to get between her and the shooter, then two things happened at the same time—a bullet slammed into her, knocking her backwards and away from me, and something whistled over my head and flew into my car and exploded, lifting the car off the ground and flipping it over.

The blast knocked me against the railing and I saw the red dot wavering on my sleeve and I vaulted over the railing and into the bushes as another bullet whizzed past and ricocheted off the concrete. I hustled out of the bushes and zigzagged my way to the car, around to the passenger side, but the door handle was too hot to touch. Through the side window I saw Andrews slumped over. I wrapped my shirttail on the door handle, popped it open. A sickening burning smell as I rushed forward and pulled Andrews out. Then Emil and his pals drove into view, sirens screaming. By the time they were out of their cars, it was all over.

For them. Not for me. I looked across the street at Bobbie's body, lying on the ground, still handcuffed to the chair, and at the burning wreckage that had once been my car, and Vance Andrews. One of Crane's men touched Andrews's throat, looking for a pulse. He looked up at Crane, shaking his head. Crane snarled at me. "You were supposed to stay in the car, Gidney. Now look at this mess."

Rage and helplessness erupted out of me, I couldn't choke it down. I nailed him with a roundhouse right. He hit the ground. An instant later, I hit the pavement, too, looking up at six of his team, their guns pointed at my head. I didn't care. I was swearing at them, telling them to let me up, I'd fucking rip them apart. Emil hustled over and pulled me out of there. The team helped Crane to his feet. He looked at me; I was hoping he'd come after me, I wanted to kill him.

But he didn't. He touched his jaw where I'd punched him, then walked away. I stood there, my body started shaking, and Emil put his arm around me. He glanced over to where Bobbie's body lay, and shook his head.

By the time I had finished giving my statement to the cops and answering their questions and skirting three TV news stations, it was three in the morning. Emil gave me a ride back to Jan and Janet's house. We didn't talk in the car. Lilly was asleep on the fold-out couch when I rolled in next to her. I lay still, too upset to sleep and too tired not to, when Lilly spoke. Her voice was thick with sleep and it snapped me back, asking if I had seen Bobbie.

I managed to say, "I saw her."

Lilly stretched and laid her arm across my chest and snuggled next to me. I liked the way her body felt, her scent, her hair against my face. But the image of Bobbie handcuffed to the chair wouldn't go away.

CHAPTER 46

Early the next morning, I stood shivering and nearly naked in a Dumpster beneath the Whitehurst Freeway.

So far, my plan was working perfectly. Well, credit where credit is due, I suppose. It was really Augustus's plan. When I asked him how he could make me invisible, he said, "Take off your clothes."

The Dumpster kept me hidden from the prying eyes of rush-hour drivers. As soon as I handed him my clothes, Augustus gave me ragged, filthy jeans, a plaid shirt with ripped sleeves, and a pair of shoes that would have won me free tuition to Clown School.

What concerned me most was the smell.

"They're loaners, I want them back when this is over," Augustus said.

"No problem." I hopped out and stood on the sidewalk in front of him.

He looked at me critically, then nodded. "You look okay."

"Thanks, but how will this make me invisible?"

"You'll see." He started walking, so I followed him. "I'm giving you thirty minutes inside."

"Good," I said. "Hey, Augustus, what's with the parking meters? You never told me."

He gave me a look I couldn't read. "Goes back to Nam," he said.

"What'd you do there?"

"I released things."

"Come again?"

"Bridges, buildings. They all hold potential energy—that's the energy that's stored when they get built. Find the points to release that energy, a little explosive charge, and it all comes tumbling down. You know what you're doing, it doesn't take much. So anyhow, I'd finished two tours in Nam and come home. I had trouble adjusting." He stole a look at me. "Lotta vets have trouble. My disability ran out and so did my friends. Then a grunt sent my belongings from overseas, my books and stuff. Inside one of the paperbacks was a check Uncle Sam'd issued me in Nam that I never got around to cashing, for two hundred thirty-nine dollars and seventy cents."

"Lucky."

"No, because I couldn't find a bank to cash it. Perfectly good check, from the government, but it was"—and here he shot me a look of pure hatred—"awkward, that's what the bank manager told me. It was fucking awkward. Then the ass wipe says I should go back to Nam to cash it. You believe that shit? Back to Nam." He shook his head.

"And the parking meters?"

He looked at me like I was a little slow. He spread his hands and said, "Well, something like that happens, obviously the entire system is fucked. Only way to fix it is to destroy it from within." He nodded his head once. That explained everything.

"Oh," I said.

Walking with him, I thought maybe he was right about the whole system. Bobbie Jackson was dead. Vance Andrews was dead. I had awakened that morning in a sweat, hearing the screams, my heart pounding from running through the maze. Same as always. Then I remembered that last night my dream had been different. Something had changed. Someone—I couldn't see who—ran ahead of me, their hand held out to help me through the maze. I didn't find a way out, I'd awakened before that, but the feeling I'd had at the end of the dream was different, somehow. Hopeful. I hadn't found a way out, but I woke thinking at least there *was* a way out.

It was possible.

I'd lumbered into the kitchen, where Jan and Janet were eating breakfast and Emily and Sarah were watching TV. Lilly had already left, to run errands, Jan told me. After coffee—thank God it wasn't green tea—I'd told them what had happened last night.

Jan said, "I'm so sorry, Willis," and Janet added, "It's all over the news this morning." She showed me *The Post*, where the article appeared below the fold. No names mentioned, pending the notification of kin. I saw precious little substance in the article, in the sense that you could read it through and still not know two people had been assassinated. And yet, this was far from over. Four people dead and Mal still on the loose.

Jan said, "You'll need to call Steps, tell him Bobbie's dead."

"I have something first this morning." Breaking into Varga's office.

"Just don't forget you're taking the baby in today," Janet said.

"Nice you can keep your perspective about all of this," I had told her.

Now my perspective was about to change. Augustus led me up the street, out of the shadow of the Whitehurst Freeway and into the glaring sunlight. He was heading right for Kerberos's front entrance. Were we just going to walk in? Was he crazy? Did he have a bomb strapped to his body? Ready to blow us up to make some vague political point he couldn't even articulate? *Maybe Augustus wasn't the best choice for this type of action*, I thought, stealing a glance at him.

He took me past the entrance. Around the corner stood a second door, painted gunboat gray, flush to the brick wall. Apart from a keyhole, it was featureless. He nodded at the sidewalk by the door.

"Lie down."

Okay, this was his plan. I lay down. "Now what?"

"Stay there. Be ready." And he turned and walked away.

They keep the sidewalks clean in Georgetown, I'll say that. But it was hot in the sunlight and, after a while, I found myself pining for the Dumpster. I started watching the people walk past. Mostly young people, Georgetown students who were wealthy and seemed to be born with an innate sense of how to enjoy themselves. At least they appeared to be having a good time. All the young men were robust and trim, all the young women were shapely and smiling. And if they had a thought among them, it was on a time-share basis.

There were business guys, jolly and well fed, smoking cigars and cigarettes. And business gals, dressed to the nines. I saw healthy people jogging by and old people leaning on walkers; a news cameraman and a correspondent clutching a microphone ran past; deaf people signing to one another; four girls singing a cappella; bright orange buses shaped like trolleys chock-full of *tourista*s snapping cameras.

They ignored me. I was looking right at them, but they never saw me. I was just another homeless person, another bum. At first I couldn't believe it. Then I got pissed off. But when one human after the next walks right past you, hour after hour, pretending you're not there, it has a weird effect. You start wondering if you're really there or not. After a few thousand people go by, acting as though you don't exist, you begin to feel, well, invisible. I felt as though my identity were leaking away, leaching into the sidewalk on which I lay.

The gray door snapped open and shut a few times, with black-booted Kerberos employees going on and off their shifts. They didn't look at me, either. I saw the executives leave for the day. Well, it was almost four, time for that well-deserved first drink. Varga was among them. He didn't see me. A few minutes later I saw Augustus and three of his friends walk past me. I nodded to them, but they ignored me, too.

That hurt.

Three minutes later, I heard the sound of glass breaking. A lot of glass. I mean, it wasn't just a brick going through a window. It *sustained*, this crashing, for a good ten seconds. I couldn't see what had happened from my vantage point, but later I found out that one of Augustus's friends had stolen a car and pointed it into that glass wall that made up the front of the building.

The gray door near me burst open, and a dozen or so Kerberos employees rushed out. They didn't see me. Before the door snapped shut, I slipped inside. From the hallway in front came voices shouting and echoing off glass and brick walls. There was a service elevator near the now-deserted security station, and I took it up to Varga's floor. I followed the winding corridors around to his office, wishing I had a spool of thread to play out to help find my way back. His door was unlocked, and so was his file cabinet. I guess Varga had figured that with security that good downstairs, why bother locking anything upstairs?

I went through his files, opened books on his bookshelves, all the time feeling exposed, what with those floor-to-ceiling windows. My watch told me I had used twenty of my thirty minutes.

My palms were wet. I thought about Augustus and the second diversion he'd promised. I had to finish soon. I started going through Varga's stainless-steel desk. That's when I tugged at the bottom drawer. Locked.

Must be something good there, but who had time to break into a steel desk? I thought about Varga, the kind of guy he was. Arrogant, but not too thorough, or he wouldn't have hired guys like Westy and Mal. Would a man like that have locked the drawer above the bottom drawer?

He hadn't. I slid it all the way out, then reached down into the locked drawer beneath it. Empty except for a small Ziploc bag containing a tiny cassette, about the size of a digital audio tape. Which in fact is what it was. Augustus would move any second now. I didn't know if this tape was the leverage I needed, but as I put the bag with the DAT in my pocket, I suddenly thought of the second diversion—Augustus had been in Vietnam. He blew things up. I hefted Varga's chair and crashed it through the floor-to-ceiling window. The chair sailed into the Potomac River and I jumped out after it, hearing a series of explosions behind me.

The Potomac River hit me like a giant blue-green wall. The water shocked me as I crashed into it, but even more shocking was the sight of several tons of much-acclaimed brick overhang about to fall on my head. I swam. Michael Phelps had nothing on me. The current helped me make it downstream in one piece. Then I burst back up for air just in time to see the Kerberos building overhang plunge into the water.

It made quite a splash.

CHAPTER 47

There's nothing like a few tons of floating debris sweeping toward you to get your blood pumping. I tore through the water downstream, ending up near the boat landing by the Kennedy Center. My heart was pounding like Gene Krupa's bass drum. I dragged myself out and lay gasping on the ground. Crowds had gathered up and down the Potomac on both sides, pointing and shouting.

Some diversion. Once I'd caught my breath, I started back to the Dumpster. Fire trucks and ambulances and TV vans went speeding past. Under the freeway, Augustus was waiting for me. He saw that my clothes were wet. "What happened?"

"What happened? It's a nice day and I went in for a dip," I shouted at him.

The surprise left his face, and he looked at me poker-eyed. "You said you'd be on the first floor."

"No, I didn't."

He stared at me for a moment. Then he said, "Oh. I thought you said you'd be on the first floor." That was as close to mea culpa as he was going to get. Concealed by the Dumpster once more, I handed out the old clothes and shrugged back into my own. The little digital audio cassette seemed to have survived in its watertight bag. I placed it in my pocket. When I hopped out of the Dumpster, Augustus was gone.

I took a cab to a high-end stereo store near the Safeway on Wisconsin Avenue so that I could copy the DAT cassette. When

I reached into my pocket for my wallet, I pulled out a TV remote control. Emily strikes again. Then I pulled out the cassette and, as I listened to it, I made a copy. It was worth copying.

I'd describe it as your basic sell-your-soul scenario, with McHugh and Trace playing the supplicants and Varga representing the guy with the pitchfork. Nice of them to mention other bought members of Congress, the upcoming vote on the ag subcommittee, and Blake's enzyme formula. I'm no lawyer, but it seemed to me that there was a lot of incriminating evidence here, at least as far as McHugh and Trace were concerned. Why else would Varga have kept it locked in his desk?

As conspirators, they were a jolly bunch. At the end of the recording Varga says, "Well, Congressman, if you can stand to leave those dumb bastards down South, I'm sure we'll see you as chief executive in a few years."

McHugh replies with mock righteousness, "They may be a bunch of stupid inbred three-toed bastards, but they're *my* stupid inbred three-toed bastards." Then they all have a good laugh. I tell you, it brought a tear to my eye. I paid for the DATs—they came in packages of four—slipped the copy and blanks into my pocket, and dropped off the original tape at FedEx, two-day delivery back to me.

Now I had to talk with Steps. I got a rental car, then met Steps at the Zamboanga Café, where this had all started. He sat in a booth with *The Post* in front of him. He'd been reading the article about Bobbie and Vance Andrews. I slid into the opposite seat. Chella had just brought him a steaming plate of toast, grits, bacon, and eggs.

"You read this?" He pointed at *The Post*.

"I was there. Steps, I'm sorry, but Bobbie was the woman

who died last night, along with her stepfather. And I can tell you, Bobbie wasn't your daughter."

He set his fork down slowly, nodding while I told him about Bobbie, Alvin, Colette, and Vance. He didn't say a word. Just sat looking at the speckled pattern of the tabletop, then turned his wide brown eyes on me. "That poor girl."

"Which one? Bobbie? Or Colette?"

He shook his head. "Both of 'em, I guess. I never knew about Alvin—not about him and Colette, I mean. I guess it makes a kind of sense, why she cut him that way. And why he was so . . . territorial with her, I guess."

"You felt something was haywire."

"Yeah."

I looked down and let the moment linger, like a prayer. Then I got up to go.

I was exhausted—from the killings last night and my near-death swim this morning. I trudged along F street, through the heat, and collapsed into my car. An ambulance screamed past, the traffic making the barest gesture of letting it through. The sidewalks bulged with camera-snapping *touristsa*s, threading their way through the warren of downtown streets. A bicycle messenger shot past, his tires whistling on the pavement. I closed my eyes. The tires sounded like the bullets from last night, whistling past me, the bullets from last night and the ones at Bockman's, the memory of that night like an oil slick, spreading across my thoughts until I could find no way around it. Spreading like the sea of kids had spread around Eddie and me as we ran through them, our last night at Bockman's, making progress toward our money stash, the guards firing warning shots above our heads. Kids screamed and scurried around us, hundreds of them, searching for a way out. Some were crying, others shouting. Fighting each other, trampling the little ones. Gunshots ricocheted off the guard towers, and the moan of police sirens grew loud. The gates were shut and guards in their towers were making sure the kids stayed inside. I saw a roving group of kids lugging gas cans. Howling police cars skidded up to the gates. Eddie and I raced past a tower when, from a group of kids to the right, I heard a gunshot. A guard in the tower clutched his shoulder and fired his automatic. Eddie got hit.

I didn't know it at first, I'd just kept running. I looked beside me, then behind me and saw him on the ground, a bloodstain growing just above the knee on the inside. He gazed at his leg, then up at me. "I'm down," he said with disbelief.

"Let's get outta here."

"Get me on my feet." Together we hobbled toward the administration building. It was only twenty yards away, but we weren't making what I'd call rapid progress. Meanwhile the cops had opened the main gate and flooded inside. Most were working the crowd, trying to calm the kids and search for weapons, but the sight of the cops made the kids more anxious. The gunfire started again.

"Guess where the cops're going," I said.

"We gotta get there first," Eddie said. His breath was short and he was leaning on me more and more. A few more yards and he said, "Wait, just set me down here for a sec'." I let him slide to the ground, his back resting against the wooden siding of dorm C. His pants leg damp with blood. He looked up at me, then took a deep breath and closed his eyes. "I'm gonna sit this one out."

268

"I'm not leaving you."

"You got that right. Get the cash, then get back here and we'll take off."

"Let's just split."

"Not without the money, kid." He smiled. "Get going. I'll be waiting."

So I sprinted toward the stash we kept, the money, the god-damned money. I turned and stole a backward glance at Eddie. He waved slightly, more of a shooing gesture than anything else.

It was the last time I saw him.

Later I found out that the kids with the gas cans were planning on burning Bockman's to the ground, and the snitch house was merely their first target. But arson is tricky. The seasoned arsonists get big bucks—and the rookies get burned. These kids started pouring about five times as much gas as they needed on a pile of furniture inside dorm C.

Meanwhile I headed for the money, the money Waters wanted, which we'd hidden under his office. I shifted one of the boards beneath his window, wondering what he'd say if he knew the cash he demanded had been right beneath him. I reached in for package, twenty thousand, just as some of the top cops got the front door of the building open and made their way inside, heading straight for Waters's office. A noise from above—I looked to see Waters's leg and arm extend out the window. He had a gun. He looked toward the door as the cops broke it down, he hadn't seen me yet and I was terrified that he would. Yet I was planted there, I couldn't move.

Then a voice I knew shouted "Halt!"—Shad, playing it by the book. Except Waters wasn't halting, he was sliding out the window. Shad shouted again and fired a warning shot, but by now Waters had hit the ground.

That's when dorm C blew up in a fireball, taking the would-be arsonists with it.

Eddie had been right outside.

The blast slammed me to the ground and rocked Waters against the building. He looked up and bared his teeth at me and I could see the firestorm reflected in his glasses. He was pointing his gun—he was going to shoot me simply because I was in his way, I don't think he even knew who I was—when Shad shouted, "Freeze!" from the window, and Waters spun and shot him in the chest. Five cops fired back and Waters spun around and down.

I looked up at the cops in the window and saw Emil, his gun smoking, looking down at Shad. He looked at me and shook his head.

Shad was gone.

My eyes opened. I looked down at my hands; they were clamped on to the steering wheel. Right then I flashed that it was Lilly—she had been the one in my dream the night before. In my dream, Lilly had helped me through the maze. That's what I was thinking when my phone rang.

"Gidney," a distorted voice said.

My hand tightened on the phone. "Mal."

"You're a hard man to track down."

"Glad to be of trouble."

"But your friend, Ms. McClellan, she just showed up at her apartment this morning. Wasn't that nice of her? To save us the trouble of finding her, I mean."

"She's a nice person," I said, feeling the panic start to rise.

"And you know, she has beauty inside her."

"If you even think about touching her—"

"What, you mean sexually? She's not my type."

270

"You mean she's still breathing."

His voice made that weird scraping laugh. "For now. The question is, do you want her to keep breathing?"

"What do you want?"

"Well, there's a little matter of a recording you took from Varga's office. Which was really *dramatic*, Gidney. Did you know a tourist filmed the whole thing? With one of those little video cameras? We saw it on the news, Varga and me. You can even see someone jumping from his office just before all hell breaks lose. And you know who that someone looks like, don't you? I wish I could have been there."

"I wish you could have been *under* there."

"Oh, you don't mean that. But we really want that tape. So let's make an exchange—the tape for Ms. McClellan."

"When and where?"

"Oh, that commanding tone of voice. I just love it. Let's meet at the Lincoln Memorial."

Good. If he wanted a public meeting, so much the better. "I'll see you inside."

"Oh, not *in* the memorial. Underneath it."

"What?"

"The Park Service has a tour below, and the next one starts in twenty minutes. No time to get all your cop friends together, I'm afraid. So come as you are, Gidney. The girl and I will see you underneath. Remember, no cops, or she dies."

CHAPTER 48

I made it just in time. Under the Lincoln Memorial, with a guide and tourists and Lilly and Mal.

Mal grinned. Lilly moved toward me, but the bastard tightened his grip on her arm and she winced. I went toward him. He just smiled and shook his head. He held her arm with one hand and the other rested in his pocket. Flanking him were the two heavies I had spotted from the Q Street house. I wondered if Mal would actually risk shooting her with so many witnesses. The guy *was* a few colors short of a palette—I couldn't risk it.

The Park Service ranger led us down through a winding passageway that opened onto an enormous corridor with support columns that reached up into darkness. The ranger explained how the columns supported the memorial above us. He showed us a damp wall, told us it was moisture from the Potomac River. And he pointed out a kind of firefly that lived down there, its light much weaker than the fireflies above ground.

Then the ranger snapped off his flashlight. Total darkness fell. Nervous laughter twittered around me. The cool black air swept around me, tightening, wrapping me so I couldn't breathe. When the light came back on, Mal caught my eye and motioned for me to wait behind. The group left. The two heavies were the last out. Just before the overhead lights clicked out, I saw Mal slip on night-vision goggles. If I could reach him quickly—

Too late. By the time I made it over to where he'd been standing, he was gone, leaving Lilly behind. I put my arms around her. "You all right?"

"Will he shoot us?" She was shivering.

Nearby, the *click* of a chambered round. "He wants to have some fun first. Come on," I whispered. I had memorized the pattern of the columns during the tour and moved through it, holding Lilly's hand. If I had to be a target, I preferred to be a moving one.

"Gidney, you're a dead man," Mal said. As if explaining something very simple. *Keep talking.* The more noise he made, the more we could move without his hearing us. "Oh, and the tape," he said. "I'll get it after I kill you, okay?"

If we could only get back over to the door, we could—what? It was locked, I'd heard it shut. Even if we made it past Mal, all we could do was turn on the lights, and we'd still be targets. And Mal wouldn't need the night-vision goggles to shoot us.

I was wishing I had one of the many guns I'd been running across. But even that wouldn't have helped me, I'd just have been shooting into darkness. I needed Mal to fire his gun, see the muzzle flash, to be able to locate him. I didn't think he'd oblige me unless I was in front of him.

I heard Mal wander away from us, his voice edgy with excitement. He'd be back. I thought about his goggles. Night vision. It used infrared light, amplified the available light thousands of times. But it needed to have *some* light to amplify. Where was the light source? Then I remembered the fireflies. Their light must have been enough for Mal to track us. But they weren't spread evenly under ground, they kept close to the wet wall abutting the Potomac. Which meant that we had to stay away from there.

I whispered, "We're gonna get out of here, but I need you to be quiet and follow me, okay?"

She whispered back, "You're expecting an argument?"

We made our way through the maze, Mal's voice never too far away. Part of the problem was the way the support pillars of the memorial were laid out: if we weren't careful, we'd get cornered. Then it would all be over. Lilly put her lips to my ear. "Aren't detectives supposed to carry guns?"

"All I have is a TV remote control."

"Well, shit. I wish we could change the channel right now."

All of a sudden I got it. "You're so smart it's scary."

"Why?"

Suddenly I heard Mal close-by. I pulled Lilly away from there. We made our way through the columns. I led her around one, then placed the TV remote in her hand. "Stand behind this column, and point this around the corner. When I signal you, press a button."

"What? Why?"

"It shoots out a beam on infrared light. Shine it at Mal, the light'll startle him and he'll shoot. Scream like you've been hit and pull your hand away. Don't drop the remote and don't expose yourself, stay behind the column."

"How will I know when?"

I felt the cassette in my pocket. "I've got a tape box. When you hear it hit the ground, push the button."

"What if he shoots my hand?"

"Pull it away as soon as you hear the shot. I'll hide behind the column across from you. He doesn't have any peripheral vision with those goggles. He won't see me."

"Okay." She sounded less than 100 percent confident.

"This is gonna work."

She pulled me close and kissed me hard. "Be careful," she whispered. Then I sensed her moving away. I stood behind the opposite column. Now we had to wait for him. We were in a corner of the maze, there was no way out. Eventually he'd come this way.

I could hear him, of course, walking along with all the time in the world, explaining to us that these columns were one enormous canvas, it was too bad there were only two people he could use.

He drew closer. Down the corridor. Hard to judge the distance in the dark. He stopped talking—he knew we were near. Lilly and I had run out of room, and if we were unlucky now, we'd run out of living. I had the cassette case in my hand, between my index and middle fingers. My hand was sweaty. I tightened my grip on the case. Be a shame to drop it. I switched hands and wiped my fingers on my pants. *A little more, Mal. Just a few steps.*

I heard him move and I flipped the cassette. He sucked in his breath when it landed. I couldn't see Lilly or her hand but suddenly Mal started firing and Lilly screamed. Her scream sounded real. I pushed off the column toward the flashes from his gun. Each flash illuminated the scene like a bolt of lightning. The sounds of the shots rolled off the columns, incredibly loud after all the silence. I didn't see Lilly. She could've been on the ground beside me for all I knew. This all happened in an instant, but I remember hoping that he'd empty the clip if he was spooked. In the dark I rushed into him and grabbed at anything I could, my hands working frantically. My right hand found his goggles and I drove my fist into his temple, twisting his head around to the left and away from me, towards the column, using my elbow against the back of his head to bang his face into the concrete, goggles and all.

But he used my movement against me, kept turning to his left, in less than a second he'd be facing me, gun in hand. I ran my right hand down his arm toward the gun and he kept turning. We struggled, and a close muzzle flash blinded me and something tore into my left arm. I grabbed the gun with my right hand and forced it up and away from me. The gun went off again. *How many shots left?* I wondered. I'd lost count. Mal was stronger than I'd expected. My left arm went numb. But I was still able to make a fist with it, and I drove it into his Adam's apple.

He gasped and I felt his right hand loosen on the gun. I rabbit-punched him in the neck again and heard the gun hit the ground as his left hand grabbed for my face. I dodged under his hand, coming up close inside, and stomped down on his instep while slamming his chin with the heel of my right hand, but he twisted away from me and punched my arm where he'd shot me. I literally saw stars, there in the darkness. My left hand felt wet. He punched my arm again and I staggered as a wave of nausea rolled over me. I felt his breath on my face as he closed in, his hands tightening around my throat. Then something flitted past me, a breeze, and Mal said "oh" as though he'd just remembered something. His body moved and his hands relaxed and he shuddered and slid down to the floor. The floor seemed like a good idea, but the room was spinning in the darkness and I couldn't find the floor so I leaned against the column and it started tipping backward.

It was still dark, but much later, years later, it grew light again and I came to sitting on the ground while some cops were picking Mal up off the dirt and a medic in a white jacket was tying a tourniquet on my arm. Emil was standing next to him, flipping through Mal's stack of photos. His portfolio. Lilly was squatting in front of me, brushing the hair off my forehead with one hand and holding Mal's gun in the other.

She smiled. Her lovely eyes flitted over me, surveying the damage. "Hi," she said.

"Nice scream you made."

"Thanks. You feel okay?"

I felt so happy that she was alive, I didn't trust myself to speak. "I'm good. You?"

"I'm all right," she said. "Willis?"

"Yeah?"

"Next time, let me make the plan, okay?"

CHAPTER 49

The next morning my arm was throbbing, despite the dressing and the painkillers. The medics said I was lucky, the bullet had gone through my arm without hitting any blood vessels or bones. Easy for them to say. I didn't feel lucky.

The news media didn't as yet know about the Lincoln Memorial or what had gone on below. They focused Jason McHugh's 3:00 P.M. announcement about running for Broadfield's Senate seat. The thought of McHugh in the Senate made me want to crawl back beneath the Lincoln. Instead, Lilly drove my rental car downtown so we could give our statements to the cops. She got a nice cop. I got Heinrick. He listened to me without comment as I told the story. The only sounds in the office were my voice, the whine of the voice recorder, and the steady *tick* of the clock on the wall.

When I finished, Heinrick said, "That woman you found dead, the one you phoned in?"

"What about her? Did you ID her?" If they had, I could kiss Sarah goodbye.

"Her prints aren't on file. There're no matches in the NCIC. So no one's looking for her. We may never ID her. But the baby, we're checking her footprint with the local hospitals, we might come up with a match that way." He watched my face, then started to smile. "You're wondering how we can do that, if we don't have the baby. But we found her, at your friends' house. The dykes."

I knocked over the chair getting up. I'd reached the door, so angry that I didn't even know where I was going or what I was doing, when Heinrick grabbed me by my good arm and spun me around. His grip was strong. "Listen up, Gidney. You want that kid, you go through channels and adopt her. You don't just grab kids off the street. Understand?" His pale, post-chemo face was empty, all but the eyes.

If he hadn't been dying I would've killed him. He looked at me, nodded without warmth. "Good. And one other thing—toughen up. You did okay against Mal and Varga because they underestimated you. They were too busy laughing to take you seriously. But the word's out, Gidney. No one's going to make that mistake again. Next time they'll kill you first and have a good laugh later."

"Thanks for the encouragement," I said through my teeth. "Now take your hand off before I break it off."

He looked at me, his tired eyes searching for something. Then he nodded once more. "See you, Gidney."

Outside, Lilly and Emil were waiting for me. I wondered if he knew that Heinrick had taken Sarah away. He came over. "Well, boy, you look like shit this morning."

"Thanks. How's Mal?"

Emil smiled. "Got a nasty bump on the head, but he'll live. For a while. Quite the photo collection he's got. Ties him in to that homicide you phoned in. That and the film canister you found. He left a thumbprint on it."

"How did you find us beneath the Lincoln?"

"Heinrick's been keepin' tabs on you since he let Andrews bail you out. Figured you'd stir things up, bring the killers out in the open. Why he recommended you to Andrews. So when Kerberos made their move, we'd have them."

"And just how long were you going to let Mal chase us around the underside of the Lincoln?"

"Easy, son. We were just outside, takin' care of Mal's buddies. 'Sides, you know as well as us that if he hadn't shot you, we'd have a weaker case."

Lilly stared at Emil in disbelief. "Cop logic," I told her. "Makes sense to them only."

He shrugged and said to Lilly, "We save his fool life and he whines at us."

Lilly took my arm in hers. "I believe he was whining at you."

Next we headed to the Hill to give back Chilcoate's yearbook. After that, I could concentrate on picking up the pieces of my life. The ones big enough to pick up. The past day had shattered entire sections. That should have depressed me, but it didn't.

Lilly pulled as close to the horseshoe entrance of the Rayburn Building as the cops would allow. I had arranged with Stephanie to meet her outside. While we waited, Lilly tuned the radio to WPFW. Jonte Short sang that all she wanted was something that lasts forever. I was thinking about what I should do with the DAT cassette when Lilly asked, "So what will you do with the DAT cassette?" Spooky.

I looked at her. "Cops don't need it, they got Mal and Mal gave them Varga. Their masters at Chirr will simply deny everything. And taking on a multinational corporation is a job for an army of lawyers, not a single PI. So I'll file the tape away for safe-keeping."

She nodded. "There's a lot I missed. I haven't read a paper since Mal . . ."

I touched her hand. "We'll take some time, I'll tell you all about it." I'd need some time, I couldn't tell her about Bobbie, not yet. I felt comfortable with Lilly there, letting the music play. Tina Turner belted out "You're Still My Baby" as the Hill people hustled past, lobbyists and aides hurrying this way and that, all their motion purposeful, nothing wasted. But all of it somehow incomprehensible, like watching ants trail along the ground.

Finally I saw Stephanie come out into the bright sunlight, with Azalea Trace. They were talking and Stephanie spotted me and waved. When I reached them, I handed Stephanie the yearbook. "Thank you, Ms. Chilcoate." She smiled and nodded as she took the book. I looked over at Trace, who was wearing a purple silk jacket with matching slacks and black pumps. "And you, Ms. Trace, how are you and the congressman today?"

She gave me a brief smile, as warm and soft as a snowball. "Busy."

"Exciting day, though. Congratulations on your upcoming wedding to Jase."

"Thank you." She turned to Stephanie. "We'll be working on the speech."

Trace went back inside. Heads turned and watched her. She seemed not to notice, though I'm sure she was aware of the stir she caused. Stephanie was speaking to me, and when I asked her to repeat herself, she gave me a wry smile, as though she knew exactly where my mind had been.

"I was saying, I'm so sorry about Bobbie."

Yesterday's *Post* hadn't printed the victims' names, pending the police notifying their families. But this morning's edition listed Bobbie and Andrews as the two who had died. I told her what had happened that night but I didn't go into details. I'd be repeating all of it to Lilly soon enough. When I finished, Stephanie looked shocked, but seemed to recover quickly. After all, she said, she hadn't seen Bobbie in years and years, and it just goes to show how drugs are destroying our society.

I thanked her again and went back to the car. Lilly pulled away from the curb. "Now what?"

"Let's find a place, sit for a while."

"And talk, I'd like that. You must be feeling pleased with yourself, finding Bobbie."

How did she know about Bobbie? "Well, no, I don't feel pleased with myself at all."

"Well, she seemed to take it in stride." A strange thing to say. She looked at me briefly. "I mean, she didn't seem angry you found her."

"What are you talking about?"

"Bobbie Jackson. What are you talking about?"

"Lilly, you're not making sense."

She said, "Those two women, the one you gave the book to and Bobbie."

"Who?"

"Don't shout at me. Her, the woman in purple."

"What about her?"

"She's Bobbie. That's Bobbie Jackson."

CHAPTER 50

"Sir, you can't go in there. Sir!"

I pushed past McHugh's secretary and through the door to his office.

McHugh was perched on the edge of his desk, his shirtsleeves rolled up, a sheaf of papers in his hand. Trace was beside him, and in the corner a woman was setting up a folding director's chair. Next to the chair was a red plastic tackle box filled with makeup supplies.

Trace was about to say something but McHugh beat her to it. "Why, Mr. Gidney, what an unexpected treat." He nodded to the secretary in the doorway, who closed the door with a look of uncertainty on her face.

"For me too, Congressman." I turned to the makeup woman. "Why don't you take five?"

Trace said, "Who the hell do you think you are?"

"A guy with something to say. I don't think you want her to hear it."

McHugh glanced at Trace, who kept her blue eyes steady on me. She kept looking at me while she said, "Kathy, why don't you get a cup of coffee."

Kathy smiled tentatively at Trace and McHugh, put down her powder and brushes, and walked past me. None of us spoke until the door had closed.

McHugh had recovered enough to bluster. "What's this all about?"

"It's over, Congressman."

McHugh gave me a confused look as Trace muttered, "I'm calling security." She picked up the phone.

"That would be a mistake." Something in my voice stopped her. She still had her hand on the phone, but she kept the handset cradled, staring at me.

McHugh said, "We'll see about this," and headed toward the door.

"I can see who has the brains. Wanna tell him what's going on?"

"Jase, wait a minute."

McHugh stopped. "You better explain yourself, Gidney."

I shrugged. "It's over."

Trace asked, "What's over?"

"Well, let's see." I started ticking them off on my fingers. "Your deal with Chirr, the formula for altered hemp, your careers in Congress." I held up my palms. "Over."

McHugh snorted, his face red. Trace looked calm. "Why is it over?" she asked.

"For one thing, a recording Varga made of you two." I turned to McHugh. "Not very nice, Congressman, selling out Griffin Blake just to get in Chirr's good graces."

"Goddammit, I'll have your ass."

I smiled. "You know, I really admire you, Jase. Okay if I call you Jase? Using those foundations to launder drug money." I mimicked his southern drawl: "It exemplifies that spirit of American entrepreneurship that makes our country great." I took a step toward him. "But how would your constituents feel about it? Just how does racketeering fit in with your message about stopping America's mongrelization?"

Trace said, "What do you want?"

"What do I want?" I turned to her. "What you can't give me. I want four people breathing again. I'll have to settle for both of you out of here, out of this office and off the Hill. Permanently." I shot a glance at McHugh. "Your speech today? It's your resignation."

Without a word, Trace left the room. McHugh said, "You can't prove a thing."

I laughed. The laughter sounded a little crazy to me. "Prove? I don't need to prove a thing, just give this tape to the media." I showed him the cassette. "This is Washington, where political correctness isn't just a way of life, it's a form of indoor competition."

Trace came back, a black leather handbag on her shoulder. "I've dismissed the staff," she said calmly, and pulled out a tiny .22 automatic. She aimed it at me. "Hand it over."

"Kill him, Ayzie," McHugh said.

"Give me the tape," Trace said.

"You'd shoot me? Here?"

"Self-defense. And don't worry about the sound, these walls are incredibly thick," she said.

"Christ, so are you. What, you think I'd just waltz in here? You want the tape?" I tossed the cassette, it landed by her feet.

"Have another," I said, throwing one at McHugh. It bounced off his chest and hit the floor. "I've got plenty. And a friend's ready to send them to half-a-dozen news bureaus, if I don't come out in ten minutes." Trace looked down at the tape at her feet and lowered her gun. I took it from her. "And you know what would happen if that tape got out—your careers would be finished. Forever. The lobbying, the consulting. You'd be untouchables. The obits—that's the next time you'll get your names in *The Post*."

"My people will stand by me," McHugh said without conviction.

"You mean those 'inbred three-toed bastards' you represent?" I rubbed my chin. "You know, they just might forgive you the money laundering and corruption," I said, looking at Trace, "but not the mongrelization."

The color drained from her face.

I asked, "How do you think McHugh's people would feel about that, Ms. Trace?"

"About what?" McHugh asked.

"About how Ayzie here is the daughter of Steps Jackson, jazz saxophonist and card-carrying Afro-American."

McHugh was frozen, no reaction at all.

"Might be hard to explain, Jase. I mean, wouldn't you be kind of contributing to America's mongrelization? What about 'America for the Americans'?"

He stared at me. Trace said, "I'm not . . . *his* daughter." Her voice was quiet.

"Of course you are. You have to be, it's the only way any of this makes sense. And after all that trouble you went to, to bury your past."

"No," she said.

"Varga told me that the two guards from Targus overheard me tell Chilcoate I was looking for Bobbie. But they couldn't have, not stationed outside McHugh's office door. But you did, Ayzie. You stood right next to Chilcoate when I told her. Then two hours later I get called to Varga's office, where I'm warned to keep away or else. It confused me at first, the rough and soft. Getting the offer to join your team while Varga's boys were hunting me." I turned to McHugh. "I'd bet the job offer was your idea? To buy me off?"

"That was a valid offer."

"And you wanted me dead," I said to Trace. "You two need to communicate; there's been a lot of wasted effort. Like the striptease in your limo. You didn't care about me ogling you, it was the tan lines you really wanted me to notice, wasn't it? I've heard a laser can do that. I bet it hurt."

She barked out a laugh. "You know nothing about hurt."

"Then at The Palm, you told McHugh I'd pretended to be from the Perth Gallery when I'd visited Colette. But I hadn't told you the gallery's name."

"Stephanie told me."

"I hadn't told her, either. I told Colette, she called Bobbie, Bobbie called you."

"I've never spoken to either of them," she said.

"You want to know what got me started thinking about you? As Steps's daughter? At The Palm, when you went ballistic at the black waitress. Big reaction for a small mistake. And it made me wonder, why does a successful white woman get so upset at a black waitress? Because she's a bigot? But that wasn't it, was it?" They were silent, so I plunged ahead. "You know what's funny? About all of this? Anyone but you, Congressman, no one would care. But you made it a campaign issue, didn't you?"

McHugh looked from me to Trace. "Ayzie, I—I've known it a long time now, baby. And I don't care, it doesn't matter. All I care about is you." There was something in his voice that I hadn't heard before. He turned to me. "Gidney, listen. We can still make some kind of arrangement. Don't you see? This is your chance, your chance to be somebody, someone important. Ayzie's told me about your past. Well, here's your chance to put it all behind you."

I turned to Trace. "So if Steps is your father, who's your mother?"

Some of the fire had washed out of her. She kept her eyes on McHugh. "Does it matter? She OD'd when I was nine, white trash who liked jazz and drugs and couldn't control her cunt." She laughed. "Nine, that's how old I was when I lost her. I grew up in state institutions. Like you, Gidney. But I remember her, I can remember her telling me about Steps, she was actually proud." Her voice took on a hard edge. For a moment, her face flushed red.

"You must hate him," I said.

Then, as suddenly as it came, the intensity drained away. "It doesn't matter," she said.

"Like Colette didn't matter. Or Bobbie. You told them both to sit tight. Then you phoned Varga and Mal. Did Mal give you some kind of package rate?"

"He was just supposed to scare Colette."

"You don't actually believe that. You met Bobbie through Griffin Blake. Bobbie hated Alvin, and told her high school friends her father had died. Then when she heard about Colette and Steps, in Bobbie's mind Steps became her father, a much better explanation than being the child of incest. Did she tell you Steps was her father?"

She laughed. "Practically the first words out of her mouth, when Blake introduced her."

"You knew it was a lie, one you could use. Like you used Bobbie. Must've been easy."

"It's always easy," she said, moving toward me. Easy. Like an accommodation with McHugh, that'd be easy too. I looked back at my life, all the decisions and paths taken that had brought me here. And I wondered, what defines people? Like Colette and Vance Andrews—their money? Their good taste? Or like Alvin and Bobbie—what or who made them? Or like being on the street, with no notion of who you are, just following the pack, surviving.

Now the pack was McHugh and Trace. Inviting me in. But maybe the past doesn't matter. Maybe what defines you is not your social class, education, clothes—maybe you're defined by your actions. What you do right now. Maybe you can control who you are.

Right then, in that office with Trace walking toward me, for the first time in my life I felt a strange, sudden rush of identity. I knew what I was going to do. "Bobbie was a shill," I said, "so anyone looking for Steps's daughter would find her. But that wasn't enough for you. You posed as Bobbie when you hired Lilly McClellan to write the computer program and embed it at Vital Records. Once you knew I was looking for Bobbie, you sent Varga and Mal after me, and now four people are dead."

She stopped, her face inches from mine. "Why not go to the cops, then? You must want something."

"Two things. First, the congressman's resignation. He's quitting."

"Like hell I am."

"It's the only chance you have. Be grateful. Stick to the script, you should know how to do that. Resign gracefully. You can still work as a lobbyist. Refuse and I'll ruin you. It's a simple choice." I shook my head. "Even a moron like you should be able to figure that out."

McHugh looked at me slack-faced.

"And the second thing?" Trace asked me, her breath hot on my face.

"You. Now." Again, the tidal surge of identity as I put my fingertips to the back of her head and felt her cheek against my palm. "McHugh is finished. But I'm forcing my way in with Griffin Blake; I'm gonna make his operation bigger than ever. We're talking millions. And I want you with me."

I grabbed a handful of hair at the back of her head and kissed her. She pressed her body against me as she opened her mouth. I felt her arms twist around me. She moved, the raw sexual energy from her body like a vibration. In that moment, I knew with all the conviction I'd ever felt that we would be great together, that she would be the only woman I'd ever need. And I put every ounce of that conviction into our embrace. I pulled away from her, finally. We were both breathless. I said, "Well?"

She nodded, panting. "Yes."

"McHugh is finished."

"Yes."

"Say it."

"McHugh is finished."

I looked at McHugh. He stared at us like a chicken at a gator convention. "You traitorous little slut," he said.

Her lips twisted in a smile. "All of a sudden," she agreed.

I took her chin in my hand and turned her face to me. "And you'll come with me."

McHugh shook his head in disbelief.

She smiled up at me. "Yes," she said.

I looked at McHugh—his pocked face raw with rage and pain—then back at Ayzie. I pushed her away. It felt like pushing my hand through a wall, like pushing a planet off its orbit. It was the hardest thing I've ever done, shoving her away from me. She caught herself at the desk, her eyes hard.

I could still feel her near me, but also a new sense of awareness. I'd discovered a way of finding out who I was. It had nothing to do with the past.

"You know, I think I've changed my mind."

Her face mottled. "You son of a bitch." Her voice was thick, strangled; she made a claw of her hand and flashed her nails at my face. But I had seen that coming and was out of reach. I headed for the door, smiling to myself. My self.

"Thanks for the hospitality," I said.

CHAPTER 51

That evening, Lilly and I went to Jan and Janet's house. We'd packed up our belongings and were having dinner in the backyard. Emily was running in circles, singing the score to *Guys and Dolls*, getting about half the words right. Everyone was feeling cheerful but me. Janet stood next to me, watching Lilly play with Emily.

"I like her," Janet said. "I like seeing the two of you together."

"I'm not getting used to it."

She nodded. "That something you'd like to talk about?"

"You mean friend-to-greeting-card-writer? Not really. It's just that my whole life seems to have fallen apart in the last week."

"Maybe it wasn't held together very well."

"Hey, I feel better. That's why you get the big bucks, huh?"

"What I mean is, maybe that wasn't your life."

I looked into Janet's gray eyes. "Come again?"

She touched my face. "You look different." I shrugged. "I think you're trying to live in two worlds, Willis. Trying to be two different people. Striving for some kind of perfect normalcy—whatever that is—on one hand, and being a detective on the other."

"You're saying I should quit the detective business?"

"I'm saying to forget normalcy, let it go. Like Shelly and the polka records, your marriage to Karla." She smiled at me. "Come on, Willis, you must have hated your life with her."

"It wasn't terrific," I said.

"It was a punishment. So you acted out. Like hitting on The Doves for a free meal, saying you were from Esther Claire. That's where you proposed to Karla, right? Maybe your unhappiness makes you keep trying to change the world to suit you. But, honey, life is imperfect. The world will always screw up. Maybe you should learn to appreciate its imperfections. Sometimes there's no sugar and the tea tastes bitter." She put her arm through mine. "And sometimes it's better just to shut up and drink it. But don't stop the detective work."

"Just now I'm not feeling like much of a detective."

"You found Bobbie. Willis, are you going to tell Steps? Tell him about Trace?"

I'd thought a lot about that. Steps was my friend. Did that mean I had to bring him face-to-face with a child who would've surely killed him if she'd felt she needed to?

"No," I told her. "Steps wanted a daughter. I'm not even sure Trace is human."

A few weeks later I opened an office on F Street, a couple of blocks from the Zamboanga Café. Having a real office and paying rent worried me. But I figured I needed to start taking myself seriously as a PI if I expected anyone else to. And I was living there, too, I had a cot and a microwave. So I was saving on rent. The block also had shops selling doughnuts, corsets, used blue jeans, and wigs with prices starting at one dollar. I expected an elegant clientele.

So far, all I had collected was a daily mound of junk mail. While waiting for today's pile I worked my way through the D.C. forms to be a foster parent, my first step toward adopting Sarah. I had been visiting her each day, and finding out which classes I had to take. Whether the District deemed me a suitable foster parent was another question altogether.

And Lilly? The last time I'd seen her was at Steps's final set at the Willard. He was playing "Stolen Moments" when I told her about the baby. Then I saw the look on her face.

She said, "It's a little too much for me. And babies? It's, like, too domestic. See, I took care of my two little sisters, I'm the first of Irish triplets? That's three kids over three years? And I should tell you," she said, touching the hairs at the base of my neck, "I have a brief affection span."

"So that's it? We're quits?"

She shook her head, her long dreads swaying. "By now we

should be, and I don't know why we aren't. See, a long-term relationship for me is, like, a week. I think part of it, I've never met anyone like you. But I need to figure this out. I mean, all the time we've been together people have been, like, chasing us, shooting at us. Now they're not. That takes getting used to." She got up to go. "I want to be with you, but I'm not sure I can. Can you understand that?"

"Sure."

She paused, her fingertips touching the top of the table. Then she turned and hurried out.

Since then I'd had no nightmares, about the maze or anything else. Waking up rested was a new experience. Plus, Lilly was no longer around to needle and annoy me; I should have been glad.

Instead, I found myself missing her.

Just then someone knocked on the frosted glass door that read WILLIS GIDNEY, PRIVATE INQUIRIES. I opened the door and found a FedEx envelope. Inside was a check from the Democratic Campaign Committee. Seems they were paying me for McHugh's resignation. The check was for twenty thousand dollars. I was standing in the doorway, recounting the zeroes, when a little old lady with sharp features and a kindly expression ambled up to me.

Glorioski, a client! She rested her hands on the silver handle of her cane.

"Are you Mr. Gidney?" she asked, her voice as warm as a grandmother's calling the kids as she took cookies from the oven.

"Yes, can I help you?"

She was fast. The silver handle arced and smacked into the side of my knee. Next thing I knew, I was on the floor, looking up at her. She leaned close and squinted at me, as though I were some peculiar and loathsome insect. Now her voice sounded like a tree chipper. "I'm Esther Claire, you little shit. Use my name to get food again and I'll rip your heart out."

She slammed the door behind her. A moment later, it opened again.

Lilly came in. She kneeled down to my eye level.

"And that was?"

"A satisfied customer," I said, putting my elbow on the floor and resting my head on my hand. "Hi." The picture of casual.

"Hi, yourself."

"Are you back?"

She had looked so serious coming in, but now she smiled. "Well, who's gonna protect you from the old ladies?"

I was happy to see her, of course, but I wondered what kind of future she would have with me. She deserved someone better. "Lilly, I don't know. Maybe we're not what each other needs just now."

"Well, someone once told me, we have to figure out the difference between what we want and what we need."

"Who told you that?"

"Oh," she said, sitting beside me, "just a guy."

I put my hand on her arm, gently pulling her to me. "Sounds intelligent."

"Some of the time," she said, coming into my arms.

"And the rest of the time?"

"The rest of time," she said, pushing the door shut with her foot, "he's damn lucky I'm around."